Isaac Mayer Wise

Pronaos to Holy Writ

Establishing on documentary evidence

Isaac Mayer Wise

Pronaos to Holy Writ
Establishing on documentary evidence

ISBN/EAN: 9783337282516

Printed in Europe, USA, Canada, Australia, Japan

Cover: Foto ©Andreas Hilbeck / pixelio.de

More available books at **www.hansebooks.com**

PRONAOS TO HOLY WRIT

ESTABLISHING, ON DOCUMENTARY EVIDENCE, THE
AUTHORSHIP, DATE, FORM, AND CONTENTS
OF EACH OF ITS BOOKS

AND THE

AUTHENTICITY OF THE PENTATEUCH

BY

ISAAC M. WISE

PRESIDENT OF THE HEBREW UNION COLLEGE, CINCINNATI

CINCINNATI
ROBERT CLARKE & CO
1891

PREFACE.

MOST critics read little more than the index or table of contents of the books which they criticise; few of them study an author before they attempt to laud or blame him. The author of this Pronaos to Holy Writ criticises the literature of the ancient Hebrews, and has read all those books and every word thereof in the original for a term of sixty-six years, *i. e.*, from boyhood up to his seventy-second birthday, and has attempted to acquaint himself with all ancient versions and commentaries, and a large portion of the modern translations and commentaries of the Bible. Besides, he expounded Holy Writ these forty-eight years in the synagogues and school-rooms, and before academical classes in the college these sixteen years.

Therefore he ought to have written a much better book than this Pronaos to Holy Writ. He should have dived into the depth of this spiritual ocean, and brought up for the reader the priceless pearls of divine wisdom and salvation, the gems and beauties of inspired eloquence, the grandeur and sublimity of divine truth. Domineering realism, however, in Biblical criticism as in all other realms of science, forbade him to make such an attempt before the authority and authenticity of the holy writings are established. God only did create light out of darkness; man can not produce truth out of fiction, unless in his self-delusion problematic truth satisfies him. All so-called gems of truth buried under the quicksand of fiction and deception are problematic at best, if not supported by authoritative

corroborants. None can speak conscientiously of Bible
truth before he knows that the Bible is true, and especially
in its historical data. The science commonly called Modern Biblical Criticism, actually Negative Criticism, which
maintains, on the strength of unscientific methods, that the
Pentateuch is not composed of original Mosaic material, no
Psalms are Davidian, no Proverbs Solomonic, the historical
books are unhistorical, the prophecies were written *post festum*, there was no revelation, inspiration or prophecy, must
also maintain that the Bible is a compendium of pious or
even impious frauds, willful deceptions, unscrupulous mis-
representations; whence comes the Bible truth of which
they speak? It was necessary, therefore, the author thinks,
first of all things, to meet Negative Criticism with the documentary evidence—and this is undoubtedly the legitimate
method of criticism—which establishes the truth of the
Bible, before he could speak intelligently of Bible truth. So
he could offer to the reader a mere Pronaos to Holy Writ,
which will assist him in convincing himself of the truth of
the Bible, and point him to the door leading into the
interior of the sanctuary, which is the system of Bible
truth. To this end we must know first and foremost when,
where, by whom and to what end these various books were
written, in order to judge correctly the quantity and quaiity
of truth contained in them. It is this which this Pronaos
chiefly offers.

The author has paid particular attention to the most
ancient records of Israel's history, contained in Pentateuch,
Joshua, Judges, Kings and Ruth, and to the semi-propheti-
cal books, called Hagiography, for the following reasons:

1. If the historical veracity of the post-Pentateuchal
records is established, as he verily believes he has done, all

arguments against the Mosaic origin of the Pentateuch are untenable, inasmuch as in all matters of fact the direct testimony of veracious witnesses or the documentary testimony of authentic records, are conclusively demonstrative opposite all circumstantial evidence of the *a priori* or *a posterori* category, which after all can prove probability or possibility only, and not certitude, which the direct or documentary testimony establishes. If the advocates of Negative Criticism urge that the author's arguments are insufficient to establish certitude, they must admit their sufficiency to controvert their own. This places the problem upon the *statu quo* of the uninterrupted tradition, and this testifies to the Mosaic origin of the Pentateuch.

2. The same argument holds good with the Davidian Psalms and the Solomonic Proverbs. They not only testify directly to the existence and acknowledged authority of the Mosaic documents in the time of those kings as a heritage then of the congregation of Israel, but also to the veritable contents of those ancient documents being identical with the Pentateuch now before us. We find then in Psalms the Theology of Moses, in Proverbs the Ethics of Moses, in Job and Ecclesiastes the Apologetics of both, in Chronicles, Ezra and Nehemiah the necessary addenda to the ancient canons; so that the entire Book is a logical organism, with every part in its right place.

3. The authenticity of the Mosaic records is the foundation of all Bible truth. The whole system of righteousness, justice and equity for public government and the conduct of the individual, virtue and holiness as a form of divine worship, monotheism itself with all the doctrine derived from this principle, the entire canon of divinity and humanity depends for evidence on the authenticity and

veracity of the Pentateuchal records; every other evidence has been at different times refuted and is subject to skepticism now, perhaps, more than ever. If these records are fraudulent, there exists no proof that whatever the chroniclers, prophets and psalmists said or sang is not of the same kind of fraud and imposition, and there is no Bible truth. This explains the author's attempt to save the records which establish Bible truth. The kind reader will decide how successful or unsuccessful this attempt was, and at least give credit to the author for honesty of purpose.

THE AUTHOR.

CINCINNATI, the 3d day of the month of Nissan, 1891.

TABLE OF CONTENTS.

8 TABLE OF CONTENTS.

8444PAGE.

VIII.	Characteristics of the Book,	43
IX.	Characteristics of the Appendices, being of later origin,	44
X.	Samuel the author of Judges (note on "Dan"),	46
XI.	Joshua, being older than Judges, was written in the Phineas age dates for both books,	47
XII.	SAMUEL. Characteristics,	48
XIII.	Divisions and Contents,	49
XIV.	Authors, Samuel, Gad and Nathan and date fixed,	51
XV.	Proofs for the Samuel portion,	52
XVI.	The objections reviewed,	53
XVII.	KINGS. Divisions and Contents,	55
XVIII.	Four Authors in Kings,	55
XIX.	The last synoptic could not have written the former portions, nor could the first have written the last portions; dates fixed,	56
XX.	Historical value and authenticity of the four books,	57

CHAPTER IV.—THE LATER PROPHETS.

I.	The second part of the Second Canon, the names of the authors,	59
II.	Uninterrupted succession of Prophets to Malachi, 425 B. C.,	59
III.	JOEL. Divisions, Contents, Time and Characteristics of the book,	65
IV.	Objections considered,	66
V.	The four cotemporary prophets, dates of their prophecies,	67
V.	AMOS. Divisions, Contents and Characteristics,	69
VI.	HOSEA. Divisions, Contents and Characteristics,	69
VII.	ISAIAH. Divisions, Contents Characteristics and Unity,	70
VIII.	Isaiah xl. to lxvi. Contents, Date and Characteristics,	72
	MICAH in paragraphs v. and vi.	
IX.	NAHUM. Divisions, Name and Place, Date and Contents,	74
X.	HABAKKUK. Divisions, Contents and Date,	75
XI.	ZEPHANIAH. Divisions, Contents and Date,	76
XII.	OBADIAH. Divisions, Contents and Date,	77
XIII.	JEREMIAH. Name, Place, Date, Political Status, his relation to the Reforms of King Josiah,	78
XIV.	The Book of Jeremiah, Divisions, Contents and Characteristics,	80
XV.	Imitation in Jeremiah xlix.,	82

CHAPTER VI. — THE AUTHENTICITY OF THE PENTA-TEUCH.

CHAPTER I.

THE religion of the Hebrews is commonly called Judaism, instead of Abrahamism or Mosaism according to its founders, Israelism or Hebrewism, according to its original votaries, or ירָאת יהוה *Yirath Jehovah*, "the Worship of Jehovah," as it is called in its own sources,* and which is its main characteristic; because the Græco-Roman writers had no knowledge of this system of religion prior to the time of the Hebrews' Second Commonwealth, and then the land was called Judea and its people Judei, and consequently its teachings were called Judaism. The word Judaism, however, being popularly understood to designate the religion of Israel, it was deemed advisable to use it also in this treatise.

2. The substance of the theology of Judaism is contained in the THORAH, called in the Bible, תורת יהוה "the Thorah of Jehovah," and in the Talmud, תורה שבכתב "the written Thorah," or also חמשה חמשי תורה "Pentateuch," in Aramaic, אוריתא "the divine Canon." It contains not only the revelations of God's nature and will, his essentiality, and attributes conceivable to man, but also the body of ethical doctrine, following with logical necessity from the cognition of the one, only and true God, to guide man and mankind to happiness. In this second sense of "the Thorah of Jehovah," the Greeks called it *Nomos*, "the Law;" for whatever follows with logical necessity from the cognition of God is canon and law to man. The Thorah is expounded, expanded, amended, and the history of its development and progress recorded in the other books of

---

* Isaiah xxxiii. 6; Proverbs i. 7, and many other places, especially in Psalms and Proverbs, always improperly rendered " Fear of the Lord."

the collection called the Bible, by inspired teachers, and by
uninspired savants, or sages in the post-biblical literature of
Israel; for all of whom, however, the Thorah was and must
unexceptionally be taken as source and standard. It is
presumed that the revelations of God's nature and will in
the Thorah are the ultimate for man's comprehensibility
and his attainment of happiness in time and eternity.
Therefore, the Thorah is eternal. This always was universal
doctrine among orthodox Israelites.

3. The collection of sacred books called by Græco-Latin
writers *Biblia*,* "*the Book*," "the Bible," as it is now before
us, consists of the following forty-three books:

Five books of Moses, one of Joshua, one of Judges, two
of Samuel, two of Kings, one each of Isaiah, Jeremiah,
Ezekiel, and twelve of the Minor Prophets, connected under
the Aramaic name of תריעסר; five of Psalms, one each of
Proverbs, Job, Song of Songs, Ecclesiastes, Lamentations,
Ruth, Esther, Daniel, Ezra and Nehemiah, and two Books
of Chronicles. Each of these books is mentioned in a
source of the Talmud called *Beritha*. (*Baba Bathra*, 14*b*.)
Quotations from each of these books occur in the Talmud
and its sources.† The main commentaries accepted by the
Israelites are contained in the Talmud, of which there exist
two collections; one compiled in Palestine at the end of the
fourth Christian century, is called the Talmud of Jerusalem
(*Talmud Yerushalmi*), and the other, compiled in Persia
at the end of the fifth Christian century, is called the Talmud of Babylon (*Talmud Babli*). The extant written
sources of both collections, besides the Bible, are the six

---

* Originally the plural "books," used as a singular in Latin to
denote *the* Book emphatically.

† See "Toldoth Aaron," by Aaron ben Moses, of Pisaro, and
"Toldoth Jacob," by Jacob Sasportes, Amsterdam, 1652, added
also to some editions of the Rabbinical Bible. These books furnish a complete index of Bible passages quoted in the Talmud, also
in *Zohar*, *Akedah* and *Ikkarim*. These quotations are of the same
importance for text criticism as would be a manuscript of the whole
Bible from the second and third centuries.

volumes of statute law called *Mishnah*, on which the Talmud chiefly comments, *Tosephta*, *Mechilta*, *Safra*, *Sifri*, *Pirkei Rabbi Eli·zer*, *Seder Olam* and *Meguillath Taanith*, all of which except *Mishnah* are called *Beritha* or "outside" of Mishna, and were written in the first half of the second Christian century, with additions from the beginning of the third. Other and less authoritative commentaries are the *Targumim*, Aramaic and Syriac versions and paraphrases of Scriptures; the post-Talmudical homilies contained in the various collections called *Midrash* and *Pesikta;* the Moorish-Spanish and French Rabbinical commentators and philosophers between the tenth and sixteenth centuries; and above all the *Massora*, which rendered the text legible and intelligible to the common man by providing it with vocal and accentual signs according to authoritative traditions.

4. As far back into antiquity as the post-biblical literature of the Hebrews reaches, no book of the Bible, Nehemiah excepted, was added, omitted, or changed from its original name. Also, the twelve Minor Prophets are mentioned as one book in the *Beritha*, the Septuagint and in the book of Joshua ben Sirah (xlix. 35, in Greek 10); except the Book of Nehemiah, which was still a part of the Book of Ezra when the Talmud was written (*Sanhedrin* 93b). Samuel and Kings may have been considered one book by the Greek translators, but there is no trace of it in these sources. The three books, Samuel, Kings and Chronicles, were divided each into two by Hieronymus (*Prol. in Reg.*). In the first Bibles printed in Socinio (1488) and in Brescia (1494) the ancient divisions are retained. In the Basel edition of 1534, and also in the Bomberg Rabbinical Bibles, the subdivisions of Hieronymus were adopted, to be thence copied into subsequent prints. In order to retain the traditional twenty-four books of the Sacred Scriptures, the division of Ezra into Ezra and Nehemiah was accepted, and the five books, viz.: Ruth, Song of Songs, Lamentations, Ecclesiastes and Esther—read in the synagogue on five different days of the year—were reckoned one book. A Book of Daniel, wherein it was presumed Daniel had prophesied that one of the Greeks should destroy the empire of the

Persians, is mentioned in Josephus (Antiq. x. viii. 5) as having been shown in the Temple of Jerusalem to Alexander the Great.

Psalms is divided into five books, viz. :

1. Chapters i. to xli.
2. Chapters xlii. to lxxii.
3. Chapters lxxiii. to lxxxix.
4. Chapters xc. to cvi.
5. Chapters cvii. to the end of the book.

Each of the four books closes with a doxology, "Amen and Amen," or "Amen Hallelujah," similar to Nehemiah viii. 6, and I. Chronicles xvi. 35. 36, to which is added at the close of the second book כלו תפלת דוד בן ישי. "Finished are the prayers of David, son of Jesse."

Not all Psalms are Davidian, as their headings show. The ancient rabbis mention nine older poets, like Moses in Psalm xc. and contemporaries of David.

There can be little doubt that Psalms were written much later, or even up to the time of Simeon the Asmonean, and that the five-book division refers to five collections made at different times, all of which were accepted in the Canon without re-arrangement. Still, as part of the Canon, Psalms is counted as one book only, even in the most ancient notices; it is evident, therefore, that those collections were made prior to the establishment of the third Canon. The division of chapters are different. Psalms had 147 chapters with them. Psalms i. and ii. were naturally counted as one, on account of the beginning of the first and the closing of the last being similar. It is uncertain which other Psalms were originally connected.

5. The forty-three books of the Bible were connected in twenty-four volumes, as they are now before us in the Massoretic text. Josephus (Contra Apion, i. 8) reports twenty-two books of Scriptures, "which are justly believed to be divine," viz.: five books of Moses, thirteen books of the Prophets, from Moses to King Artaxerxes, and four books containing "hymns to God and the precepts for the conduct of human life." Taking into the second class of Scriptures "all that was done between Moses and Artax-

erxes," his thirteen books must have comprised Joshua,
Judges, Samuel, Kings, Isaiah, Jeremiah, Ezekiel, twelve
Minor Prophets, Chronicles, Daniel, Ezra and Nehemiah,
Ruth and Esther. His third division must have consisted
of Psalms, Proverbs, Job and Ecclesiastes, either with the
Song of Solomon or without it, as he never refers to it.
Lamentations, called in the Talmud *Kinnoth*, "elegies," was
counted with Jeremiah

Hieronymus, although he mentions the   twenty-four
division (*Prol. in Reg.*),* and also the Hebrew names of the
various parts thereof, yet adopted the twenty-two division
of Josephus. The Church, according to the *Index Scrip-
turarum Nicephori*, and the Anathasian Index,† retained the
Hieronymus division, also in the reconstructed Septuagint.

In all rabbinical sources the twenty-four division only
is mentioned. It is noted first in the Talmud (*Taanith 8a*),
in connection with Rabbi Adda bar Ahabah (second Christian century) as an existing fact. Ben Asher‡ reports this
rabbi as the first Massorite who came after 138 (Christian
Era) from Palestine to Babylonia.§ It seems possible,
therefore, that the twenty-four division was established in
the Academy at Jamnia, under Rabbon Gamliel II.‖

6. The twenty-four books of Scriptures are divided into
three canons, *Thora*, *Nebiim* and *Kethubim*, "Law," "Prophets" and "Hagiography." This division is as old as the
post-biblical traditions of the Hebrews. The books belong-

---

* See also Wolff, "Bibliotheca Hebraica."

† Credner, "Zur Geschichte des Canons."

‡ Dikdukei Hat-Taamim, Strack Edition, p. 56.

§ It is maintained in *Tosephoth* to *Baba Bathra* 22*a* and *Rashi* to
Kiddushin 72*b*, that there were two rabbis of this name and the
older one was an older cotemporary of the author of the Mishnah.

‖ It is evident from the Talmudical statement בקשו לגנו that a
revision of the Canon and the elimination of the books of Solomon
and Ezekiel from it was proposed and discussed in that academy
under Gamliel or his immediate predecessor, Jochanan ben Saccai,
but was not accomplished, perhaps by the opposition of the then
most important teacher of that day, Akiba ben Joseph, who
declared even Song of Songs most holy.

ing to each canon are named in the Talmud (*Baba Bathra* 14). The order of the books following each other in each canon, as given in the Talmud, with but one exception, was preserved intact by the rabbinical casuists.*

In Prophets a difference of opinion prevails only as to the position of Isaiah in the prophetical canon before Jeremiah or after Ezekiel, which begins in the Talmud (*in loco cit.*) and reaches down to the seventeenth century. In Hagiography a difference of opinion in the order of the books prevails with the Talmud and the casuists on the one side and the authors of the written Massora on the other.†

The printed Bibles (Hebrew) follow the order laid down by the rabbis in Talmud and casuists, and place Isaiah before Jeremiah. These differences being of no particular importance, any further investigation is unnecessary in this place.

The high antiquity of this three-division is evident from the preface of the Grecian translation of Ben Sirah's book, about 125 B. C.; from Josephus (*in loco cit.*); and from the rabbinical records of the post-biblical traditions,‡ although it was not adopted in the Septuagint, Peshito, Vulgata, or in the Christian Church. Also in Maccabees II. 13 it is maintained that in the library founded by Nehemiah there were the "books" of the Kings and the Prophets, also the "writings" of David and the "letters" of kings who sent presents to the temple. This shows that the "writings" even of David were a different class of scriptures from the books of the Kings and Prophets, supposed to have been the case in the days of Nehemiah. Ibid. xv. 9, the Law and Prophets only are mentioned in connection with Judah Maccabee, perhaps because the third Canon was not established yet in his days.

---

* See Maimonides, *Hilch. Sepher Thorah* vii. 15, and Joseph Caro, *Joreh Deah, Sepher Thorah*, 283, 5.

† See Amsterdam Rabbinical Bible *Koheleth Shelomo*, of 1724, pp. 10, 11; also Wolff in Bibl. Hebr. Part II. p. 51, col. 5: Hieronymus, *Prol. in Reg*

‡ For instance *Taanith 8a; Baba Bathra 9a and 13b; Sabbath*, 14, and ibid. Talmud, 116*; and ibid. *Yerushalmi* xvi. 1; Nedarim, 111, 9; Meguillah I. and elsewhere.

7. This involves a doctrine. The rabbis claimed plenary inspiration for Moses only (*Babu Bathra* 15a, and *Menacoth* 30a הקב'ה' אומר ומשה אומר וכותב), and not also for the Prophets. In the synagogue Moses only was read and expounded, and sections from the Prophets were read in conclusion of exercises in the synagogue or academy to be expounded by the *Meturgam.* (See Rapaport's *Erech Millin*, Art. אפטרתא). In regard to the Hagiography, the ancient *Halacha* was אין קורין בכתבי הקודש אלא מן חמנחה ולמעלה "We read not in the Hagiography except from and after the afternoon service," although it was permitted to take texts from them for the morning homilies.* So Hagiography was considered of inferior holiness to Prophets (See Yerushalmi *in loco cit.*), and Prophets inferior to the Pentateuch; so much so that it was maintained that Prophets and Hagiography may in future be abolished, because the Prophets have not been permitted to add a new law to that of Moses; and also, "If Israel had not sinned he would not have been given more than the five Books of the Law, and the Book of Joshua (*Nedarim* 22b and *Yerushalmi Meguillah I.* 7).

It appears that prior to Rabbi Jehuda the *Nassi*, it was held that the three divisions of the Bible must not be written in one scroll, so that they appear not of equal holiness.† Moses Maimonides, according to his responses, as given by his son Abraham, in the beginning of *Maaseh Rokeach*, would not permit the three divisions of the Bible to be written in one book, because reading in the Prophets or Hagiography, parts thereof would be placed upon the Thorah, which is not permitted, on account of the superior holiness of the Thorah. " Prophets and Hagiography must not be placed upon the Thorah." (*Megillah* 27a) ואין נותנין נביאים וכתובים על גבי תורה.

The rabbis of the Talmud called the Prophets דברי קבלה

---

*Compare Tosephta *Sabbath* 14 to Talmud Yerushalmi, ibid. xvi. 1, and Babli ibid. 116b.

† *Mescheth Sophrim III.* and the Talmudical passages noted there by Naumburg in his *Nachlath Jacob*, and by Asulai in his *Perush.*

"Words of Tradition," and not תורה שבכתב "the written Thorah" or אוריתא, and advanced the hermeneutic rule, *רברי תורה מדברי קבלה לא ילפינן "We teach not matters of the law (basing upon) words of the Prophets."

The Tiberian Massorites also call the Thorah *Oritha*, "Canon," and the other books of Scriptures *Ashlamta*, "supplement or addendum." The Karaites rejected this doctrine, and consider the whole Bible equally holy, as the Christians do.

8. Maimonides expounds the respective passages from the ancient rabbinical literature to this effect.† The prophetical power of Moses, like his mission and his power to work miracles, was unique and superior to all prophets who lived before or after him. Therefore the Thorah is the holiest book; it never was and never will be changed or replaced; it is eternal. Among the other prophets there were higher and lower degrees of perfection, so that not all passages of prophetical Scriptures are of equal divinity; they are clearly distinguished by their various introductions. He speaks of eleven degrees of prophetical inspiration, all inferior to the inspiration of Moses and superior in nine degrees to the authors of Hagiography, including Daniel, the Judges and Kings of Israel, with David and Solomon. These Hagiographists wrote, spoke or performed deeds of valor by a divine impulse and assistance called רוח הקודש "the Holy Spirit," which comprises only the first and second degrees of inspiration, leading to the prophetical degrees. Therefore, Hagiography is less divine than Prophets, and both less divine than the Thorah.

In *Moreh* I. 27, Maimonides points to Onkelos, the first Aramaic translator of the Pentateuch (beginning of the sec-

---

*(Hagigai 10*b*, Niddah 23*a*, Baba Kammah *b*), on which point see *Shene Luchoth Habberith* (ש ל״ה). They also called the whole Bible מקרא the "Reading," the literature which is read, in contradistinction of the oral laws and traditions, which were spoken and not read.

†Moreh, Part II., chap. 32, e. s.; *Yesodei hat-Thora*, chapters 7 to 10.

ond Christian century), as an additional authority for the distinction made among the prophetical passages of Scriptures according to the higher or lower degree of the prophet in the scale of inspiration. Then in Part II., chapter 45, where he describes the various degrees of prophecy, he sets down the Scriptural terms which distinguish the various passages and characterize them.

9. The division of the Thorah into five books is mentioned continually in the Talmud and its sources (*Mishna Yoma*, viii. 1), and especially in *Yerushalmi Sotah* v. 6: "Moses wrote five books of the Thorah, and then again he wrote the section of Balak and Balaam." Its antiquity is demonstrated by the most ancient translations of the Pentateuch—the Greek, Syriac and Aramaic—by Josephus and Philo, and especially by the Samaritan Pentateuch, all of which are precisely the same five books, with some slight inversions in the Samaritan Pentateuch in favor of Samaritan doctrine.

(*a*) בראשית (*Bereshith*), which is the first word of the Bible, called by the Greeks "Genesis," consists of fifty chapters (modern division), forty-three *Sedarim* (ancient division) and 1,534 verses, the midst of the book in verses is xxvii. 40. Genesis contains the history of creation, the first parents and their three sons, the genealogy of the ten antediluvian patriarchs, the Noachian deluge and covenant, the post-Noachian genealogy, origin and location of the seventy nations, including the building of the Tower of Babel, the subsequent dispersion of the families and the origin of languages; and begins in the twelfth chapter with the life, covenant and circumcision of Abraham, which together with the history of the three generations of his descendants, make the contents of the whole book. It is all simple prose except iv. 22, 24, Lemech's address to his wives, and chapter xlix., the blessings of Jacob, which are primitive poetry in a peculiar form.

(*b*) שמות (*Shemoth*), which is the first noun in this book, called by the Greeks "Exodus," consists of forty chapters (modern division), 29 *Sedarim* (ancient division), 1,209 verses, the midst thereof is xxii. 27. It contains the history

of the Israelites in Egypt, the birth, early fate and calling of
Moses (*Mosheh*) and Aaron, the struggle for liberation, the
miracles, the exode from Egypt, the passage through the Red
Sea and the Song of Moses, voyage from the sea to the wilderness of Sinai, including the organization at Marah,* and the
war against Amalek, water from the rock and the manna;
then the revelation on Mount Sinai, the primeval cult (xx.
21–23) and the first Mosaic legislation, including in xxiii.
10, 11 Leviticus xxv., the laws of the Sabbath and Jubilee
years; and in Exodus xxiii. 14–19 the laws from ibid. xii. 14–
27, 33–49, and chapter xiii. 1–16, concerning Passover, other
holy days, and the sanction given to the first-born as the
priests of the people. Chapter xxiv. closes the history of the
revelation and the establishment of the covenant. From
chapter xxv. to the end of the book, with the exception of
chapters xxxii., xxxiii. and xxxiv. contains all appertaining to the construction of the national sanctuary and its furniture, the priestly garments, and the form of worship in the
tabernacle, being evidently an introduction to Leviticus,
while the chapters xxxii. to xxxiv. are evidently the conclusion of Exodus. The whole book, with the exception of the
song at the Red Sea, is prosaic.

(c) ויקרא (*Vayikra*), which is the first word of the book,
called in the Talmud *Thorath Kohanim*, "the Thorah of the
Priests," and by the Greeks " Leviticus," consists of twenty-
seven chapters (modern division), 23 *Sedarim* (ancient
division), 859 verses, the midst thereof is xv. 7. It contains
from chapter i. to vii. ordinances and prescriptions concerning sacrifices not properly belonging to the tabernacle cult.
From chapter viii. to x., to which belongs also chapter xvi.,
is the detailed history of the dedication of the tabernacle,
which actually belongs after Exodus xl., between the verses
33 and 34. It was placed here as the proper introduction to
the ritual laws from chapters xi. to xxiv., outlined in chapter
x. verses 10 and 11 as the duties of the priests, "to distin-

---

* Exodus xv. 22–26, which appears to be identical with the organization in ibid. chapter xviii., following the advice of Jethro. The
ancient rabbis are of another opinion.

guish between the holy and the profane, the unclean and the clean, and to teach the children of Israel all the ordinances which God hath spoken concerning them by the hand of Moses." Chapter xix. specifies particularly the material for this third priestly duty. Chapter xxii. contains the laws concerning the priests personally and exclusively. Chapters xxiii. and xxiv. repeat the commandments of the holy days to specify the prescribed sacrifices for those days and the priests' duties concerning them. This last chapter concludes with the story of the blasphemer in the wilderness and the laws connected therewith, and this seems to be the proper conclusion of the book. Chapter xxv. on Sabbath and Jubilee years and the poor laws connected therewith, and chapter xxiv. containing prophecies of Moses, as the heading of the former and the conclusion of the latter shows, belong to the close of Exodus, the first Mosaic legislation. Chapter xxvii., containing the laws of valuation and ransom of persons, animals and things vowed to the sanctuary, in which the priest is concerned and the year of Jubilee referred to, is a proper conclusion of both the first legislation of Moses and the laws of the cult, and concludes well the book of Leviticus.

(d) במדבר (*Bamidbar*) which is the first word in the book after "The Lord spake to Moses," called in the Talmud חומש הפקורים one of the five parts of the Pentateuch referring to the numbering, and by the Greeks "Numbers," consists of thirty-six chapters (modern division), 32 *Sedarim* (ancient division), 1,288 verses, the midst thereof is xvii. 20. This book is fragmentary. It begins with the census and organization of the camp in the wilderness, in which the Levites are taken separately, which could have been ordained only after the appointment of the Levites instead of the first-born, hence after the revolt of Korah, narrated in chapter xvi., to which is clearly referred in iv. 28. This part, including ordinances concerning the Levites, closes v. 1–4, an ordinance concerning the hygiene of the camp, to which is added an additional law concerning trespass, which actually belongs to Leviticus. Then follow in chapters v. and vi. the laws concerning the suspected woman, *Sotah*, and the Nazirite (*Nazir*), one who vowed abstinence from wine and observed special cleanness and purification. From vi. 22 to the end of vii. follows a sequel to the dedication of the tabernacle, the gifts and sacrifices of the twelve princes of the tribes, headed by the oldest liturgical formula on record, the priestly benediction. Chapter viii. begins with an additional prescription concerning the candlestick in the tabernacle, followed by ordinances for the Levites. Chapter ix. contains the ordinance of a substitute Passover in the second month for those who were not in condition to observe it properly in the first month, and concludes with the signals given in the camp by the pillar of cloud upon the tabernacle. Chapter x. begins with the signals given in the camp with two trumpets, also their use at the sacrifices; continues with the marching regulation, and the names of the captains of the tribes, and of the four divisions; then follows the engagement of Chobab as a guide in the wilderness, and in conclusion two brief prayers of Moses, one starting the host and another calling it to rest. Chapter xi. contains the story of the quails, and the constitution of the council of the seventy elders. Chapter xii. narrates the murmuring of Miriam and Aaron against Moses, and the definition of true prophecy. Chapters xiii. and xiv. narrate the story of the twelve spies; chapter xv. is an addition to Leviticus, then the story of the Sabbath-breaker in the wilderness, closing remarkably with the ordinance of the national fringes and colors. Chapters xvi., xvii. and xviii. narrate the story of the Korach revolt and its consequences, together with additional ordinances for the Levites; xix. tells the ordinances concerning the red heifer and its ashes of purification. With chapter xx. begin the historical notices from thirty-seven years later, interspersed in chapters xxii. to xxiv. by the account of Balak and Balaam and his poems. Chapter xxv. contains the appointment of Phineas to the high priesthood. With chapter xxvi. begins the second census and the second legislation of Moses, which is continued and closed in Deuteronomy. Except the poems of Balaam it is all prosaic.

(*e*) דברים (*Debarim*), which is the first noun of the book, called also תורה מישנה (*Mishneh Thorah*), "Review

of the Thorah" (Deut. xvii. 18), and by the Greeks "Deuteronomy," consists of thirty-four chapters (modern division),
twenty-seven *Sedarim* (ancient division), 955 verses, the
midst thereof is xvii. 10.

It contains from chapter i. to xi. and xxvi. to xxxi. 9, the
last speeches and prophecies of Moses; from xii. to xxv. the
continuation of the second legislation of Moses expounding
and amending the first as required for the practice in the
land which the Israelites now approached. Chapter xxxi.
contains the inauguration of Joshua and the delivery of the
former Thorah to the custody of the Levites, to be kept at
the side of the ark of the covenant, and the delivery of
Deuteronomy to the Levites and all the elders of Israel,
commanding also that it be read in public during the closing feast of the Sabbath year. Chapter xxxii. contains the
last song of Moses; the first is in Exodus xv. Chapter
xxxiii. contains the blessing and departure of Moses.

The whole Thorah contains 5,845 verses, the middle of
which is Leviticus viii. 8. The middle of all its words is in
Leviticus x. 16. *Darosch* closes the first, and *Darash* opens
the second half. The middle of all its letters is the *vav*
of the word נחון in Leviticus xi. 42.

10. There can be no doubt that the divisions of the Bible,
according to the traditions and documents of the Hebrews,
reach up to the time of the original establishment of the
three canons. There exist no traditions and no documents
in this matter in antiquity or explicitness approximately
equal to those of the Israelites.

It is no less certain that the subdivisions of every biblical
book into major and minor paragraphs, verses, words and
the counting of letters, were fixed and carefully noted by the
ancient scribes. It seems, therefore, impossible that the
text, at least in its consonantal letters, could have been
amended or interpolated at any time within the two thousand years of Hebrew post-biblical traditions and documentary records. But the question in criticism goes far
beyond that, and the critics rely more on *a priori* argument
than on documentary evidence, a species of reasoning which
appears illegitimate to us, if applied to the investigation of

facts and traditions based on the testimony of documents. Therefore, before we can discuss the question of the authenticity of the Pentateuch, the authorship of Moses and the kindred topics, we must first ascertain all the facts from the documents which have a bearing on the main question. This, and this only, can lead to approximate certainty. It is the entire Hebrew Bible we must know first, to collect therefrom the system of facts by which certitude in this matter can be obtained.

CHAPTER II.

THE term Canon is of Greek origin, and is, in its ecclesiastical application, merely an equivalent for "Thorah," the emphatic teaching or instruction, the authoritative guide in religion and morals. The term was applied, however, to the whole collection of the Hebrews' sacred books, and extended also to the Apocrypha of the Old Testament by some early Christian writers. The Hebrews always counted the Apocrypha among ספרים חצונים, "outside books" (*Sanhedrin* 100b), and no quotations from either, except from the book of Ben Sirah, occur in the Talmud. The position of Prophets and Hagiography in the Canon has been defined. Although accepted as divine, yet they are אישלמתא, "appendices or supplements," to the Canon or Thorah. We consider them canons with these restrictions, because such is the common conception of the term.

2. The reason for classifying the sacred books besides the Thorah, as the Hebrews always did, appears to be chronological. They were canonized or edited for the use and guidance of the people in different times. Joshua, Judges, Samuel and Kings are called נביאים ראשנים, "Former Prophets," while Isaiah, Jeremiah, Ezekiel and Minor Prophets are called נביאים אחרנים, "Latter Prophets," although the prophecies proper are contained in the latter collection, and Daniel is omitted altogether. So are Lamentations, Ruth, Psalms, Proverbs, Song of Solomon and Ecclesiastes. According to the chronological order of the supposed origin of these books, they could not have been classified as they are. The distinction between prophetical books and others could not have guided them, as Former Prophets contains only prophetical fragments, while Daniel claims to be entirely prophetical. We are forced, therefore,

to accept the theory that these traditional divisions of the Canon had their origin in the relative chronological succession of their canonization. Therefore, the historical books canonized at an early date are called Former Prophets. The whole of Prophets having been canonized prior to Hagiography, assumed a higher and holier character than the latter in the estimation, tradition and veneration of the people, upon which the Scribes based the dogma of its superiority. It is, therefore, evident that the Thorah, occupying the highest position in the people's estimation, tradition and veneration, must have been Canon in Israel long before the other books of the Bible. We know to a certainty that this was the case in the time of Judah Maccabee, when the Scroll of the Law was the only holy emblem of the Synagogue (I. Maccabees iii. 47, 48) ; that the official translators of Ptolemy Philadelphus were required to Grecise the Thorah only ; that the Samaritans adopted only the Thorah and no other book of the Hebrew Scriptures, and that Ezra and Nehemiah placed the Thorah only before the assembled people on that solemn occasion, and this only was accepted as the Canon. (Nehemiah viii. and ix.) In the Temple of Jerusalem the reading of sections from the Thorah only was part of the divine service (*Mishnah in Yoma*), and the official correctors of manuscripts in the Temple *Azarah*, as far as we know, limited their labor to the Thorah chiefly or exclusively, for which they were paid out of the tithe fund.

Besides all these points, it is a fact that every one of the prophets points to the Thorah Canon, and none to the teachings of his predecessors as being of an equal authority, as shall be proved hereafter.

3. The very first canon, for the existence of which we possess documentary evidence, was that of the Patriarchs, contained in Genesis, viz. : the Thorah of Adam, the Thorah of Noah, the Thorah of Abraham and the other Patriarchs.* Basing upon the Thorah of the Patriarchs and progressing from the rules of conduct ordained for the individual and family to those of a nation and nations, follows the second

---

* See Albo's *Ikkarim*, III. 13, 14.

part of the first canon, viz.: (a) the Sinaic Thorah, contained originally in the ספר הברית "Book of the Covenant,"* now contained in Exodus and Leviticus; † and (b) תורת כוהנים the Thorah of (or for) the Priests, establishing the polity and ritual in harmony with the teachings of the Thorah, now interconnected with the "Book of the Covenant" in these three books of the Pentateuch. Basing upon these two canons, reviewing, expounding and amending, follows the fourth part of the first canon, viz. (c): תורת משה the "Thorah of Moses,"‡ now contained chiefly in Deuteronomy, and parts of it also in Numbers. A fifth class of writings entering into the composition of the Thorah as a whole, and especially in Numbers, consists of the "Scrolls," also believed to be of Mosaic origin, mentioned in the Talmud, תורה מגלה מגלה נתנה the "Thorah was given (or preserved) in various scrolls" (Guitin 60), for which also we possess documentary evidence.

4. The following Mosaic scrolls are noticed particularly:

(a) The story and poems of Balaam (Numbers xxii. and xxiii.), concerning which it is maintained in the Talmud quoted above (Bab. B. 14, and Yerushalmi Sotah v. 6), "Moses wrote five books of the Thorah, and then again he

---

*Exodus xxiv. 15; 2 Kings xxii., xxiii.; 2 Chronicles xxxiv., xxxv.

†In regard to the contents of the Book of the Covenant, see *Mechilta* in *Bachodesh*, section 3. One of the Tana'im (his name is given differently here and in Yalkut) holds that it contained all from Genesis i. to Exodus xxiv. Rabbi Jehudah, the Prince, holds it contained the commandments only which were given to Adam, the children of Noah, Abraham, in Egypt, at Marah, and the other commandments. Rabbi Ishmael holds it contained also Leviticus xxv. and xxvi., as the first verse of xxv. and the last of xxvi. plainly show. It appears most likely that originally Exodus xxiv. was the end of the book, to which Moses later on added Leviticus xxv. and xxvi.

‡See 2 Kings xiv. 6; the quotation from תורת משה is from Deut. xxiv. 16; 2 Kings xxi. 8; one Thorah is referred to in צויתם and then another in התורה אשר צוה אותם עברי משה Compare also Deuteronomy xxxiii. 4; Joshua i. 7, 8; viii. 30; xi. 15.

wrote the chapter on Balak and Balaam," and mentioned again in Deuteronomy xxiii. 6; Joshua xxiv. 9, 10, and Micah vi. 5, as a well-known fact.

(b)   The Book of the Journeys.   It is mentioned especially that Moses also wrote by divine command the history of the exode from Egypt and the sojourn of Israel in the wilderness, as stated in plain terms, Numbers xxxiii. ויכתב "משה את מוצאיהם למסעיהם על פי י׳׳ "And Moses wrote their goings out according to their journeys at the command of Jehovah."   This document may have originally contained the historical notes connected with these stations in the wilderness, as is evident from verses 3–5 and perhaps also various laws made known on such different occasions, all of which may have been afterward detached and placed elsewhere, as the plan of the whole book required.

(c)   There is noticed in Numbers xxi. 14 ספר מלחמות "The Book of the Wars of Jehovah," and a passage is quoted from it.   This, critics maintain, must be a book older than the Thorah.   We maintain that no war of Jehovah could have existed prior to Moses, and Moses was particularly commanded to write, or rather to start, such a book right after the first war of Jehovah, which was waged against Amalek, as recorded in Exodus xvii. 14.*   "And Jehovah said, write this as a memorial in THE book." etc., which could mean a special book only, a book for that purpose, viz.: to record the Wars of Jehovah.   It stands to reason that Moses obeyed the divine command, consequently he was the author of the Book of the Wars of Jehovah, as far as his time was concerned.

(d)   There existed another ancient book ספר הישר "The Book of Jashar," quoted in Joshua x. 12–13, and 2 Samuel ii. 17–27, which also appears to have been started by Moses, or found by him among his people and continued; as some of the rabbis in the Talmud maintain that *Jashar* stands for *Jesharim,* and it signifies the Book of the Righteous, viz.: Abraham, Isaac and Jacob.   According to the extant quota-

---

*This is suggested by Abraham Ibn Ezra and Targum Yerushaimi to this verse.

tions from that book, it must have been a collection of the people's didactic and epic poems, to which the song at the Red Sea, beginning *Oz Yashir*, as does also the quotation in Numbers (xxi. 17) and another in Joshua (x. 12), may have given the name of *Jashar*. It is stated expressly (Deuteronomy xxxi.) that God commanded Moses to write the last song (Deuteronomy xxxii.), and that he did write it that day. It seems to be reasonable to suppose that this and other songs of Moses started the Book of Jashar as he did the Book of Wars. על כן יאמרו המושלים "Therefore the *Moshelim* said," in Numbers xxi., being a poem, *Moshelim* signifying "poets," as well as "rulers," and in that book "mashal," in the case of Balaam וישא מישלו signifying "poetry," it is very likely anyhow that the passage is a quotation from the same Book of Jashar, whose authors were called *Moshelim*.

(e) "The Book of Generations." ספר תולדות (See *Lekach Tob* to Genesis v.) This book is mentioned first in Genesis v., although neither the term writing nor book occurs again in Genesis.* Genealogies reoccur in Exodus and chiefly in Numbers, called in later times ספר היחש (Nehemiah vii. 5), and must of necessity always have been kept among the ancient Hebrews, as all titles to landed property and most important political rights depended on the individual's authentic family and tribal records. This term ספר could have been added at that particular place only to inform us that the Israelites, prior to Moses, possessed a written genealogy reaching back to Adam, or that Moses started also this official book; anyhow, it is of Mosaic or pre-Mosaic origin, as are other documents accepted into Genesis.

From time to time important national matter may have been added to these various scrolls or books. Moses may have entered into the Book of the Covenant in his last days, the Covenant in the Plain of Moab (Deuteronomy xxviii.), or it may have been a separate scroll added to Deuteronomy afterward. Joshua may have entered his covenant with

---

* Except in the case of the Egyptian חרטמים Genesis xli. 8.

Israel at Shechem in this scroll or book, as is mentioned especially (Joshua xxiv. 26) ויכתב יהושע את הדברים האלה בספר תורת אלהים "And Joshua wrote these words in the Book of the Thorah of Elohim," not in the Thorah of Moses, as usual in this book. Samuel may have entered his constitution of royalty in the same book, as it is stated there (1 Samuel x. 25): ויכתב בספר "He wrote (it) in THE book," and not in a book, as this was also a covenant, viz.: with royalty. So likewise all the wars of Joshua and after him, down perhaps to Samuel, may have been recorded in the Book of Wars, and all national hymns, like that of Deborah, and David's song, *Kesheth*, perhaps many now incorporated in the Book of Psalms, like Psalm cxiv., may have been entered in the Book of Jashar, as these were the official records of the nation started by Moses. Other special laws of Moses and records of his time, like the description of the tabernacle and its furniture, the appointment and functions of the Levitical priesthood, the particulars about the sacrificial polity, may just as well have existed in different smaller scrolls from the hands of Moses.

5. Deuteronomy was originally written and delivered by Moses to the priests and all the elders of Israel (Deuter. xxxi. 9). It was intended to be the popular canon in the hands of all who could read; to be read publicly at stated times (ibid. 10–13; 2 Chronicles, xvii. 7–9); to be the text-book for the young (Deuter. vi. 7; xi. 18, 19); to be copied by the king and to be continually before his eyes (ibid. xvii. 18, 19; 1 Kings ii. 3; Psalms i. 2); to be written on the twelve stones taken out of the Jordan* (Deuter. xxvii. 1–8; Joshua viii. 30–35). This Thorah of Moses was never forgotten and never set aside in Israel, not even in times of prevailing Pagan corruption, also not in the kingdom of Israel, and was always read at stated times in the temple as late even as in the time of Agrippa I. (Mishnah in *Sotah* vii. 7.)

---

* Only that portion, perhaps, which is contained in Deuteronomy xxvii. and xxviii., as appears from Joshua viii. 14, where הברכה והקללה is mentioned with particular stress in explanation of את כל דברי התורה.

The assumed difference of diction which critics suppose to distinguish Deuteronomy and characterize it as a work of later origin than the former books of the Thorah, is imaginary only. The laws in Deuteronomy differ in nowise from those in the former books. Wherever any former law is repeated, it is amended with some additional provision, as Rabbi Ishmael has put down in the Talmud (*Sotah* 3a) as a hermeneutic maxim. The speeches and prophecies of Moses differ from his juridical diction, as the orator's style must, but they differ not from his previous rhetorical passages, as for instance, Exodus xxxii. to xxxiv., Leviticus xxvi., and especially Numbers after chapter xx. The last Song of Moses differs from the first as the rigid moralist's didactic poem differs from his triumphal lyric effusion. But suppose there was such a difference, it must be admitted that forty years' literary and oratorical practice changes the diction of every man of genius. Besides all that the critics possess no reliable standard by which to fix the age of any portion in the ancient classical Hebrew.

6. Being once admitted that Moses was the author of the Book of the Covenant, the various scrolls mentioned, and Book of Deuteronomy, it must also be admitted that he was the author of the Book of Genesis, for (*a*) it is no more and no less than a historical introduction to the Mosaic Scriptures, as the first eleven chapters are the introduction to the history of the patriarchs. It establishes the main doctrines of the Mosaic dispensation, such as God being supermundane, Creator, Preserver and Governor of the world, the Providence, sovereign law-giver and supreme judge of man; man being the highest, spiritual, physical and God-like being on earth, standing in perpetual connection with the Deity by his understanding and conscience, if he obeys the commandments of his Maker; and especially the covenants between God and Noah, God and Abraham, to be inherited by their posterity. (*b*) The next object of Genesis is to establish the title of the children of Israel to the land of Canaan, which is the very foundation of the Mosaic policy. (*c*) The whole plan of Genesis is to present the regular development and steady progress of the revelation of Deity in the

human consciousness, and the consequent generation of the ethical principles from the progressive cognition of God's nature and will. None of the patriarchs is ethically as perfect as Joseph, for he is the last in the upward scale of the development, preceding the Mosaic dispensation. (*d*) Without this introduction, this knowledge of preceding development, the doings and writings of Moses would appear an unintelligible mystery, inexplicable and incomprehensible, a state of culture and a stage of reason and ethics issuing suddenly from dead rocks, and Moses would appear like a wizard wrapped in the deceptive mantel of darkness. (*e*) In all his writings Moses continually points back to the events, doctrines and promises recorded in Genesis. It might be maintained that somebody prior to Moses wrote the Book of Genesis. This, however, is refuted by the constant use of the tetragrammaton in the book, which, according to documentary evidence, is of Mosaic origin (Exodus iii. and vi. 2–9). The portions of Genesis in which God is called *Elohim* or *El Shaddi* are ancient documents, which its author accepted and incorporated literally, but on no occasion omits to state that Elohim or El Shaddi is identical with his Jehovah, and does not signify any other Deity. Genesis, like the whole of the Hebrew Bible, except some psalms between Psalms xlii. and lxxxiii., which are Elohistic, is entirely Jehovistic, only the ancient documents are not : hence Genesis could not have been written prior to Moses.* Again Genesis contains a number of indications that it was written outside of Palestine, by one who knew most about Egypt, and for readers best acquainted with this country. Genesis xxiii. the author finds it necessary to explain Kirjath Arba. "This is Hebron in the land of Canaan," which he repeats in verse 19 of the same chapter, and again in chapter xxxv. verse 27, which only an author outside of Canaan could have written. This is also the case in Numbers xiii. 22, where

---

*This, of course, is to maintain that the various hypotheses of fragments from different authors, distinguished by different names of the Deity employed by them, called Jahvistic and Elohistic writers, is, aside of the Elohistic portions mentioned above, entirely false. The Elohistic Psalms will be noticed under Psalms.

Hebron is again referred to as having been built seven years
prior to Zoan of Egypt. The land between the Euphrates
and the Isthmus of Suez is called in Genesis the land of the
Eberites, or Hebrews. Abraham is called the Ibri (xiv. 13).
Joseph is called an *Ibri* man (xxxix. 14); tells of himself
that he was stolen from the land of the Ibrim (xl. 15), and
is called by the royal courtier an Ibri slave (xli. 12). So the
Ibrim are constantly mentioned as being called so by the
Egyptians. This was certainly not written in Canaan, nor
was it written east thereof, where the people west of the
Euphrates were called "Western" Arabi, Arabs. The
Egyptians naturally changed the "Western" Arabi, Arbi, or
Erebi into Ebri or Ibri, the people or land "on the other
side" of the Isthmus. The term Ibri, or Hebrew, can be of
Egyptian origin only. The author of Genesis never explains
the names or offices of Egyptian persons, although they
have no equivalents among the Hebrews, as Pharaoh, Poti-
phar, the Sar Hat-Tabachim, Sar Ha-Ophim, Sar Ha-Mash-
kim, and the location or history of Egyptian places, as he
often very carefully does with names of places and persons
outside of Egypt; evidently because he wrote for a people
well acquainted with Egypt and Egyptian affairs. This is
evident from the entire history of Joseph and partly also
from the history of Abraham. These are points of circumstantial evidence proving that Moses, after the exode and in
the wilderness, must have written the book of Genesis. If
there occur in it passages which seem to be of a later origin
than the time of Moses, they must be accounted for from
another standpoint than the Jahvistic, Elohistic fragment
hypothesis or any other theory which places not the authorship of this book at any time after the death of Moses.

7. The Book of the Covenant and perhaps also all the
other Mosaic documents, called ספר התורה הזה (Deuter.
xxxi. 26) and not התורה הזאת (ibid. verse 12), as Deuteronomy is called, was delivered to the Levites to be placed *at
the side of the ark of the covenant of the Lord*, as part of עדות
"The testimony" upon which the whole of Deuteronomy is
based, and to which it constantly refers, and not in the

hands of all the Levites and Elders; hence it could be
known and examined by the expounders of the law and the
priests, but not also by the whole people (Deut. xxxi. 24–26).
It is quite natural, therefore, that the earliest prophets
whose books we possess, like Joel, Amos and Hosea, arguing
against the corruption of religion and law in the kingdom
of Israel, spoke and wrote in the style of Deuteronomy, and
referred to it most frequently; it was the canon of the people, and known as such to everybody, while the other portions of the first canon—perhaps Genesis excepted—could
not have been known so popularly.*

8. Documentary evidence not merely entitles but compels
us to maintain that all these manuscript scrolls, preserved
and zealously guarded in the national sanctuary, may have
been connected with the Mosaic books of Genesis, Covenant,
Leviticus and Deuteronomy, and shaped in the present form
of the Five Books of Moses, if not Moses himself performed
this task in the last days of his life; and that material
which, after Moses, was added to any of those books or
scrolls was incorporated in the later books of Joshua and
Judges, although some of it may have been retained in the

---

*It seems that קרא מקרא, in Isaiah i. 13, does not refer to מקרא
קרש in the Thorah, because in the next verse Isaiah calls the holy
days מועריכם, and so or חגים the prophets usually call the feasts ordained in the Thorah; none refer to them as קרא מקרא. Nor is this
phrase in this sense found anywhere in the New Hebrew. It appears
that it must be understood literally "Reading Scripture;" in this
sense only the term מקרא went down into the New Hebrew. Isaiah
referred to the then already prevailing custom of reading canonical
Scripture as part of the divine service of Sabbath and New Moon.
That he had in this chapter the last song of Moses before his eyes
is evident from יִשְׁמְעוּ and הַאֲזִינוּ in verses 2 and 10, and in the previous chapter (Deut. xxxi. 11) he saw the commandment of " To read
this law," which according to verse 9, refers to Deuteronomy. This
is also evident from Isaiah lxvi., which is chiefly an imitation of
Isaiah i.; and there, verse 21, occurs the phrase הכהנים הלוים, which
is taken from Deuteronomy. It appears, therefore, that Deuteronomy chiefly was read as part of the devotional exercises on Sabbath and New Moon.

Pentateuch, as for instance Genesis xiv. 14, xxxvi. 31 ; * Exodus xvi. 35, 36 ; Leviticus xxi. ; Numbers xiii. 24, xxi. 3, 25, xxxii. 34–42 ; Deuteronomy xxxiv. Unless it be maintained that such anachronistic passages came in the Thorah as marginal notes first, which transcribers erroneously incorporated into the text, for which we possess no proof whatever.

This must have been done at an early date of Israel's history, long before the first books of the Prophetical Canon were recognized as holy Scriptures. Still, whenever this was done, there exists no reason to suppose that the compilers of the Mosaic Canon accepted anything into it which they did not verily believe to have come from the hands of Moses or his immediate disciples. We have no right to suspect fraud or imposition where the object of any book is the highest good of mankind, which is the case with the Pentateuch, unless forced to do so by the undoubted dicta of reason. It is a self-contradictory assumption, that any man or any body of men whose sole object is truth and righteousness should resort to fraudulent means to reach his or their aim. The so-called pious fraud is not applicable to such stern preachers of righteousness as Israel's prophets were. In order, however, to approach argumentatively the time when the Pentateuch received its present form, we must first ascertain when the books of the Prophetical Canon were written, and when they were considered Holy Writ. This is attempted in the next chapter.

---

* It is possible enough that this passage was written by Moses, and the eight kings of Edom, all foreigners—no Edomites reigned in the land of Edom before the sons of Esau—assumed the reins of government in that country and before the Israelites had an organized government, i. e., in the time of Moses. The *Melech* in this passage, as in Deuteronomy xxxiii. 15, refers to Moses (Sepurno).

THE eight books of the Prophetical Canon, viz.: Joshua, Judges, Samuel, Kings, Isaiah, Jeremiah, Ezekiel and Minor Prophets, were esteemed among the ancient Israelites of equal holiness, inferior only to the Thorah, at as early a date, indeed, as the reading of holy Scriptures besides the Thorah, as part of the divine service, was introduced in the synagogues and academies. According to most ancient regulations prescribed sections from any of these books were read in conclusion of the morning service of every Sabbath, biblical holy day, the ninth day of the month of Ab, and in conclusion of the afternoon service of any public day of fast. Passages from the Prophetical Canon only and not also from Hagiography were prescribed to this end. But it made no difference from which of the eight prophetical books such selections were made, which certainly shows that they were esteemed of equal holiness. And yet the four books called the Former Prophets, because they are called so must have been esteemed Holy Writ prior to the four called Latter Prophets. This point deserves particular attention, especially as radical criticisms, in order to bring down the origin of the Pentateuch to a comparatively recent date, entirely misconstrue these historical books.

2. Outside of the Bible we possess but one document on the dates, when, and the authors by whom the various books of the *Bible* were written, and this is the record of ancient tradition in the Talmud, *Baba Bathra,* 14b and 15a, which, literally rendered, reads thus:

"Moses wrote his own book, the section of Balaam, and the Book of Job. The latter is contradicted by various teachers, and finally by the principal Massorites of Tiberias, Rabbis Jochanan and Eleazar, who maintain איוב מעולי גולה היה

"Job was among those who returned from the Babylonian captivity," as appears also from Job xlii. 10, and from its position in the third Canon.

"Joshua wrote his own book and the last eight verses in the Thorah." This is amended on the next page in the Talmud to the effect that the last verses of Joshua were written partly by Eleazar and partly by Phineas, the high priests.

"Samuel wrote his own book, also Judges and Ruth;" which is amended on the next page of the Talmud to the effect that the Prophets Nathan and Gad wrote parts of the book Samuel, as stated expressly in 1 Chronicles xxix. 29.

"David wrote a book of Psalms, in which he incorporated the psalms of ten older authors.

"Jeremiah wrote his own book, Kings and Lamentations.

"Hezekiah, the king, and his associates wrote Isaiah, Proverbs (see Proverbs xxv. 1), Song of Solomon and Ecclesiastes.

"The Men of the Great Synod wrote Ezekiel, Twelve Minor Prophets, Daniel and Esther."

"Ezra wrote his own book (including Nehemiah) and the genealogies of Chronicles up to himself יחס של דברי הימים עד לו" (see RASHI).

It must be understood that כתב or כתבו, "he wrote or they wrote," in this or other Talmudical passages, does not always refer to authorship; it refers, also, to the editorship, the parties that collected and compiled the manuscripts of any author.

3. It is evident from the books of "Wars of Jehovah," "Sojourns," "Genealogies," and "Jashar or Moshelim," that official and cotemporary chronography was one of the public institutions in Israel. This appears also from Joshua and Samuel, of whom it is reported that they wrote into such existing books, and from the above Talmudical tradition, which admits that Joshua wrote into the Thorah (see also *Ramban's* commentary to Numbers xxi. 1), and that the two high priests added to the records of Joshua. No such official records are mentioned in the period of the Judges, although frequent references to them occur in the

Book of Judges (v. 4, 5; vi. 7–10; xi. 14–27). Still, in that
very ancient song of Deborah (chapter v.), a host of en-
gravers of the law on stone or metal, מחוקקים, presiding
judges, יושבים על מדין, and expert scribes, מושכים בשבט
סופר, are expressly mentioned,* so that cotemporary chronography also in that period can hardly be doubted, especially as the variety of styles in the different accounts in the
book point distinctly to various larger chronicles from which
the narratives were epitomized.

From and after King David the Scribe (סופר) and Chronographer (מזכיר) or Chancellor were members of the
royal council. Solomon had even two scribes (1 Kings iv.
3), and that official is there yet in the time of Jeremiah
(xxxvi. 9, 12; lii. 25), to the very end of the two kingdoms.
Both the chronicles, and in many instances also the chronographers are mentioned. In the Book of Kings only three
such official and cotemporary chronicles are referred to, to
the very end of the book, viz.: "The Book of the Words of
Solomon" (1 Kings xi. 41); "The Book of the Chronicles of
the Kings of Israel" (ibid. xiv. 15; xv. 31), and "The Book
of the Chronicles of the Kings of Judah" (ibid. 1 xiv. 18).

In Chronicles the two latter sources are referred to (1
Chronicles ix. 1 and 2 Chronicles xxxvi. 8), that is up to
King Joiakim, exactly as the author of Kings does, to which
he also refers in the terms "The Book of the Kings of Judah
and Israel" (2 Chronicles xvi. 11), also in the terms ספר
המלכים and calls it (xxvi. 27) "A *Midrash* of the Book of
Kings."† Besides which the author of Chronicles refers to
the books of prophets who wrote the cotemporary history
of certain kings. He mentions Samuel, Nathan and Gad as
writers of the history of David (1 Chronicles xxix. 29);
Nathan, Abiah Hashiloni and Eddi having written the history of Solomon, (2 Chronicles xi. 29); Shemaiah and

---

* Also 1 Chronicles ii. 55.   ומשפחת סופרים יושבי יעבץ

† It is evident that *Midrash* refers to the synopsis and not to the
primary sources, in this case to our Book of Kings, as in the place
referred to and beginning of next chapter, the author of Chronicles
copies literally from 2 Kings xii. 20 and xiv. 1–7.

Eddo—the latter perhaps identical with Eddi—having written the history of Rehabeam (ibid. xii. 15) ; the same Eddo wrote also the history of Abiah, the son and successor of Rehabeam, in a separate book called " MIDRASH Eddo." The history of the other kings was not preserved in separate books known to the author of Chronicles ; it was recorded in the official chronicles by cotemporary prophets, as special mention is made of Jehu, son of Hanani, who inscribed from his own book the history of King Jehoshaphat in the official chronicle (2 Chronicles xx. 34), and the prophet Isaiah wrote the history of Uziah in the same manner (2 Chronicles xxvi. 22), and the history of Hezekiah, in the Book of Isaiah, then called חזון ישעיהו בן אמוץ according to the four words at the head of this book, and also in the official chronicle (ibid. xxxii. 32). The history of King Menasseh was written by various prophets, one of whom, called Hozai, is mentioned in Chronicles xxxiii. 19. All these historical sources must have been extant to the end of the fourth century B. C., as the author of Chronicles makes copious abstracts from them, including many names and sayings of prophets and other prominent persons not mentioned in the preceding historical books, as for instance in the genealogies up to chapter ix. and the various historical notes connected with them, all of which he states (ix. 1) " are written in the Book of Kings of Israel and Judah." So the same author continually refers to books from which he copies, and not to mere traditions or opinions. The institution of cotemporary official chronography, it appears from the closing passage of 1 Maccabees, was permanent in Israel, and was there yet in the time of John Hyrcan, whose official day book is mentioned there.

4. The historical books of the Bible are synopses from official and cotemporary records in some instances, or a connection of some books into one—as is the case with Joshua and Samuel—from cotemporary writers. They were not re-written or corrected by any one man or any set of men at any time. Aside of some errors which might have crept in by copyists during thousands of years, they are be-

fore us to-day exactly and literally as they came from the hands of their respective authors, and furnish us with the consecutive history of the Israelites from 1450 to 585 B. C., as complete and truthful as no other people of that millenium has left a record. Each book continues the history from the end of the former, and each author evinces a full knowledge of his predecessors. All of them have in common the aim and object which is not only to write history, but to produce the historical evidence in support of the fact, that Israel's life, prosperity and success depended on its adherence to the divine covenant and obedience to its laws and teachings, and all national miseries and failures down to the destruction of Jerusalem and the Babylonian exile resulted from disobedience, desertion and rebellion. Therefore they are both popular text-books of history and divine canons. Each of these books is different from the others in diction, plan and terminology, consequently no one person could have been the author of any two of them. Each has its own exceptions from the rules of grammar and peculiarities of construction; hence none was re-written by critics or literary editors, none went through the hands of a corrector. These books are before us in their antique originality. Had they been revised at any time they would be uniform, correct and smooth. Had they been written or re-written at any time by any one man or any one body of men, they could not differ so entirely in plan as Judges does from Joshua and Kings from Samuel, which are as different as is the synoptic from chronographer.

5. Joshua contains three different elements from three different records: (a) The original records of Joshua, added by him to the various public records established by Moses; (b) the geographical and topographical records referring to the conquest and division of the land (Joshua xii.–xxi.), which could not have been written at any later date, as the whole claim of the families to certain lands always depended on it; and (c) the Book Jashar quoted in Joshua x. 12–14 as the source for the miracle of sun and moon standing still. The book as now before us was cer-

tainly not compiled or edited by Joshua, nor was the author of the Joshua records different from him who wrote the last chapter of Deuteronomy, as a cursory inspection of this and Joshua i. sufficiently proves.

It is certain that Joshua is older than Judges, which is chronologically a continuation of the former. The last words of Joshua are quoted in Judges (ii. 6–9), and the beginning of this chapter is in substance from Joshua xxiii., as the notice from Caleb taking Hebron (Judges i. 10–15) is from Joshua xiv., xv. 13–19.

6. The Book of Joshua is before us in twenty-four chapters (modern division), fourteen *Sedarim* (ancient division), 656 verses, the middle of which is xiii. 26. Its contents are:

Chapter I. God's charges to Joshua and to his people.

Chapter II. Sending and returning of the spies from Jericho. The story of Rahab.

Chapters III. and IV. Marching from the camp east of the Jordan, crossing that river, and erecting the twelve stones taken from its bottom at the west side thereof.

Chapter V. Circumcision and the Passover at Gilgal, and the vision of Joshua.

Chapter VI. Capture of Jericho.

Chapter VII. Reverse before the City of Ai; crime and punishment of Achan.

Chapter VIII. Capture of Ai, erection of the altar, writing the law upon the stones, and pronouncing the blessings and the curses on Mounts Gerizim and Ebal.

Chapter IX. The Gibeonites and the covenant with them.

Chapter X. War and victory over Adoni Zedek and four other kings; sun and moon standing still.

Chapter XI. Jabin, King of Hazar, and other kings defeated in battle and slain.

Chapter XII. Renumeration of Joshua's victories.

Chapter XIII. to XXI. Division of the land among the tribes, and appointing cities of refuge.

Chapter XXII. The two and a half tribes dismissed to their homes beyond Jordan, the altar they erected, and the controversy to which it led.

Chapters XXIII. and XXIV. Public meetings, addresses of Joshua, reaffirmation of the covenant. death and burial of Joshua and Eleazar the high priest.

According to tradition, the wars of Joshua lasted seven years, the division of the land and taking possession thereof, also took seven years. Then the Mosaic law was put in force and the tabernacle erected in Shiloh.

Diction and phraseology of this book are similar to that of Moses, although less nervous. It is without documentary evidence to speak of a Hexateuch instead of a Pentateuch; and linguistically, there is no more similarity between Joshua and Pentateuch than what is ordinarily the case in the writings of a weaker disciple comparing to those of his original and more powerful master.

In order to approximate the time when the Book of Joshua was written, we must ascertain first when Judges was written. Therefore, we turn now to the second book of the prophetical canon.

7. The Book of Judges is before us in twenty-one chapters (modern division), fourteen *Sedarim* (ancient division), 618 verses, half of which is x. 8. Its contents are: After the introduction (see above), the book begins iii. 7, with the exploits of Othniel ben Kenaz and his successors, Ehud ben Gera and Shamgar ben Anoth. the three judges following Joshua.

Chapter IV. Contains the story of Deborah and Barak.

Chapter V. The song of Deborah.

Chapter VI. to VIII. Is the record of the Gideon period.

Chapter IX. Contains the story of the usurper, Abimelech, and the parable of Jotham.

Chapter X. Opens with a mere mention of two succeeding Judges, Thola and Jair, and closes with reports of prevailing corruption and invasion. leading to the appointment of Jephthah.

Chapters XI. and XII. Is the record of Jephthah, with the story of his daughter, closing chapter xii. with a mere mention of the three succeeding Judges, Abzon (said to be the Boaz in Ruth), Ailon and Abdon.

Chapter XIII. to XVIII. Is the record of the Samson period.

From chapter xvii. to the end of the book two stories are appended, to which there is no reference made in the body of the book, although they narrate incidents which are supposed to have occurred at the very beginning of that period, when Phineas was high priest, and differ radically in spirit, phraseology, tone and object from the body of the book. No reader can help seeing that these two appendices are later productions, and were added for a purpose to the Book of Judges.

The author of Judges mentions neither Eli nor Samuel, although they were the very men he must have glorified, according to the plan of his book, if there existed no particular reason for ignoring them.

8. The author of Judges is an outspoken monotheistic, theocratic patriot. He evidently transcribed his narratives from the Book of Wars of Jehovah, where cotemporaries of the respective events recorded them. Therefore he has no records from the long intervals of peace and evident prosperity. He claims that all national misfortunes and miseries were divine retributions for Israel's abandonment of the true God and adopting pagan cults; and that salvation from misery was always effected by Judges who were faithful to God and succeeded in reforming the people; and this is the tendency and purpose of the entire book. He is the stern theocratic democrat. He dwells with special delight on Deborah on account of her brilliant genius and God-inspired patriotism. Gideon, Jephthah and Samson, heroic men of the people, true to Israel's cause, are his central figures, while he barely mentions the names of most of the Judges, and has more to say of the filial devotion of Jephthah's daughter than of the judges governing forty-five years prior to Jephthah. He literally pours out his abhorrence of the monarchical, anti-theocratic institution in narrating the story of the first usurper, Abimelech, the son of Gideon, and a concubine, who is the first fratricide after Cain, in sacred history, much more criminal than Adam's first-born. His supporters and partisans are paganized rebels. The treasures in support of his cause are taken from the temple of Baal. He is the first bloodthirsty despot in Israel's history;

within three years of his reign he slays thousands of his
followers, to be himself slain at last at the hands of a woman.
None of the reigning judges is. blamed by the author.
Throughout the book the theocratic democrat, the invincible
man of righteousness, speaks the blunt and stern language
of a heroic age.

9. Entirely different are the language and tendency of the
two appendices. evidently written by another author. He is
no synoptic. He writes extensive stories containing many
particulars of single events. He evinces his animosity to
the democratic form of government by saying four times:
"In those days there was no king in Israel," to which he
adds twice: "Every man did what seemed right in his sight,"
which is to say, then confusion and anarchy reigned. With
undisturbed equanimity and without a word of blame, he
tells the story of Michah's idol, how the Danites stole it and
its priest and worshiped it all the time that the tabernacle
was at Shiloh. He is evidently not the same man who wrote
the main portion of Judges.

The second story, about the concubine slain at Gibeah
and the subsequent murderous execution of justice on the
tribe of Benjamin, fully betrays the intention of the author.
Besides his anti-democratic sentiments, which he makes the
groundwork of both stories, he makes out a case of what
happened in Gibeah so similar to that of Sodom, when the
angels had come to Lot, that the story borrows both the incidents and phrases from that part of Genesis (Judges xix.
8–27). Then his evident intention is to bestow as much
praise as the situation would afford on Levy, Judah and
Ephraim, and as much blame and disgrace as could be
afforded on the tribe of Benjamin and the men of Jabesh
Gilead (ibid. xxi. 5–12). Their crime was that of Sodom,
their punishment and degradation were complete; a mere
remnant of them was permitted to live by the grace and
mercy of the people, and even those had to steal women and
take them for wives. This story has certainly not the same
author who incorporated in his narratives the words of
Deborah, "After thee, Benjamin. among thy people" (Judges
v. 14). Another remarkable point is that the Book of

Judges has no mention whatever of any high priest or Levite, while in this appendix we meet again the Levite and the high priest Phineas (xx. 28).

There exists internal evidence in Judges to the effect that the body of the book is older than the appendices. In Judges i. 20 we read, "And the Jebusite dwelt with the children of Benjamin in Jerusalem עד היום הזה to this very day," which must have been prior to the reign of David. In one of the appendices (ibid. xviii. 31) we read that the Danites worshiped the idol of Michah, as long as the house of God was in Shiloh, as a reminiscence of days past, and not עד היום הזה consequently the second event transpired long after the first, and the writers so dated it. Again, as the song of Deborah bears testimony to the Sinaic revelation, the tribal divisions and the state of culture in her days, and Jephthah in his message to the King of Ammon (Judges xi. 12–28) bears testimony to the events in the last year of Moses, so Samuel (1 Sam. xii. 8–11) and the author of Psalms lxxxiii.* confirms the stories narrated in Judges. But the stories narrated in the two appendices are not as much as referred to any more anywhere in the Bible.

These appendices must have been written at a time when it was deemed necessary to denounce the democratic form of government, the tribe of Benjamin and the city of Jabesh Gilead, to laud the monarchical institution and to compliment the tribes of Levi, Judah and Ephraim. This concurrence of events happened at no time in Israel except during the reign of King David. Then the theocratic democracy was yet strong in number and dissatisfied, as is evident from the revolutions under Absalom and Sheba ben Bichri; Benjamin was David's enemy; Jabesh Gilead was loyal to Saul; Levy, Judah and Ephraim were David's strongholds. There can be no reasonable doubt as to the time when those appendices were written, nor as to the reason why they were

* This Psalm could have been written only in the earlier time of David's reign, as is evident from the names of the hostile nations mentioned therein. Compare 1 Samuel viii. גם אשור in verse 9 of that Psalm refers to Aram Zobah, which was under Assyrian dominion then, and must have been assisted by Assyrians.

attached to the Book of Judges, which is the very glorification of theocratic democracy, credits Benjamin with one of
the earliest saviors of Israel (Judges iii. 15), and records the
words of Deborah, אחריך בנימין בעממיך

10. It is easily understood why the tradition makes Samuel the author of Judges. The book was written for the people, to whom the official chronicles were inaccessible, by an
uncompromising and zealous advocate of the theocratic
democracy, an implacable opponent of the pagan corruptions, monarchy and the priesthood, with the avowed intention to convince the masses of the real cause of all national
miseries, and to uphold and maintain in their original purity
the theocracy and the covenant.

This man could have been Samuel only; there is no other
known in history. He was the reformer of his people, with
him idolatry vanished out of Israel for a century. He was
the last pillar of theocracy and opponent of monarchy to the
very end. He was the opponent of priesthood and almost
overthrew it, to which he was forced by the demoralization
of the sons of Eli, and the fact that the first royalist rebels
were chiefly Levites, as the city of Sichem belonged to the
Levites of the family of Kehath (Joshua xxi. 21). His hand
is visible throughout the book. The authority of the prophet made the book a popular oracle. It was canon as
soon as it had reached the people (1 Samuel iii. 20). Therefore when royalty struggled against democracy, as was the
case in the time of David, it was necessary to neutralize the
effect of that book, which was attempted by the addition of
that appendix.*

The book presents also an argument *e silentio* in favor of
the authorship of the prophet Samuel, being written in the
lifetime of the high priest Eli. It closes with the death of

---

* This Dan, the name which the Danites gave to the city of Laish,
in the northwest of Palestine, in the valley of Beth Rahab, not far
from Zidon (Judges xviii. 28), is not identical with the Dan in Genesis xiv. 14 and Deuteronomy xxxiv. 1, which is the name of a moun-
tain range in the northeast of Palestine, at the head of Gilead, near
Hobah, west of Damascus.

Samson, mentions neither Eli nor Samuel, with whom the period of the Judges closes, although the author records , every name of the Judges from Joshua to Samson. Had the book been written or transcribed by a later author, he must certainly have closed it with some account of the two last Judges in Israel. If Samuel was its author he must have written it during the lifetime of Eli, whose administration being not matter of history yet. The same kind of argument points to the high priest Phineas as the compiler of the Book of Joshua in its present form. The book closes with the account of the death and burial of Joshua and Eleazar the high priest, makes no mention of Phineas, although he was acting high priest, at least in the latter days of Joshua (Joshua xxii. 13). Had the book been written, re-written or compiled by any later author, he must certainly have added some account of the third high priest in Israel.

11. Joshua having undoubtedly been written prior to Judges, it was certainly compiled and finished in its present form in the period between Joshua and Samuel. Its diction points to a disciple of Moses, and this could well have been Phineas, the high priest, of whom the tradition admits that he wrote the close of the book. There is no established rule in the canon of Biblical criticism to set aside the facts that Phineas was the last editor of Joshua, that Samuel wrote Judges, and an anonymous author in the Davidian time wrote the appendix with the avowed intention of counteracting among the people the democratic tendencies of the book, the prevailing sympathies for the tribe of Benjamin and the inhabitants of Jabesh Gilead.*

All this, however, does not prove that Joshua was not the author of the material compiled in the book. The whole record of the conquest of Canaan must have been inscribed in the national records, called " The Book of the Wars of Jehovah " (see page 28). The last speeches of Joshua were certainly added to the " Book of the Covenant " as main-

---

* See the author's History of the Israelitish Nation, Appendix to Period II., " Literature," Albany, 1854.

tained in the book (xxiv. 26). The quotation from the Book
of Jashar is marked (x. 12-14). The topographic portion
was written by the men appointed by Joshua at Shiloh
(xviii. 8, 9) and must have originally been added to the
national records in the Book of "Sojourns." All this material was taken from the original records and compiled into
the one Book of Joshua. Some notes and explanatory
remarks of the compiler may have been added, but there
exists no evidence whatever that the original material had
been changed or interpolated, nor does any rational ground
exist to suspect the compiler's stern honesty and veracity.
We may, therefore, fix the following dates:

Joshua was written by him and his scribes, and compiled
in its present form by the high priest Phineas 1400 B. C.

Judges, being an abstract and epitome from the national
records, was written in its present form by the prophet Samuel 1075 B. C.

The appendices to the Book of Judges were written —
author unknown—1025 B. C.

With the authentication of these two books we gain one
more argument, and a very important one, in favor of the
authenticity of the Pentateuch and its Mosaic origin. We
also have an intimation, when the original material was
placed in its present form, viz.: when the post-Mosaic
material was separated from the Mosaic records; hence
either in the time of Phineas or of Samuel. The former
seems most likely, for the latter the evidence of history,
especially of literature, speaks most distinctly, as we shall
ascertain later on.

12. Joshua in its first verse announces itself as the continuation of Deuteronomy. Judges in its first verse announces itself as the continuation of Joshua. With Samuel
begins a new book, in style different from Deuteronomy,
and in plan and design different from the synoptic Judges,
which resembles the first sixteen chapters of Samuel in the
one point, that the same theocratic-democratic spirit, the
same opposition to king and priest, characterizes both of
them. This outspoken tendency of the two books is suffi-

cient evidence that they were not written in the time of the kings and hereditary high priests.*

13. The Book of Samuel is before us in 30 and 24 chapters (modern division), 34 *Sedarim* (ancient division), 1,506 verses, the middle of which is 1 Samuel xxviii. 24. It begins with the narrative of the parents of Samuel coming from their home to Shiloh to sacrifice there.

Chapter II. begins with the prayer of Hannah and the history of Samuel at Shiloh, in connection with the high priest, Eli, and his two sons.

Chapter III. contains the first prophecy of Samuel and its delivery to Eli.

Chapter III. contains the narrative of the war of the Philistines upon Israel, the defeat of the latter, capture of the ark, death of the two sons of Eli, and of Eli himself.

Chapters V. and VI. describe the plagues which came on the Philistines on account of the ark, and how they returned it with gifts and sacrifices, resulting in the death of 50,000 (?) of the men of Beth Shemesh.

Chapter VII. narrates how after the ark had been twenty years at Kiriath Jearim, the people reformed ; Samuel prays

---

* The author of Samuel certainly understood the Levitical laws of Moses to the effect that the priesthood belonged to the tribe of Levi, one of them to be high priest and he to be assisted by his sons, as is expressly stated in Deuteronomy xxxiii. In Deuteronomy occurs always the phrase, "The Priests-Levites," as also in Isaiah lxvi. In Leviticus it is " Aaron and his sons," and not their descendants, to whom the priesthood is given. When this dignity was conferred on Phineas, the grandson of Aaron, it was for special cause, as narrated in Numbers xxv. 10, and not as a birthright. When, after Phineas, again a high priest is mentioned, it is Eli and his two sons and no other priest, and it is not certain even that Eli was a descendant of Aaron, although the custom may have in after times become law, that the sons of Aaron only should be priests and the high-priesthood be hereditary in one family, as was the case from and after King Solomon to the time of the Maccabees. It does not seem to be so ordained in the Levitical laws of Moses, and Samuel, who was a Levite, did perform priestly functions (1 Samuel vii. 9; x. 8; xi. 15).

for them at Mizpah, leads them in battle against the Philistines and subdues them, and he becomes the judge of the people.

Chapter VIII. The people want a king; Samuel's opposition and his warning.

Chapter IX. Beginning of Saul's history, and

Chapter X. he is anointed King of Israel and is accepted among the sons of the prophets; Samuel writes the royal constitution in one of the national records.

Chapter XI. Nahash, the Ammonite, invades Gilead and besieges the city of Jabesh. Saul comes to its assistance, defeats the besiegers and liberates the city, which causes Samuel to call the people to Gilgal to renew the covenant with royalty, to which strong opposition had been manifested.

Chapter XII. Speech and miracle by Samuel at Gilgal.

Chapters XIII. and XIV. Valorous deeds of Saul and his son, Jonathan, in the war against the Philistines with his standing army of 3,000 men, during the second year of his reign. Mistakes of Saul.

Chapter XV. Invasion and overthrow of Amalek. Samuel prophesies the mournful end of Saul and his house.

Chapter XVI. Samuel anoints secretly David, son of Jesse, King of Israel. David at the court of Saul.

Chapter XVII. The Philistines again invade Palestine. Goliath slain by David, which ends the campaign.

Chapter XVIII. David returns to Saul's court, marries the king's daughter and becomes the intimate friend of the king's son, Jonathan.

Chapter XIX. Saul attempts to slay David; his wife saves his life, and he seeks shelter with Samuel at Najoth. Saul sends messengers there to capture him, and David returns to Jonathan.

Chapter XX. Covenant of friendship between David and Jonathan.

Chapter XXI. David's flight to Nob, then to Achish, King of Gath;

Chapter XXII., and is finally compelled to seek refuge in

the cave of Adullam, where he becomes the chief of a band
of voluntary warriors.

Chapter XXIII. to XXVII. Various exploits of David, and
his persecution by Saul.

Chapters XXVIII. and XXIX. The ends of Saul and Jonathan
in another war with the Philistines, and last exploits of
David at Ziklag.

Second Samuel begins with the end of Saul and Jonathan,
account thereof being brought to David; David's elegy,
Kesheth.

Chapter II. to IV. Narrates the end of the house of Saul
while David is King of Judah, in which are prominent Ish
Bosheth, son of Saul, and Abner, his chief captain, and Joab,
with his brother, Ashhael, on the side of David.

Chapter V. to XX. Contains the history of David as King
of all Israel.

Chapter XXI. is an appendix to this history.

Chapter XXII. contains the great hymn of David.

Chapters XXIII. and XXIV. contain a collection of fragments,
historical and poetical, appertaining to the history of David.

The history of David, closing abruptly in chapter XX. with
the end of the rebellion under Sheba, son of Bichri, is brought
to a close in 1 Kings chapters i. and ii. and is supplemented
in the Book of Chronicles.

14. There exists no tenable ground to contradict the tradition that Samuel wrote his book and the Book of Judges.
1 Samuel xvii. to 2 Samuel v. 3 is from the Book of Gad,
different in style and tone from the genuine Samuel. Gad
followed David in his early exploits (1 Samuel xxii. 5), and
was undoubtedly the historian of that period in David's life.
2 Samuel v. 4 to 1 Kings iii. 28 is from the Book of Nathan,
who is named as the chronographer of both David and
Solomon (1 Chronicles xxix. 29 and 2 Chronicles ix. 29).
Gad is mentioned no more up to 2 Samuel xxiv. 11–22; but
that story, placed there among the appendices, certainly belongs chronologically to 2 Samuel vi., * and Gad is always

---

* See also 1 Chronicles xxi. 19.

called *Choseh* and not *Nabi*, the official prophet, which Nathan was after David was anointed King of all Israel (2 Samuel vii.), and he maintained himself also for some time under Solomon. The three narrators, although differing decidedly in style, diction and phraseology—the Nathan portion being the most polished and elegant—all wrote like eye-witnesses thoroughly acquainted with the most minute details in regard to persons and places mentioned. They have in common antagonism to the house of Saul, which proves that they wrote before the division of the kingdom; after this event there was no further occasion for that enmity. The last writer, the Prophet Nathan, knows King Solomon for his piety and wisdom only (1 Kings iii. 3, 5, 28), knows nothing of his idolatry (1 Kings xi. 1-13) and his despotism (xii. 1-4); nor does he know anything of the immensity of his wisdom (1 Kings iv. 9-14) and his literary productions. He evidently wrote during the earlier days of the reign of Solomon. This is undoubtedly the time when the Book of Samuel, as it is before us, was compiled. The same Prophet Nathan seems also to be the author of Psalms i., ii. and lxxii., which, in connection with the first chapters of Kings and 2 Samuel vii. 12-15, explain one another well in regard to time.*

15. Among the various internal proofs that Samuel wrote his portion of the book prior to the rise of Zion and the temple, as for instance the עַד הַיּוֹם הַזֶּה in 1 Samuel v. 5, and vi. 15, there is the frequent mention of *Bamoth*, "high places," and the building of altars to Jehovah outside of the national sanctuary, without any censure or objection, which no prophetical writer after Samuel would have permitted to pass uncensured, as is evident from the Book of Kings. Samuel builds an altar (1 Samuel vii. 17) at Ramah, has there his Bamah (ix. 12 e. s.) while there was another *Bamah* in Gilead, where the sons of the prophets worship (x. 13), and the sanctuary was in Nob (xxi.). Saul also built an altar to Jehovah (xiv. 35) near Ayalon, and Ahiah, the

---

* See our " Defense of Judaism," Psalm II., p. 109.

grandson of Eli, was there with the ark of the covenant and did not censure it. The *Bamah* at Gibeon, with the Mosaic tabernacle and altar, was there yet in the time of David. Zadok was chief priest there, Haiman and Jeduthum were the chief Levites, although the ark was in Zion (1 Chronicles xvi. 37, also xxi. and xxix.), and was there yet in the time of Solomon (1 Kings iii. 4 c. s.) and was called the great Bamah. No later prophetical writer (see 1 Kings iii. 2) would have allowed the building of altars and *Bamoth* to pass without some censuring or explanatory notice. We stand here evidently upon historical ground in the lifetime of Samuel.

16. The objections to this theory are (1) from 1 Samuel ii. 10 and 35; in both cases it is maintained the Messiah-King is mentioned, which points to a time after Samuel and to another author. In both cases, however, the passages can be taken out of their respective places without changing either the sense or the meter,* and may well have been added by Nathan, for the same reason as the appendix was added to Judges, to suggest that the theocratic-democratic Samuel prophesied the coming change from the republic to the monarchy; or as verse 10 occurs in the hymn of Hannah, and verse 35 in the prophecy of the Man of God to Eli, and not by Samuel, it may well be that this coming change was indeed predicted by various intelligent people, and was delayed only by the successful administration of Samuel. (2) 1 Samuel ix. 9 may certainly have been written by Samuel himself:

"Beforetime in Israel, when a man went to inquire of God, thus he spake, Come and let us go to the seer; for he that is now called a prophet was beforetime called a seer."

In the same chapter Samuel is called "Man of God," "Seer" and "Prophet." It appears, therefore, that the

---

* In the poem of Hannah the words ויהן עוז למלכו disturb the meter, and משיחו may refer to the high priest, who was the anointed one. The three words referring to the king are evidently a later addition. In the message of the *Ish Elohim*, verse 35, read והלך לפני משיחי "He (the *Cohen*) shall walk before me my Messiah all the days."

" Seer " was still in usage, in common parlance, while the
" Prophet " was no less the official name of the " Man of
God," at the time when Samuel wrote, which was also the
case beforetime ; and this explanation is given to show why
Saul and his companions, as also the maidens, met in the city,
persistently called the prophet seer, the latter word being
yet in popular use, while the term prophet was the correct
expression. The populace looked upon the Man of God as
being a seer or soothsayer, while in fact he was the *Nabi*,
the inspired orator.

(3) First Samuel xxvii. 7 : "And Achish gave him (David),
Ziklag ; therefore Ziklag belonged to the Kings of Judah
unto this day." According to Joshua xix. 5, 31, there were
two Ziklags, one belonging to Simeon (1 Chronicles iv. 30),
and one to Judah. The former was captured by the Philistines and given to David by Achish, and remained crown
domain to the kings of Judah, the first of which was David.
Before he was made King of all Israel, it could have well
been said, that Ziklag was crown domain of the Kings of
Judah to this day. But if this be taken as one of the explanatory notes, the like of which were added to the historical accounts by some later writer, being in all cases explanatory notes only, they can not be taken as criteria of the age
of the text itself. As an instance of this kind may be
quoted (Joshua xix. 47), which could not have been written
in the time of Joshua, and yet it occurs in the topographical portion of Joshua, the authenticity of which none could
doubt, especially as it closes thus : " These are the inherit-
ances which Eleazar, the priest, and Joshua, the son of Nun,
and the heads of the fathers of the tribes of the children of
Israel, divided for an inheritance by lot in Shiloh before the
Lord at the door of the tabernacle of the congregation. So
they made an end of dividing the country." None of these
explanatory or marginal notes could have been written after
the fall of Samaria in 720 B. C., and the one regarding Ziklag may have been written at any time after the death of
Solomon ; hence they give no support to radical criticism
anyhow.

17. The Book of Kings, as it is now before us, consists of 22 and 25 chapters (modern division), 35 *Sedarim* (ancient division), 1,534 verses, the middle of which is 1 Kings xxii. 6. The contents of this book are :

Chapter i. to ii. 11. The last days and last will of David.

Chapter ii. 12 to v. 32. The earlier part of Solomon's reign.

Chapter vi. to ix. Building and dedication of the Temple ; the king's house and the other buildings and cities.

Chapters x. and xi. The latter part of Solomon's reign.

Chapter xii. Division of the kingdom in Judah and Israel ; Rehabeam and Jeroboam.

Chapter xiii. The prophet at Beth El, his mission and death.

Chapter xiv. to 2 Kings xvii. 6 is an abstract of synchronistic history of the two kingdoms, their kings and prophets.

Chapter xvii. 7 to 41. A review of the past. The establishment of the foreign nations in the country of Israel and their conversion.

Chapter xviii. to xxv. An abstract of the history of Judah, and the destruction of Jerusalem, with a later addition of four verses on the liberation of King Jehoiachin from prison.

18. Kings consists of four sections written at different times, viz.: (1) The first three chapters are from the book of the prophet Nathan. (2) The history of King Solomon, up to chapter xi., including the building of the Temple, is from "Dibrei Shelomoh" (1 Kings xi. 41),* which may have been written by one of the two prophets named in Chronicles (2 Chronicles ix. 29). (3) From 1 Kings xi. to 2 Kings xvii. is the work of one synoptic ; and (4) from chapter xviii. to the end of the book is the work of another and later synoptic, who also connected the various sections into

---

* According to the statement in 1 Kings xi. 41 : "And the rest of the acts of Solomon and all that he did, *and his wisdom*—are they not written in the book of the acts of Solomon?"—the literary productions of the wise king, hence also his Proverbs, at least up to chapter xxv., must have been contained in that book.

one book.   There exists no reasonable objection to the tradition, that this last synoptic and compiler was the prophet
Jeremiah.   These closing chapters begin with the lengthy
account of King Hezekiah, taken from Isaiah xxxvi.–xxxix.,
after this synoptic had repeated (xviii. 9–12) what the former
synoptic had written already (xvii. 1–6), showing distinctly
that a new account, by a different writer, begins there, which
is also apparent from the different phraseology of the last
author.   In his first chapter he mentions Moses three times,
viz., the serpent which Moses had made; the commandments which God commanded Moses; according to all
which Moses commanded, the servant of the Lord (as in
Joshua).   While the first synoptic mentions Moses but
twice in his entire book, and in entirely different phrases,
viz.: "The Thorah of the Lord, the God of Israel" (2 Kings
x. 31); As written in the Book of the Thorah of Moses (ibid.
xiv. 6) as in 1 Kings ii. 3.   In chapter xxi. the style of Jeremiah is easily discernible.   In the next chapters the narrative of an eye-witness is before us, one who is well-informed
in his people's history and literature.   What he narrates
briefly after the death of King Josiah he records at length
in his own book (Jeremiah xxxix. to xlii. and lii.).   The
same hand is discernible in both books.

19.   This last synoptic, however, could not possibly have
written the section of the first, which begins with the last
days of Solomon and closes with the fall of Samaria.   It is
not the history of Judah, it is the history of Israel and its
prophets, which was his main object.   He begins by placing
King Solomon in the very worst light he could without doing
violence to facts.   He then justifies the secession of the tribes
from the house of David and betrays nowhere any desire,
except in Elijah's altar on Mt. Carmel, of reuniting them.
He attempts *sub rosa* to excuse the schism introduced by
Jeroboam by condemning the Baal worship in much stronger
language than he censured the worship introduced by Jeroboam.   While he with special care reports the names and
marvelous deeds of the prophets in Israel and the sons of
the prophets, he has little or nothing to say of cotemporary

prophets in Judah, not even of Joel, Isaiah and his older cotemporaries. He omits important facts concerning Judah, Jerusalem, the Temple and the priesthood, narrated later by the author of Chronicles, so that it appears evident that he wrote the synchronistic history of Judah only as far as necessary for a better understanding of the history of Israel. This undoubtedly was the cause which prompted the author of Chronicles to write the history of Judah, Jerusalem, the Temple and priesthood without more than absolutely necessary reference to the history of Israel. Most remarkable in this connection is the notice that the priest who, after the fall of Samaria, was sent among the aliens of Samaria to teach them the laws and religion of the land, was one of the priests of Samaria, and not of Jerusalem (2 Kings xvii. 28). We have before us in the first synoptic an anonymous prophet, who, after the fall of Samaria, wrote the history of Israel with special reference to the synchronistic events in Judah. That he was a prophet is evident from the space he allots to the prophetical history. That he was an exact and truthful historian is evident now by the corroboration of his statements in the Babylonian-Assyrian inscriptions. It is no less evident that he must have written prior to Jeremiah. According to 2 Kings xvii. 19 he must have lived in the time of King Menasseh, as appears also from " unto this day " in verses 23 and 41. The only prophet from that period who might have written it is Habakkuk or Nahum; concluding from his prophecy, it was the latter, as shall be shown further on.

The first chapters from the Book of Nathan may be dated about 980 B. C.; the chapters from Dibrei Shelomoh, 960 B. C.; the first synoptic, 700 B. C.; the second synoptic and compiler of the whole book, 580 B. C., with the last verses added by one of the last prophets.

20. In these four books—Joshua, Judges, Samuel and Kings—we have before us a complete and chronologically correct history of the ancient Israel from their coming into the land of Canaan to the very day of their exile to Assyria and then to Babylon, all written by prophets for the instruction

of the people, with the outspoken object in view, to prove, by authentic history, that Israel's salvation is in God, his covenants, his law, and all national misery is divine retribution for rebellious conduct. As soon as these facts were known, these books became canons; therefore they were called Former Prophets. It has never been proved that any of these books, or any portion thereof, was ever re-written according to Deuteronomy or any other literature, nor could it be proved. The style, phraseology and tendency of the various portions of this literature are so entirely different from one another; the irregularities and unevenness in the language in various portions of the books also have been so conscientiously preserved, that evidently no corrector's or reviser's hand ever touched them. If such an attempt had ever been made to remodel them after the so-called Jahvistic or Deuteromic legislation, the Book of Judges and portions of the Book of Kings must certainly have been eliminated or re-written first. All alleged facts, data and names of persons and places noted in these books, whenever compared with other historical material having any bearing upon them, are corroborated and confirmed. Opposite such sources all *a priori* speculations underlying the construction or reconstruction of Israelitish history, are certainly illegitimate and unreliable. Hitherto all critics failed in disqualifying these historical sources. As these sources establish the facts narrated in the Pentateuch and its Mosaic origin, all *a priori* speculations, basing upon assumptions and hypotheses, are null and void. Indeed, the radical critics never attempted to invalidate these historical sources by internal evidence or by comparison with cotemporary events, they having started out with the hypothesis that there was no law of Moses prior to Ezra or King Joshiah, sought means to disqualify these historical books, because they undoubtedly testify to the existence of the Mosaic law prior to Joshua. In the face of this historical testimony, however, all hypotheses and speculations fall to the ground, and with them the whole artificial structure of radical criticism.

THE second part of the second Canon consists of the four prophetical books, Isaiah, Jeremiah, Ezekiel and twelve Minor Prophets. The names of the authors are given in each of the fifteen books, and in some of them the respective names are mentioned more than once; as, for instance, in Isaiah three times, twice in Ezekiel, thirteen times in Jeremiah, seventeen times in Jonah, three times in Zechariah, nine times in Haggai, twice in Hosea and Amos, and once at least in every other book. Some of those prophets are mentioned in other books of the Bible, as Isaiah in 2 Kings, Michah in Jeremiah xxvi., Jonah in 2 Kings xiv., Obadiah in 1 Kings xviii., Haggai and Zechariah twice in Ezra. Only in parts of Isaiah, Jonah and Zechariah is the authorship questionable; in regard to all the other prophets it is generally admitted that they are the authors of the books bearing their names, the exceptions to be noticed below, after we have ascertained the dates of those prophets.

2. It is necessary to review the literary monuments of these prophets in chronological order, as the knowledge of the emergencies and vicissitudes of every age furnish the key to a proper understanding of its literature. It is also of special interest and importance to know that a regular and uninterrupted succession of prophets is recorded in the sacred books. This establishes two facts: (a) the uninterrupted current of tradition in Israel, which is the main fort and support of its literary material; and (b) the continuous presence in all ages of history, of a prominent and numerous class of purely Jahvistic-theocratic worshipers and patriots as the main body of the nation, among whom the semi-paganized elements, of more or less numerical strength

at different times, were the demoralized exceptions in the normal condition of the nation.

Two facts must be borne in mind: (*a*) The prophets of Jehovah were at no time isolated individuals of a visionary characterr, or teachers of religion and guardians of morality exclusively; they were the representatives and spokesmen of the party of theocratic patriots, statesmen and advocates of human rights, the covenant and the law no less than stern teachers of. righteousness. (*b*) They appear in Scriptures under different names, as *Nabi, Chozeh, Ro'eh, Ish Elohim, Malach Elohim,* also, *Malach Jehovah.** These different names may designate different ranks among those inspired men, whose common title was *Nabi.* "spokesman" (Exodus iv. 14; vii. 1).

According to the traditions recorded in the Talmud there was an uninterrupted succession of prophets from Adam to Abraham. Prominent among them were Seth, Enoch, Methuselah (who was the head of an academy מדרשו של כתושלח), Noah, Shem and Eber; the latter two are also supposed to have been at the head of an academy, from which Abraham and Jacob derived their knowledge, called בית מדרשו של שם ועבר, and where also Rebecca went to inquire of the Lord (Genesis xxv. 22). In the time of the Patriarchs, we are informed in Genesis, there lived a considerable number of such inspired messengers of God (Genesis xix. 1; xxii. 11, 14; xxxii. 21). From Abraham to Moses

---

*The term *Malach* signifies "messenger." either profane or divine; if the latter, it is rendered "angel." It is synonymous with *Malachah,* "work," and designates a person or thing doing a certain work, an active agent, a factor. In Scriptures persons are called *Malach,* as the high priest in Malachi ii. 7, the prophet in Haggai i. 13, and elsewhere. In the Talmud the grandson of Aaron, Phineas, is called an angel in explanation of Judges ii. 1: "And an angel of Jehovah went up from Gilgal to Bochim." This angel was Phineas. The angel of Exodus xxiii. 20 is considered identical with the Nabi of Deuteronomy xviii. 15–22, by Moses Maimonides and others. Elements also are called angels, Psalms civ. 4, and the wind a word of God (ibid. cxlvii. 18).

the succession was Isaac, Jacob and their wives, Levi, Kehath, Amram and Moses, which seems to be based on 1 Samuel ii. 27, 28 and this again on Deuteronomy xxxiii. 8–11. However, the idea underlying this tradition may be that of successive revelation and the conservation of knowledge by natural means.

In the time of Moses many prophets are mentioned: Aaron, Miriam, Hur, Eldad, Medad, the seventy elders, and Moses expresses the wish that all the people of the Lord be prophets. Between Joshua and Samuel, although we possess of that time mere fragments and episodes of history, for the most time a bare nomenclature of Judges, the continuous existence of the Jahvistic-theocratic patriots as the bulk and kernel of the people and the appearance of prophets are continually noticed. In Judges i. 2 appears the *Malach Jehovah*, supposed to be Phineas. Ibid., chapter iii., appears Othniel, son of Kenaz, of whom it is said, "And the spirit of Jehovah was upon him" (verse 10). Chapters iv. and v. the Prophetess Deborah appears in her full glory of monotheism and theocratic patriotism. Ibid., chapter vi., there appears first the *Ish Nabi*, "the man prophet." who speaks to the children of Israel; then the *Malach* Jehovah, who speaks to Gideon; and then Gideon himself, of whom it is stated repeatedly, "And God said to Gideon." After the death of Gideon and Abimelech follows a long time of peace and prosperity, always supposed to be a period of theocratic piety, when no prophet is heard. Right after that follows Jephthah, of whom it is stated, "And there was upon Jephthah the spirit of Jehovah" (xi. 29). Then comes again the *Malach* Jehovah to the mother of Samson (xiii. 2), who is called in the same chapter *Ish Ho'elohim*, "The man of God" (verse 8), and plainly *Ish* (verse 10); and also Samson, of whom it is stated three times that the spirit of Jehovah moved and incited him (xiii. 28; xiv. 6, 19). This brings the prophetical succession down to Samuel, and with it the permanent Jahvistic theocracy also.

With Samuel begins a new period of prophecy and literature. For a long time none was acknowledged from Dan to

Beer Sheba, a prophet of Jehovah, as he was, no revelation
from Jehovah was received at Shiloh as Samuel did (1 Samuel iii. 20, 21). Tradition credits him with the establishment of the school of prophets at Najoth in Ramah, the
disciples of which were called *Bene Hannebiim*, "Sons of the
Prophets." Choruses of these prophetical disciples existed
in the land during the latter days of Samuel (ibid. x. 9, 10),
whose inspiring influence neither King Saul nor his messengers could resist (ibid. xix. 18-24), called there plainly a
chorus of prophets. Their presence and influence are
noticed in the historical records, also in the kingdom of
Israel, down to the end of the Ahab dynasty (1 Kings xx.
25; 2 Kings ii. 3, 5, 8, 15; vi. 1). This one fact proves the
continuous prophetical succession from Samuel to Elijah
and Elisha and Joel. The succession, however, during
this whole period is marked in the historical records also
by prominent names of prophets. Shortly after the death
of Samuel we meet with David in the cave of Adullam, the
Prophet Gad (1 Samuel xxii. 5). During the lifetime of
Saul, and to his very end, the prophets are there, although
no particular names are given (ibid. xxviii. 6). At the
court of David, as King of all Israel, we meet the Prophet
Nathan, high in authority (2 Samuel vii. and xii.; 1 Kings
i.) and also Gad (2 Samuel xxiv. 11-14). At the court of
Solomon the prophetical voice was suppressed, still at the
end of his days it resounds so much more terribly by Ahiah,
of Shiloh (1 Kings xi. 29-39), to whom is added in 2 Chronicles, Jedi the Seer (ix. 29). After the demise of Solomon,
the prophetical voice of Shemaiah is heard (1 Kings xii.
22-24; 2 Chronicles xi. 2-4; xii. 5), called in one account
Ish Ha'elohim, and in the other *Nabi*. Shortly after we read
of another *Ish Elohim* coming from Judah to Beth El
exhorting King Jeroboam, who finds in Beth El "an old
prophet" (2 Kings xiii.); and Jeroboam sends his wife
stealthily to the Prophet Ahiah. This phalanx of prophets
is succeeded in the days of King Asa by Azariah ben Oded,
and later on by Hanani the Seer (2 Chronicles xv. 1-7 and
xvi. 7-9). Cotemporary with Azariah was in Israel Jehu

ben Hanani, whose message to King Bashah is noted, 2 Kings xvi. 1–4. With Hanani the Seer we come down to the thirty-fifth year of Asa. Three years later Ahab mounts the throne of Israel, and five to six years later Jehoshaphat mounts the throne of Judah. During the reign of these kings appears the prophetical pillar of fire, Elijah the Tishbite, his disciple, Elishah, Michaiahu ben Jimlah, a host of true and of false prophets, and sons of the prophets. So also by this historical nomenclature we establish the continuous succession of prophets and the Jahvistic theocracy from Samuel to Elijah, about one hundred and fifty years.

The chain of succession is no less solid from Elijah to Isaiah, with whom a new period of prophetical literature begins. During the long reign of King Jehoshaphat the records show besides Elijah, Elishah and Michaiahu, also the Prophets Jahaziel ben Zechariah (2 Chronicles xx. 14–17); Eliezer ben Dodovahu (ibid. verse 37); Jehu ben Hanani again (ibid. xix. 2) and Joel ben Pethuel, of whom we treat below. These later prophets outlived King Jehoshaphat. During the next following sixteen years, under the reign of the wicked Jehoram, Ahaziah and Athaliah, no prophets speak, still those mentioned last must have outlived the evil years, as Elishah died thirty-eight years later (2 Kings xiii. 10, 14–20); and an exhorting letter of Elijah to King Jehoram is noticed in 2 Chronicles xxi. 12–15. During the reign of King Joash, the prophets are noticed (ibid. xxiv. 19), and especially Zechariah ben Jehoiada, who was slain in the court of the temple by command of the king. Under the successor of Joash, his son Amaziah, we meet again with the *Ish Ha'elohim*, and later on with the *Nabi*, announcing divine messages of retribution to this king (2 Chronicles xxv. 7, 15); and also Jonah ben Amithai from Gath Hepher (2 Kings xiv. 25), who prophesied success to Jeroboam II., as this king mounted the throne of Israel in the fifteenth year of Amaziah's reign. This brings the succession down to the time of King Uzziah, called in 2 Kings Azariah (xiv. 21), whose prophetical adviser was another Zechariah (2 Chronicles xxvi. 5)—perhaps identical with the one men-

tioned in Isaiah viii. 2—and in direct connection with Amos
(i. 1), Hosea (i. 1), Isaiah (i. 1), and his younger cotemporary, Michah (i. 1; Jeremiah xxvi. 18).   During the reign
of Ahaz there was also in Samaria the Prophet Oded (2
Chronicles xxviii. 9), whose remarkable influence upon the
victorious warriors of Samaria furnishes no mean evidence
to the effect that the Jahvistic theocracy predominated also
in the northern kingdom notwithstanding the schism of
Jeroboam.

Tradition accuses Hezekiah's son and successor, Menasseh,
of having slain the Prophet Isaiah, which says that he outlived Hezekiah.   This seems also to be the case with the
Prophet Michah.   It seems quite likely that Isaiah xiii. and
xiv. was written when Menassah was a captive in Babylon
(2 Chronicles xxxiii. 10, 11); and Michah vi. and vii. were
written in the time of that king.   Besides this, however, during the fifty-seven years of Menasseh's and Amon's reign,
when Jerusalem and the country were so much paganized,
the prophets were not silent.   The prophets' exhorting and
threatening voices are noticed in 2 Kings xxi. 11–15, and in
2 Chronicles xxxiii. 10, 18, where one of them, called Hozai,
is specially mentioned.   Besides them, as we shall see below,
Nahum, Habakkuk and Zephaniah belong to this age.   Thus
we are led in regular succession to the prophetess Huldah
and the Prophet Jeremiah.   In the time of this inspired and
woe-stricken patriot there lived an abundance of true and
false prophets, also ill-fated Uriah, who was slain by King
Jehoiakim (Jeremiah xxvi. 20–23), besides his younger
cotemporary, Ezekiel, in Babylonia.   There also was no
scarcity of both kinds of prophets, besides Daniel and his
companions (Ezekiel xxii. 23–28; xxxiv.), so that among
the colonies returning from the exile there were prophets
even besides Haggi, Zechariah and Malachi, and they were
there yet in considerable numbers besides the Prophetess
Noadiah in the time of Nehemiah (Nehemiah vi. 7, 12, 14).
With Haggai the millenium of prophecy closes, which begins
with Moses, and up to him no ring is missing in the chain
of succession.   So the genius of the Hebrew people mani-

fested itself continually and continuously for one thousand years through those favored persons, whose knowledge, wisdom, zeal and enthusiasm outshine and overtower all products of their cotemporary intelligence which have reached us. This is certainly marvelous if not miraculous.

3. The Book of Joel (Yo'el) ben Pethuel is before us in four chapters (modern division), of seventy-three verses, the middle of which is ii. 17. The whole of Minor Prophets, of which Joel's is one of the twelve books thereof, contains twenty-one *Sedarim* (ancient division), one thousand and fifty verses, the half of which is in Michah iii. 12, which, remarkable enough, is the direct prediction of the destruction of Jerusalem and its temple, a parallel to Amos ii. 5. This Joel book, undoubtedly written by himself, according to its purely Hebraic diction, clear and unequivocal phraseology, stands nearest among all the Later Prophets to the David and Solomon age, as it is reflected in the Davidian Psalms and Solomonic Proverbs. This, it seems, led some of the ancient rabbis to confound this prophet with Joel, the son of Samuel and father of Heman, the great master of music in the time of King David (1 Chronicles vi. 18). Later expounders, however, understood this rabbinical expression, "son of Samuel," like "disciple of Samuel," or one of the school of Samuel. This seems to be correct, as that David-Solomon period of the Hebrew style originated from the Samuel school at Najoth. The fact that this prophet knows of no Assyrian, Babylonian or even Syrian invasion of Judah, speaks of no dispersion and restoration of the nation, and mentions only Edom, Ammon, Moab and the Philistines as enemies of Judah, points distinctly to the latter days of King Jehoshaphat, when, according to 2 Chronicles xx. 1 and 10, those nationalities invaded Judah, and most likely after a long period of hostilities and depredations, were checked, not by the force of the Judaic arms, but by dissensions among themselves (verse 23), which forced them to flee in wild disorder at the approach of Jehoshaphat's army. This was shortly after a period of famine in the Kingdom of Israel (2 Kings viii.) under the

reign of Jehoram, and the Prophet Joel dwells on this subject most emphatically—the singeing drought which destroys
even the trees of the field, and the army of locusts which
consumes the last blade of grass, the consequent famine and
mourning among men and beasts, the prayers, fasts and
repentance of sins among the cheerless people, the mercy of
God and his final sending of the first rain and the latter rain
together in the unusual time of the first month of the year,
which puts an end to the misery (Joel ii. 23). All this
points to the days of Jehoshaphat and Jehoram. Besides
these points, there is yet the fact that Joel speaks with
reverence and adoration of Zion, the holy mount, the altar,
the sacrifices, the priesthood and their office, as none of the
later prophets do. This state of the cult and the law could
only have been in the time of King Jehoshaphat, whose reforms were not limited to the city and temple of Jerusalem,
but permeated the masses of the people (2 Chronicles xix.
and xx.); or in the time of the high priest Jehoiadah, or
King Hezekiah. However, the style of the book and the
peculiarity of the promises connected with this prophetical
oracle pointing to a time after the David-Solomonic age and
to the lofty inspiration of the Elijah and Elishah time, as
the conjuncture of events touched upon in the book point to
the time of Jehoshaphat, we may safely assert that Joel was
written in the decade prior to 880 B. C. This is also the
opinion of the celebrated commentator, Moses Chiquitilla,
expressed in his *Perush Threi-Assar.**

4. The first verse of Joel iv. is taken as a proof that this
chapter at least was not written before the fall of Samaria,
or perhaps not before the fall of Jerusalem. For that verse
reads: " For behold, in those days and in that time when
אשיב את שבות יהודה וירושלים (usually translated) I
will bring back the captives of Judah and Jerusalem; and I
will assemble all the nations and I will bring them down
into the valley of Jehoshaphat, and I will go into judgment

---

*The Valley of Jehoshaphat (Joel iv. 2) was afterward called
Emek Barachah (2 Chronicles xx. 26).

with them on account of my people and my inheritance, Israel, which they scattered among the nations, and my land (which they) divided." This is a mistaken notion, however; because

(a) In verses 3 and 6 the prophet states plainly that the scattered of Israel were either kidnapped or captured persons who had been sold to the Greeks as slaves, to which refer Amos i. 6–13; Zephaniah iii. 10, and Zechariah ix. 13, as is also evident from 2 Kings v. 2. Besides this, it is evident that voluntary migration of Hebrews began as early as the time of King Solomon.

(b) The phrase translated, "I will bring back thy captives," is a quotation from Deuteronomy xxx. 3, where it is evident from ישבת עד '' in the preceding verse, and from ושב וקבצך following this passage, as also from the Aramaic rendition by Jonathan, Ibn Ezra's quotation from Judah Chaiyug, the Sepurni and others, that it must be rendered: "And the Lord thy God will cause to return thy penitents." So, and not otherwise, this phrase must be understood here and wherever it occurs, as in Psalms xiv. 7 and liii. 7, as proved by Psalms lxxxv., where this phrase is followed by its definition: "Thou hast forgiven the iniquity of thy people, thou hast covered over all their sins." *

(c) The Prophet Joel (iv. 4) tells who they were that scattered Israel among the nations and divided its lands. They were the men of Tyre, Zidon and Philistia, the marauders and slave-traders of those days, and not the Assyrians or Babylonians; consequently, he must necessarily have spoken of a time prior to the very first Assyrian invasions, if even the phrase in (b) is understood as in the authorized English translation.

There is evidently no trace in this whole book of any time after 880 B. C.

5. Amos was the oldest of the four prophets that prophesied simultaneously, viz., Hosea, Amos, Isaiah and Michah. According to tradition Hosea was the oldest, but not accord-

---

* See MECHILTA, Friedmann's edition, p. 16b., on וישב.

ing to the testimony of their respective books. Amos prophesied in the time of Jeroboam II., King of Israel, and Uzziah, King of Judah (Amos i. 1), and not even to the last years of King Jeroboam. If he had known of the victories and conquests of this king, the glorious achievements of his cotemporary, King Uzziah, in Judah, and the reviving hopes and prosperity of the people (2 Kings xv.; 2 Chronicles xxvi.), he must have noticed them in his speeches. Hosea (i. 1) lived from the time of Uzziah and Jeroboam to the time of Hezekiah. In his prophecies the victories and conquests of both kings, the wealth, prosperity and reviving hopes of the people, connected with unbridled luxury and moral corruption, are re-echoed in unmistakable language. On the other hand, it is evident that this prophet had no knowledge of the Assyrian invasion in the fourth year of Hezekiah, and the Shalmon Baith Arbal in x. 14 can not refer to Salmanaser, who reigned from 727-725 B. C., as he only knew of emigrants that had gone to Assyria and Egypt. He only knows of the hope and confidence placed in that power and in Egypt (Hosea xi. 5, 11; xiv. 2-10), which points directly to the time of King Ahaz (2 Kings xvi., and 2 Chronicles xxviii.). His prophecies can be placed only between the last years of Rehoboam II., and about the middle of the time of Ahaz. Isaiah (i. 1) was a younger cotemporary of Hosea. In the heading to this book the name of Jeroboam is omitted. His prophecies, however, beginning with the death of King Uzziah (vi. 1), are chiefly from the time of Ahaz and Hezekiah and reach into the time of King Menasseh. Michah must have been a younger cotemporary of Isaiah, whose diction he has acquired, and with whom he has form and contents of prophecy and even texts in common (Michah iv. and Isaiah ii.). He is noticed (ibid. i. 1) in the reign of Jotham, Ahaz and Hezekiah only. Still he has evidently not seen the fall of Samaria. His prophecies can be placed only between Ahaz and the sixth year of Hezekiah. The dates for these prophecies may be thus:

Amos, 816 to 780 B. C.

Hosea, 750 to 730 B. C.

Isaiah, 735 to 700 B. C., with chapter vi. from 757 B. C.

Michah, 735 to 720 B. C.

5. The Book of Amos, written by him, is before us in nine chapters (modern division), 146 verses, the middle of which is v. 15, remarkable for the shortness of its chapters, of 13, 14, 15, 16, 17, and but one of 27 verses. He came from among the herdsmen of Thekoa, a town noted for its wise women already in the time of King David (2 Samuel xiv.). When he was expelled from Beth El by the priest, he said of himself: "I am no prophet and no son of a prophet; I am a herdsman and a gatherer of sycamore fruit; and the Lord took me, as I followed the flock, and the Lord said to me, Go, prophesy unto my people Israel" (Amos vii. 14, 15). But once he refers to the misdeeds of Judah (ii. 4, 5), as he does to the surrounding petty nations, and twice to the punishment in store for Judah (vi. 1). All his messages, exhortations and prophecies are directed to Israel and its King, Jeroboam II., with the only exception of the closing message, in which he announces the restoration of "the fallen booth of David" and the restoration of Israel and its country after the period of devastation and desolation.

There are system and unity in Amos' book. Chapter i.–iv. consists of prophetical messages, v.–ix. of prophetical visions, with an exalted *finale*. The diction is not as simple and clear as in Joel; it contains some few orthographic irregularities, aside of which it is idiomatic and classical.

6. The Book of Hosea (Hoshea), son of Beeri, a citizen of the northern kingdom—according to the traditions the scion of an aristocratic family—is before us in fourteen chapters (modern division), 197 verses, the middle of which is vii. 13. This book, like Amos', is remarkable for its short chapters, the longest of which is one of twenty-five and the shortest one of five verses. The book begins with prophetical visions (i. to iii.) symbolizing the prevailing corruption in the Kingdom of Israel and closing up hopefully for Israel's re-elevation and its return to the only God and the Davidian dynasty, i. e., to union with Judah. This portion was evidently written in the earlier period of the prophet's life;

v.–xiv. consists of prophetical speeches of a stern character, addressed to the people, its priests and the house of its king, recounting in forcible language the prevailing aberrations and corruptions and announcing with perfect certainty the punishment, the particular nature of it, which will come over the commonwealth, and the restoration of Israel after the punishment shall have purified the remnant of the people; i.–iii. is prosiac, vi.–xiv. is rhythmical, that kind of blank verse in the various forms of parallelism which makes Hosea in diction the immediate forerunner of Isaiah. The language is antique but faultless, the phraseology frequently elliptic and enigmatical. Amos speaks like an inspired herdsman, Hosea like a trained orator of the prophetical school, not so well used as his predecessor to the popular diction.

7. The Book of Isaiah (Yeshayah or Yeshayahu) ben Amoz—according to tradition the nephew by his father of King Amaziah—is before us in sixty-six chapters (modern division) *thirty Sedarim* (ancient division), 1,295 verses, the half of which is xxxiii. 21. Besides chapter vi., which is a prophetical vision, consists, from i. to xxxv., of prophetical orations, and xxxvi. to xxxix. of historical narratives, three episodes from the life of King Hezekiah. From xl. to lxvi. are again prophetical orations, of a different nature, however, than the former. The former, except chapter vi., refer to the time of the Kings Ahaz and Hezekiah. Chapter one points clearly (verses seven and eight) to the invasion of Judea by Rezin and Pekah in the time of Ahaz. The next following four chapters can not refer to any time during the reign of King Jotham, who was a God-fearing man (2 Kings xv. 34) and an eminent ruler over a prosperous people (2 Chronicles xxvii.). They could refer only to the time of Ahaz. It seems that these five chapters were not considered by the compilers of equally high degree of prophecy with the following chapters, and were therefore placed before the beginning of his prophetical speeches. Nowhere in these chapters is it found that God said or spoke to Isaiah, as it occurs in the next following chapters (vi. 8;

vii. 3, 7; viii. 1, 5, e. s.) These first speeches are character-
ized by the terms חזון and חזה, " vision " and not by verbal
communications from God, as are other chapters of the same
book. If the amendation was not too venturous, we would
say vi. 1 should read : " In the year of the death of Jotham."
Isaiah was first an inspired teacher of righteousness, who
became a prophet in the time of the invasions, wars, national
misfortunes and catastrophes with which the eighth century
B. C. closed. The heading *Massa*, which the prophet assumes
from the thirteenth chapter, distinguishes his prophecies to
the Gentiles from those to Israel. His references to Babylon and its downfall may have been inspired by the successful
rebellion of Morodoch Baladon, in whose success he saw the
rise of another powerful enemy to the smaller countries between the Euphrates and the River of Egypt, whose final
downfall, however, he predicted, and it was fulfilled ; for
Morodoch was slain six months after his messengers to
Hezekiah returned, and under his son and successor Babylon
was retaken by the Medes. The prophet, hostile to all
reliance on foreign powers, is no less hostile to any reliance
on the then youthful and promising power of Babylon,
whose speedy downfall he predicts. Chapter xix. merely
shows that the emigration from Judea and Israel into Egypt
was as numerous then as it was into Babylonia, to escape
from the power of Assyria, as is evident from other passages
in Isaiah. He prophesied success to the emigrants in Egypt,
as he did prophesy the downfall of Babylon. Egypt is near
and Babylon very distant from Palestine. The emigrants to
Egypt, he may have thought, might return after the fall of
Assyria, or might always remain in close intercourse with
their country and people, neither of which could be expected
from those that migrated to distant Babylon. There exists
no necessity to suppose that any chapter, or part of one,
from i. to xxxix. was not written by the very Isaiah, son of
Amoz, whose name is at the head of the book. The tradition
that Hezekiah and his commission " wrote," or rather collected and compiled the book of Isaiah, might be correct if we
presume that the said literary commission, called in Proverbs

"the men of Hezekiah," was not dissolved at once after the
death of that king. The absence of dates and chronological
succession in parts of the book could only prove that the
compilers were governed by another than the chronological
principle, as is also the case in Psalms, the twelve Minor
Prophets and partly also in Jeremiah. It is yet to be
ascertained what that principle was. The Talmud admits
אין מוקדם ומאוחר בתורה "there is no chronological order
in the Thorah," without informing us of any other principle
which guided the compilers. The other tradition of the
Talmud, however, that King Menassah slew Isaiah, seems
to be a mere allegory suggesting that Menassah in his
wickedness uprooted and destroyed all the piety and patriotism which Isaiah had cultivated among his people. With
Isaiah begins the third epoch of the Hebrew language. His
vocabulary is the richest, his tropes most artistical, his
diction fully rhythmical, his poesy as mystical and sublime
as Job's or Homer's, all of which he outshines by the total
absence of fiction in his speeches and the unparalleled
power of formulating most sublime truths in the briefest and
most expressive words. He, like Joel, is a prophet of Judah
especially. Israel in his time was an enemy of Judah, and
later on it fell with the destruction of Samaria by Salman-
asar. Then came the invasion of Judea by Sennacherib and
his discomfiture before the walls of Jerusalem. These are
the main events which engaged the mind of Isaiah, except
where he casts the seer's glance into the distant future of
Israel and the human family, full of hope and cheer, also
under the most distressing vicissitudes of the present, with
unlimited confidence in the course of Providence, the future
of mankind, the final triumph of truth, righteousness and
goodness among all nations.

8.   Isaiah xl. to lxvi. is the product of another prophet, or
other prophets, that lived from near the close of the Baby-
lonian captivity to a time after the dedication of the Second
Temple, 540 to 510 B. C. This is partly admitted by that
Talmudical tradition which, in the order of prophets, places
Isaiah after Ezekiel. Besides it is maintained in *Leviticus*

Rabba, chapter xv., that two prophecies of Bari, father of Hosea, were attached to the book of Isaiah; hence it is admitted that not all of that book is of Isaiah. Abraham Ibn Ezra, in his commentary to Isaiah, maintains that Jekaniah, or Jehoyachin, the King of Judah, who was carried captive to Babylon in the ninteenth year of his life (2 Kings xxiv. 8), and kept there imprisoned thirty-seven years, till released by Evil Morodoch, was the very prophet who produced those chapters of the Isaiah book.* This ingenious hypothesis accounts well for the classical Palestinean diction and many obscure passages in the book, but not for all. Zerubabel could not well have become Governor of the colony as long as the legitimate King of Judah lived, and part of the Deutro Isaiah was certainly spoken after the return from Babylon. The fifty-third chapter of Isaiah, like chapter fifty-seven, seems to be the funeral oration over that very king, whose self-sacrifice, sufferings and final triumph are well described there. Anyhow, the diction shows that it is not the product of the same prophet as the other chapters. The same is the case with the closing chapter of Isaiah and several passages in other chapters. This forces us to admit that we do not know who was the author or authors of Isaiah xl. to lxvi., although it is evident that they were written in the time between Darius I. and Darius II., between 540 and 510 B. C., in the century prior to Ezra and the close of the prophetical cycle. It seems from the double tradition in the Talmud in placing Isaiah before Jeremiah, or after Ezekiel, that there were two different books of Isaiah before the compilers of the Canon, an older and a younger Isaiah, which at a later date were connected in one book, as was also the case with the five chapters of Lamentations, which are certainly not the product of one author, or with the Book of Psalms, of which we treat later on.

---

*According to rabbinical tradition (*Echah Rabba*) " Lamentations" was written in the time of this king, and by Jeremiah; hence Lament. iv. 20 refers to this king, and there he is called "Messiah of the Lord; " and the terms, *nilkad bishchithothom,* rather point to Jekaniah than to Joshiah, who was slain and not put in chains.

The diction of Deutro Isaiah is entirely different from the first in the vocabulary, metaphors, vocatives, tone and tendency. He is less poetical and more rhetorical and compares rather to Demosthenes than to Homer. He is most vehement and agitating, rousing to immediate action. His tropes, similes, apostrophes or personifications are mostly taken from the celestial sphere, always grand and universal, or from the most tender sentiments of the human sexes, the bride, the mother, the daughter of Zion, the confiding child. He always speaks of Jacob, Israel, the servant of the Lord; never of Judah, Zion, or even Jerusalem, except when he refers to its ruins and desolation. He adresses some of his messages to Cyrus, whom he calls the Messiah of the Lord, is less national and much more universal than any one of the older prophets. He is in style, tendency and fundamental thought so entirely different from Isaiah and the spirit of his time, that he could not possibly be indentified with his older namesake and his age, although that great unknown may have borne the same name (See Ezra viii. 7) or assumed it. The contents of his prophecies identify him with the age of Zerubabel.

9. The Prophets after Isaiah to the Babylonian captivity are Nahum, Habakkuk, Zephaniah, Jeremiah, Obadiah and the unknown author of the book of Jonah. The book of Nahum (Nachum) is before us in three chapters (modern division), seventy-four verses. The name is unique, although it is evidently formed of Genesis v. 29 and became the parent to the later name of Nehemiah and Nehuniah. In the Talmud the name recurs, and passages from this prophet are quoted without any reference to his person or to the place "Elkosh" added to his name. There was in Palestine a place called *Kephar Nahum,* or Capernaum. This may have been the Elkosh, called afterward after this prophet, but there exists no proof for it, no more than that it was the El-Kauzah near Ramah in Naphthali. He certainly was a citizen of the northern kingdom whose downfall he had witnessed. The diction of Nahum is so similar to that of Isaiah and Micah that he may be easily recognized as their

disciple. He prophesied the downfall of Nineveh and the Assyrian Empire, therefore his book is a *Massa*, like Isaiah's prophecies to the Gentiles. His prophecy was announced after the fall of Samaria (*Nahum* i. 4-6), and after the retreat of Sennacherib from Judah (ibid. ii. 1-3). This occurred in 710 B. C. Between this and the year 706 B. C. the Assyrian Empire was in a state of dissolution; many provinces besides Media revolted; Sennacherib raged furiously among his own subjects till he was finally slain by his sons. This was the time when Nahum prophesied the destruction of Nineveh, which, however, did not come to pass till a century later, in the year 612 B. C., although the Assyrian Empire soon fell into the hands of the Babylonian dynasty. The prophet, still aglow with the vengeance which he thought God would execute on Nineveh, opens his message thus: "God is jealous, and the Lord revengeth; the Lord revengeth and is furious; the Lord will take vengeance on his adversaries, and he reserveth *wrath* for his enemies." No other prophet ever presented God in such a state of fury. As these expressions can not be understood to convey the idea of what God is or was at that time, being contrary to Moses in Exodus xxxiv. 6, they can only inform us of the prophet's state of mind at that particular time, which could have been the case but shortly after the fall of Samaria and the invasion and downfall of Sennacherib before Jerusalem, all that misery being still present to the prophet's mind, with the faith in God's justice firmly established in his soul. We may, therefore, fix the date of Nahum's prophecy between 710 and 705 B. C. The book has no proper close and appears to be the fragment of a larger work.

10. Habakkuk, also consisting of but three chapters and fifty-six verses, is in diction the same as Nahum. He sees the Chaldeans approach (i. 6), speaks of their conquests, audacity and the slaughter of multitudes of human beings, like the fish and the creeping things abandoned by Providence (i. 7-17). He prophesies, however, salvation and reformation to Judah, knows of no destruction of Jerusalem

and no downfall of the nation (ii. 3, 4), and predicts the
downfall of the Chaldean invader almost in the same words
as Isaiah prohesied the fall of Babel (xxi. 5–8). Then he de-
nounces the moral corruption and the idolatry in the highest
places of Jehuda's government (ii. 9–20). He refers to the
crushing defeat of Sennacherib, his miserable end and the
salvation of Hezekiah (iii. 12–14) as an encouraging precedent of God's help in the time of distressing need, and
closes up his inspired message with joyous hope and unshaken trust in Providence. It is evident, therefore, that
Habakkuk did not refer to the last invasion under
Nebuchadnezzar, but to an invasion prior to this, one which
did not result in the overthrow of the Kingdom of Judah.
This could be either in the time of King Jehoiakin (2 Kings
xxiv.), in the fourth year of his reign, or in the time of
Manassah, in the year 677 B. C., when Esarhaddon, the
Asnapper of the Ezra book (Ezra iv. 10), being king of both
Assyria and Babylonia, invaded Palestine, placed foreign
colonies in Samaria (2 Kings xvii. 24), defeated the army of
Manassah and sent him in chains a captive to Babel. The
latter date is most likely. For Habakkuk speaks distinctly
of a prevailing idolatry in Judah (ii. 19), which certainly
had no existence in the land after King Joshiah's thorough
reforms, so that both Kings and Chronicles denounce the
successors of Joshiah as wicked kings, but not as idolators,
nor does the prophet Jeremiah speak of any prevailing idolatry at any time after the Joshiah reformation. The visions
of Ezekiel refer to the time of Manassah and Amon. It is
safe, therefore, to place the prophecy of Habakkuk between
680 and 677 B. C.

11. Zephaniah, whose book consists also of three chapters, fifty-three verses, informs us (i. 1) that he prophesied
in the time of King Joshiah, after the destruction of Nineveh
in 612 B. C. (ii. 13–15). Idolatry had disappeared from
the public places, only the "remains" thereof among the
higher aristocracy, including the princes and the king's sons,
were left. The ex-priests of Baal are mentioned by them
with equal reverence with the *Kohanim*, the priests of the

temple. " Upon the roofs " of their private houses only they bow down to the host of heaven, and in their private parlance they swear by the name of God and their chief idol. They are the class that deserted God, or that never sought to know him or inquire of him (Zephaniah i. 4-8); or the class that did not believe in the prophets and would not inquire of them. The principal persons accused of wickedness and corruption are the *Saarim*, "princes," and the sons of the king, "that leap on the threshold," are the frequent visitors in the royal palace and " fill their master's house with violence and deceit." The master's house in this case is evidently the king's palace, as the term master in the Hebrew is in the plural number (as in Genesis xlii. 30). All this points to the last days of King Joshiah, as is evident from the youth of his immediate successors as well as by a careful comparison of 2 Kings xxiii. 26-28; 2 Chronicles xxxvi. 27, to Josephus' Antiquities X. v. 1, and Talmud *Shabbath* 40 and *Thanith* 22, which shows that the king in the last years of his government was not as pious a ruler as in former years. Zephaniah gives as the cause of this change the princes and the sons of the king. The last year of Joshiah being 610 B. C., it is evident that Zephaniah prophesied and wrote 612 to 610 B. C. He was a senior cotemporary of Jeremiah.

12. Obadiah, of whom we possess one message of twenty-one verses against Edom, is identified in the Talmud with the Obadiah in the time of Ahab (1 Kings xviii. 3).* Abraham Ibn Ezra raises objections to this identity, and places this Obadiah in the time of Nebuchadnezzar, which is supported by internal evidence. For the diction of Obadiah is not the poetic, artistical style of Isaiah; it is in meter and metaphor much more like Jeremiah. The whole speech prophesies the downfall of Edom and the final triumph of Mount Zion.† It is no longer Zion in its glory and its

---

* He may be identical with the Levite Obadiah from the fourth year of Joshiah (2 Chron. xxxiv. 12).

†See also Lamentations iv. 21, 22, which seems to be the text to Obadiah's speech.

power—it is Mount Zion, which " will be holy " when " the house of Jacob shall *again* possess their possession " (verse 17).   Edom is still powerful and prosperous (verses 3 and 4), it possesses yet its rock-bound capital (verse 3), has yet its savants, sages and heroes (verses 8 and 9).   Evil is predicted to the dominion of Esau : " For thy violence against thy brother Jacob, shame shall cover thee and thou shalt be cut off forever" (verse 10).   And now follows the specification of that violence (verses 11–14) :

" On the day that thou stoodst on the other side, on the day that strangers carried away captive his army, and foreigners entered into his gates, and cast lots over Jerusalem, also thou wast as any one of them.   But thou shouldst not have looked on (pleased) at the day of thy brother, on the day that he was delivered up to strangers ; neither shouldst thou have rejoiced over the children of Judah on the day of their destruction ; nor shouldst thou have spoken proudly on the day of distress.   Thou shouldst not have entered into the gate of my people on the day of their calamity ; yea, thou shouldst not have looked (pleased) on their affliction on the day of their calamity ; nor have laid hands on their army on the day of their calamity.   Neither shouldst thou have stood in the crossway, to cut off those of his that did escape ; neither shouldst thou have delivered up those of his that did remain on the day of distress."

No such a time of extreme calamity to Jerusalem and Judah is recorded in history prior to the destruction of the city by the host of Nebuchadnezzar.   It is evident, therefore, that Obadiah prophesied the downfall of Edom after the destruction of Jerusalem, 586 B. C., although the prophecy was fulfilled four and a half centuries later under John Hyrcan.   It is no less evident, as in the case of Nahum, that the prophet did speak shortly after the catastrophe, as he knew all the particulars of Edom's wrongs perpetrated on Jerusalem and Judah in that catastrophe.

13. Jeremiah, son of Hilkiah, a priest from the priestly city of Anatoth, in Benjamin, northwest of Jerusalem and within ten miles of it, was the inspired patriot of a heroic

age. From the Tigris to the Nile all countries were in a state of turmoil and incessant warfare—offensive and defensive. Palestine and Phœnicia were the special objects of contention between the two powers, Egypt on the west and Babylon-Assyria on the east. Independence of any nationality between these two countries had become impossible; every one of them had to submit, either to Egypt or to Babylonia. The land of Judah, from and after the capture of King Manassah, had been subject to the eastern empire, and remained in this state of dependency, also, after the restoration of Manassah, under Amon and Joshiah, with whose death the active hostilities of those two empires reopened, and ended for Judah with the memorable catastrophe of Jerusalem's destruction and Judah's exile to Babylonia, 675-586 B. C. Jeremiah's prophecies began with the thirteenth year of the reign of Joshiah, which was 631 or 630 B. C.; the year can not be exactly fixed. The first reforms of Joshiah occurred (2 Chronicles xxxiv. 3) in the twelfth year of that king's reign, hence, simultaneously with Jeremiah's first prophetical speeches. Joshiah's first reforms could naturally extend only to Jerusalem, and culminated in the renovation of the temple, and the finding of the original copy of the Book of the Covenant (2 Chronicles xxxiv. 14); and then his second reforms, in the eighteenth year of his reign, or shortly thereafter, extended to the country and the territory of the Kingdom of Israel. This invasion of the northern kingdom could certainly not have occurred as long as Assyria was in its full power; hence it must be placed after the fifteenth year of Joshiah's reign, when Nabopolassar rebelled against the King of Assyria, and made himself King of Babylon. This again culminated in his third reform, the great Passover celebration, in which it is maintained (2 Kings xxiii. 21; 2 Chronicles xxxv. 18) all Judah, the remaining multitude of Israel and the inhabitants of Jerusalem took part. Jeremiah's name is not mentioned in connection with any of these reforms, nor does he anywhere identify himself with them. When the Book of the Covenant was found in the temple the king inquired of the prophetess Huldah, and not of Jeremiah, whether the punishment predicted in it would be inflicted on Judah; hence Jeremiah's authority was not yet established.   He must have preached for some time in Anatoth (Jeremiah xi. 21, 22; xii. 5, 6) before he went to Jerusalem (ibid. ii. 2), and his first speech there (ii. 2 to iii. 5) was evidently made after the death of Joshiah (ii. 17, 36).   It appears, therefore, certain that the reform of King Joshiah and the discovery of the original Book of the Covenant fired the soul of that young priest to prophetical inspiration, and he preached and prophesied entirely in the spirit of that reformation and on the principles of that Book of the Covenant, without being an acknowledged authority among the numerous true and false prophets of those days.*   His authority grew after the death of Joshiah, when the reaction set in, and corruption and demoralization increased with the growing power of the foreign potentate, as patriotism, self-reliance and faith in Providence decreased.   It seems he was not generally acknowledged as a true prophet prior to the catastrophe, when his predictions had been so terribly fulfilled.   Then, and perhaps as late as 550 B. C. (Jere. lii. 32), his manuscripts were collected and connected in a Book of Jeremiah.   The compiler may have been Baruch, the scribe of Jeremiah, or the liberated King of Judah himself.   His prophecies became then the pillar of hope to the exiled (2 Chronicles xxxvi. 21, 22; Daniel ix. 2), and roused that hopeful and joyful enthusiasm which re-echoes in the Deutro-Isaiah, Haggai, Zachariah, Zerubabel and Joshiah, the high priest.

14.   The Book of Jeremiah is before us in fifty-two chapters (modern division), thirty-one SEDARIM (ancient divis-

---

*The supposition that then and there Deuteronomy was forged upon the name of Moses is as contrary to the historical sources, which plainly and repeatedly state, that it was the "Book of the Covenant" which was found in the sanctuary, as is that other hypothesis which gives to Jeremiah the authorship of Deuteronomy; both are the illegitimate products of those who were misguided by the prior hypothesis, that Moses could not be the author of the Pentateuch.

ion), 1,365 verses, the middle of which is xxviii. 11. The fifty-first chapter closes: "Till here are the words of Jeremiah," while the fifty-second chapter is an addendum, part of which is taken literally from the closing chapters of Kings, omitting the story of Gedaliah, which is narrated at length in Jeremiah xli. That it was taken from Kings, and not *vice versa*, is proved by the corrections in Jeremiah. But the closing passage concerning the release of King Jehoiachin from prison was copied from Jeremiah into Kings. This seems to confirm the hypothesis that this King was the compiler of the Jeremiah prophecies. The body of the book contains three elements, viz., admonitions, predictions and cotemporary history. The admonitions are all of the same character, the people, priests, princes and kings are forcibly reminded to submit to the Thorah, the law of God, and be saved in the coming catastrophe, or disobey and perish under the coming wrath. The prophet is fully convinced that the punishment is sure to come. His predictions are no less categoric. He spoke invariably the same: "You submit to the dominion of Nebuchadnezzar and save your lives, country, city and temple from destruction, or you resist and lose everything. Babel will fall and Babylonia will be dissolved. Egypt also will perish; so will Philistia, Tyre and Zidon, Moab, Ammon, Edom and Damascus. Then Judah and Israel may regain their independence, former splendor and power, if you only hold fast to your God and his Thorah, adhere to your cause and the divine covenant. But even if you remain rebellious and lose everything, the nation and its cause will not perish. After seventy years your offspring will return to their country and continue the preservation of your nationality and your cause as better men and women than their rebellious ancestors." In the midst of all distress and calamity Jeremiah ceased not to predict a gracious future for coming generations in Israel, which will outlive all its mighty adversaries; and in all that, in the threatened punishment and promising future, Jeremiah only enlarged on the predictions of Moses (Deut. xxviii. to xxxii. and Leviticus xxvi.), whose words, phrases,

doctrines and precepts fall continually from the lips of
Jeremiah. His diction and rhythm are original, having
nothing in common with the poetical sublimity, beauty and
polish of the Isaiah period, or with the Samuel school.
Speaking continually of facts which exist or are to come,
and hurried by a rush of exciting events and calamitous and
terror-striking emergencies, Jeremiah speaks evidently without bestowing any care on the form, "as God put it into his
mouth," yet at times loftily poetical. He quotes from
older prophets or imitates frequently more ancient phrases,
as we shall show elsewhere. Still, in the main he speaks
like a disciple of Moses, without, however, the brevity and
conciseness of Moses, so that Rabbi Judan ben Simon (in
Pesikta Rabbathi) could maintain Jeremiah was a prophet
like Moses in admonitions, and some critics suspect him to
be the author of Deuteronomy, although it is of an entirely
different spirit, form, contents and diction, except perhaps
Deuter. xxviii.; and this is too frequently used by Ezekiel to
be the work of Jeremiah.

15. The most remarkable imitation occurs in Jeremiah
xlix. 7–22, where the prophecy of Obadiah is transcribed
and enlarged upon. It can not well be maintained that Obadiah imitated Jeremiah, for if so, his one-chapter speech
would certainly not have been accepted among the minor
prophets compiled some time after the Jeremiah book. Besides, all the prophecies to the Gentiles from Jeremiah xlvi.
to l. are of a different cast. They are more compact, betray
less excitement, and are full of consolation to Israel and
Judah. However, being in tone and spirit of the same cast
with his other speeches, it proves only that they were written after the destruction of Jerusalem, after the prophet's return from Egypt, when his mind was calmer than it was during the war, and, all being lost, he had retired from public
life (except chapter li., which he wrote in the fourth year of
Zedekiah), to write his last prophecies in some retired and
isolated spot, far away from the turmoils of life. Passages
like chapter x., supposed to be imitations of Deutro-Isaiah,
are certainly original with Jeremiah and imitated by the

Deutro-Isaiah, who succeeded him in time. The variations in the Greek translation embodied in the Septuagint prove nothing against the authenticity of the Massoretic text, as the Septuagint was several times remanipulated, and could also be accounted for by the presumption that the translator had before him the defective copy of an unknown and unauthorized compiler. It is, therefore, safe to maintain that Jeremiah wrote and spoke between 630 and 580 B. C., and his productions were compiled 550 B. C. in one volume, as is now before us in the Book of Jeremiah. It is evident from the numerous Massoretic annotations in this book, more than in any other, that nothing was changed in the original manuscripts by the compiler. The exactness and truth, also, of the contemporary history recorded in the book testify to its authenticity.

16. The Book of Jonah is before us in four chapters (modern division), forty-eight verses. Jonah (Yonah), son of Amithai, is the name of a prophet from Gath-Hepher, in Zebulon, who flourished in the earlier days of Jeroboam II., 812 B. C., and prophesied the victories which this king achieved (2 Kings xiv. 25). It is possible enough that this prophet went on a divine mission from Samaria to Nineveh, preached there repentance and moved the heathen (and Hebrew?) population of that ancient capital to penance and reformation, and that this story was preserved traditionally in Israel, especially because at home the prophet did not succeed in the same kind of work. But it is not probable that the same prophet was the author of the Book of Jonah. It contains terms and phrases of much later Hebrew. The prayer of Jonah in chapter ii. is mostly an imitation of other Bible passages.* The idea of a prophet attempting to escape from before God is taken from Jeremiah, who assiduously attempted not to prophesy and to speak in the name of God, and did not succeed (Jeremiah xx. 7–18); the idea is allegorized in Jonah, and the irresistible force in the soul

---

*The whale is not mentioned in the original, it is a "large fish." of which the Septuagint and Josephus made a whale.

of Jeremiah, compelling him to speak, is represented here by the storm and the fish which swallows Jonah. Also the idea that God would forgive the penitent sinners, the punishment would not overtake them, and the prophet would appear a false prophet, is outlined in Jeremiah (xxviii. 5–9). So is Jonah iv. 3, 8 almost literally from Jeremiah, so that there can be hardly any doubt left that the Book of Jonah was written after Jeremiah. Other ideas contained in this book point distinctly to the cosmopolitan time which had its start in the exile. God cares also for the sinful heathens, and extends his mercy to them. God's mercy extends even to the cattle of Nineveh. God forgives the penitent without any sacrifices or intercession. The heathens are even better than the Israelites who would not listen to the admonitions of their prophets. The office of the prophet is not to work miracles and to prophesy; it is to announce the will of God to his erring children. Conceptions like these will fit only into that century, and are worthy of the prophet in whatever form he expressed them—in legend, allegory, myth or fable. The book could not have been written much later, as it was accepted in the Propheticel canon, and its author constantly uses the tetragrammaton. It was evidently not written after the close of the prophetical era. It is safe, therefore, to maintain that the Book of Jonah was written about 540 B. C. Its pseudonymous author elaborating the Jonah tradition, must have been one of the Hebrew exiles in Assyria, as his diction is foreign, he knows more of Nineveh than of Palestine, and calls himself an *Ibri*, a Hebrew, as none either in Judah or in Israel called himself. It is evident from Ezekiel that in his time a great revival of faith took place among the Assyrian exiles. It was to them that Jonah preached this divine message on the efficacy of repentance, as a continuation of Ezekiel's message to them. (See Ezekiel xx.)

17. Ezekiel (*Yechezkel*), the son of Busi, a priest dwelling in a colony of the exiles on the Chebar River, east of the Euphrates, then belonging to the land of the Chaldeans, was the only prophet of the period of the Babylonian exile. His

prophecies were collected and compiled in one book by the Men of the Great Synod, a century or longer after his demise. For this Synod was instituted by Ezra about 445 B. C., continued its existence to at least 300 B. C., as Simeon the Just, who died 292 B. C., was its last President. If Ezekiel was thirty years old in the fifth year of King Jehoiachin's captivity (Ezekiel i. 1, 2), 592 B. C. and lived forty years thereafter, he must have died 552 B. C. These dates, however, are uncertain. The prophet may have had this vision on Chebar River after he had lived thirty years in that colony, may have prophesied prior to that in the twenty-seventh year of his stay among the exiles (Ezekiel xxix. 17), and may have been well advanced in age when he had that great vision of the throne of God, by which he considered himself initiated in the highest prophetical degree. The fourteenth year after the destruction of Jerusalem (Ezekiel xi. 1) may have been his last prophecy, and mark, also, the last year of his life, 572 B. C. This date seems to be correct, for he says nothing of the liberation of King Jehoiachin, which occurred about 561 B. C., and produced a thorough change in the condition of the exiles, one which the patriotic prophet could not possibly leave unnoticed. He speaks of no king of Babylon besides Nebuchadnezzar, refers to nothing which transpired in the last decade of this king's reign, and sees his own people only in a state of despair, as they must have been in the decades immediately after the destruction of Jerusalem. Therefore, if we presume that Ezekiel lived his threescore and ten, it is safe to place him from 640 to 572 B. C. He migrated, perhaps voluntarily, to the Chebar River in the eighteenth year of King Josiah, and in the thirtieth year of his abode there, which is in the fifth year of King Jehoiachin's captivity (see Rashi to Ezekiel i. 2), he began his prophetical career, about 592 B. C., when about forty-four years old.*

---

*According to *Seder Olam* (Rashi to Ezekiel) the eighteenth year of King Josiah was the jubilee year, therefore Ezekiel dates from that year. He mentions the jubilee year also in chapter xlvi. 7, as שנת הדרור" exactly in the sense of Moses.

18. The book of Ezekiel is before us in forty-eight chapters (modern division), twenty-nine *Sedarim* (ancient division), 1,273 verses, the middle of which is xxvi. 10. Dates are at the head of some chapters from the fifth to the twenty-fifth year of the captivity of King Jehoiakim. In diction and the main subjects of prophecy it is like the Book of Jeremiah, with some Aramisms which betray its author's residence in the land of the Chaldeans. The latter is also the case with the allegories of his visions, especially his descriptions of the throne of God, which, in addition to the original (Isaiah vi.), are reflexes of Chaldean astrological conceptions. He is unlike Jeremiah in his originality; besides Moses, he imitates none. He wrote like one who knew no literature besides the books of Moses. He knows Noah, Job and Daniel as righteous men (xiv. 13, 19), the latter also as a wise man (xxviii. 3), but betrays no knowledge of a book of either Job or Daniel. He elaborates the same ideas (ii. and iii. 8–10) with Jeremiah i. on entering the prophetical office and his unwillingness to prophesy (iii. 11–15) like Jeremiah, but shows no further acquaintance with his older cotemporary's literary productions. He refers (vi. 5) to King Josiah's work at the altar of Beth-El, from memory, it appears. Except his last prophecy on Seir (xxxv.), which sounds like Jeremiah's and Obadiah's in the main, he evinces no knowledge of any literature except the books of Moses. He not only reproduces largely terms, phrases and sentences peculiar to Moses, but amplifies laws of Moses and expounds them at length in the very phraseology of Moses. So, for instance, iii. 16–21, he advances the idea of the *Zopheh's*, or prophet's responsibility for the well-being of the congregation, which is an amplification of Deuteronomy xiii. 2–6 and xviii. 15–22. Again, Ezekiel xiv. and xviii. are amplifications of Deuteronomy xxiv. 16, in connection with Exodus xxxiv. 5–7 and Numbers xiv. 19–20. Again, Ezekiel xxxvi. is a reproduction of the above chapters, and all four of them are completely in the phraseology of Moses. It appears that the prophet, far away from his home, had no other literature of Israel at his command. His thorough

knowledge, however, of the nations from Ethiopia to the Caspian Sea and the Hindus River, their history, political conditions, industries, commerce and products of the soil (for instance, chapters xxvii. and xxviii.) is plain evidence of his vast information and access to the world's literature, such as no other writer of those days does show, not even Herodotus and Xenophon in the century after Ezekiel. Judging Ezekiel from the poetical standpoint his affluence of words and metaphors is admirable. His allegories and symbols are frequently most sublime, although in several instances grotesque and even coarse, as in chapter iv. He speaks, more than any other of the prophets, like a teacher rather than an orator, so that it seems that teaching was his profession in the colony. Judging him from the ethical and national standpoint, Ezekiel occupies the highest position among the great prophets. Among a people inclined to Paganism, with causes then deemed sufficient to doubt their God's power and willingness to save them, and, stunned by the nation's downfall, given to despair, ready to yield to the victor's faith and wisdom, Ezekiel rises like a pillar of fire on a dark night, a mighty and successful pleader of Israel's imperishable cause and God's inviolable promises, a terror to the wicked and wickedness, a reviving sunshine and refreshing shower to the moral sentiments, the national faith and hope, and he did resurrect the dead in the valley of Dura. In that chapter (xxxvii.) he merely describes his mission and his work.

19. The book of Ezekiel contains three distinct parts : (1) from chapters i. to xxiv.; (2) chapters xxv. to xxxix.; and (3) from chapters xxxix. to xlviii. In the first part he prophesies, in substance the same as Jeremiah, the approaching end of the kingdom of Judah either by submission to Nebuchadnezzar or by utter destruction and exile, always maintaining that the end is not the final end, but is to lead to a higher state of national life and prosperity after the sins shall be expiated by the national sufferings ; also always maintaining that the righteous and the penitent shall not perish in the catastrophe. In the second part he is the

prophet of consolation; the trumpet of resurrection, the comforter and harbinger of glad tidings to his people, the pleader of Israel and the advocate of God's tender mercies. All his messages to the Gentiles, including the "Gog" prophecies in chapters thirty-eight and thirty-nine, have the same object in view as with Jeremiah. They are to announce that all those nations and governments, however mighty and vigorous, will perish, and Israel in consequence of the covenant will outlive them; that the name of God be proclaimed and hallowed by them.* A special feature of Ezekiel's work is his teaching among the exiled Israelites from the Northern kingdom. It seems that the Thel Abib colony was composed of the older Assyrian exiles from the Kingdom of Israel and the later emigrants from the Kingdom of Judah. The elders of Israel, like the elders of Judah, come to the prophet to seek instruction (Ezekiel xiii. 24; xx. 1). He announces to them the divine oracles, pleads their cause, prophesies salvation to them, predicts their reunion with Judah, sees the land of Israel repopulated and prosperous (chapter thirty-six) and knows of no distinction any longer between the two kingdoms (chapter thirty-seven). In the third part, Ezekiel lays down a plan for a new temple, service, city and geographical division of the whole land of Palestine, for the twelve tribes, retaining the sacrificial polity and Levitical priesthood of Moses with some minor changes, and changing entirely the old division of the land.† This document and, it appears, the whole of Ezekiel was unknown to Zerubabel, and it appears also to Ezra, as none of those provisions were adopted in the second temple and commonwealth. Like other prophets, Ezekiel's authority

---

*The "Gog" prophecy is in substance no more than an amplification of Jeremiah xxx. 10, 11, whether he did or did not think of the Scythians.

†It did not appear to Ezekiel or to the other prophets that the Mosaic provisions for the sacrificial polity were originally intended to be unalterable, or else he could not have proposed changes as he did.

during his lifetime was but local; he was one among many cotemporary prophets (Ezekiel xiii. and xx. 25). It was difficult to distinguish the true from the false prophet. In his locality, it appears from the general tone of his speeches, and especially from xii. 27 and xxi. 5, he met with many unbelievers. Besides, Ezekiel never left the colony, and this was too far from Babel to be known there. His name is not mentioned in any other book besides his own. So it appears certain that the prophecies of Ezekiel were not generally known before the Men of the Great Synod, perhaps after the death of Ezra and Nehemiah, collected and compiled the manuscripts in the present book. Centuries later, it is reported in the Talmud (*Shabbath* 13*b*), the learned men wanted to take the Book of Ezekiel out of the Canon, "Because his words contradict the words of the Thorah." * This contradiction can refer to Ezekiel's third part only, as in all his other prophecies he re-echoes Moses, and often literally. Ezekiel's temple, city and division of the land were intended for the reunited twelve tribes, which did not come to pass prior to the victories of Alexander the Great.

20. Three prophets of whom literary productions are extant appear in Israel's history after the return from the Babylonian captivity, Haggai, Zechariah and Malachi. Their common sepulcher on Mount Olivet, near Jerusalem, is yet venerated by the men of the three monotheistic religions. With these three hesperi closes the prophetical Canon, and also the code of the Twelve Minor Prophets, the fourth book of Later Prophets, which contains the prophecies of twelve prophets, divided, like Isaiah, into sixty-six chapters, one thousand and fifty verses. The Talmudical tradition reports many prophets coming back from Babylonia with Zerubabel and with Ezra, who were members of the Great Synod. Prophets are mentioned also in Nehemiah, together with the

---

* One Hananiah ben Hezekiah saved the book and the honor of the prophet.

prophetess Noadiah (vi. 7, 14)*. Besides those three and
this prophetess, none is mentioned by name in Scriptures.
In the historical sources Haggai and Zechariah only are
named (Ezra v. 1). Malachi appears nowhere outside of
his book. The Talmudical tradition, therefore, reports Malachi as an appellative, and his proper name as Mordechai,
or Ezra (*Meguillah* 15), the latter being generally accepted.†
It is maintained, therefore, that with Malachi or Ezra closes
the prophetical millennium beginning with Moses, in round
numbers 1450–450 B. C. This "Twelve Books," according
to the Talmudical tradition, being written, or rather compiled, in its present form by the Great Synod, the prophetical Canon could not have been completed before the fourth
century B. C.

21. The Book of Haggai (*Chaggai*), consisting of two
chapters, thirty-eight verses, is dated from the sec ond year
of Darius II., in the sixth month of that year, the three
oracles respectively the 1st, 21st, and 24th days of that
month, 519 B. C. He mentions the fact, that the twenty-
fourth day of the ninth month, the same year, building on
the temple was resumed (ii. 18). All his oracles except one
passage are admonitions to Zerubabel and Joshua the high
priest to resume work on the temple before permission was
given by Darius II. One passage (ii. 11–13), addressed to
the priests, is casuistic, and sounds like similar passages in
Zendavesta. This may be the reason that Haggai has be-

---

* Only four prophetesses are named in Scriptures, Miriam, Deborah, Huldah and Noadiah. They belong to four periods of history, and are intended to suggest the principle that in the highest
spiritual sphere also woman always was the equal of man.

†*Zebachim* 62a it is stated from Mishnath Rabbi Eliezer ben Jacob that three prophets came up with them from Babylon, one to
testify to the exact spot where the altar was, another to testify
that sacrifices might be offered up before the temple was built,
and a third one to sanction the re-writing of the Thorah in the
Assyrian characters (as it now is). No names are given there, although it appears that the two former were Haggai and Zechariah and the latter Malachi or Ezra himself.

come so prominent in the Talmudical traditions, more so than his contemporaries (*Yebamoth* 16; *Kiddushin* 42). There can be no doubt as to the literal authenticity of this book, although its diction, rhythm and prophetic address distinguish its author not from the prophets of the previous century.

22. The Book of Zechariah (*Zecharyah*) is before us in fourteen chapters, 211 verses. He was the son of Berechiah, from the descendants of Eddo, the prophet. Eddo flourished in the time of the first Jeroboam and his son, Abiah, in the tenth century B. C., and could not be the grandfather of Zechariah in the sixth century, hence we understand that Eddo was the ancestor by whom his family was distinguished. It was deemed necessary to add to the prophet's name, "Son of Eddo, the prophet," because there was another Zechariah, son of Berechiah (Isaiah viii.), who was also a prophet (2 Chron. xxvi. 5) in the time of King Uzziah, evidently an older contemporary of Isaiah. Zechariah opens his prophetical career in the same year, and but three months later than Haggai, continues the same on the twenty-fourth day of the eleventh month (i. 7) and then gives us no other date until vii. 1, which is dated the fourth month of the fourth year of Darius, although chapter vii. was certainly written after the rebuilding of the temple, which occurred 515 B. C. Thus we know that his prophetical time was but five years, 519 to 515 B. C. The substance of his oracles is the same as Haggai's, encouraging Zerubabel, Joshua and the people to complete the sacred structure. There is also a piece of casuistry in Zechariah (vii. and viii.) referring to the abolition of the four national fasts. Zechariah is more eloquent and poetical than his cotemporary. He marks the decadence of prophecy into the apocalyptic visions. He is frequently visited and spoken to by angels, sees allegoric visions which represent no truths in themselves and become instructive by the explanations only. With him Satan appears for the first time as a figure of prophetical vision. The same decadence of the prophetical power as observable from Jeremiah to Ezekiel is observable

also from Ezekiel to Zechariah. Haggai speaks more like Jeremiah; Zechariah betrays the Babylonian influence, while Haggai speaks like a Palestinean that had not left his native country — as if the former had been a disciple of Ezekiel and the latter of Jeremiah. If the same Zechariah wrote also the fourteenth chapter of this book—which is doubtful—then he may certainly be taken as a disciple of Ezekiel. For this chapter xiv. is in substance identical with Ezekiel's Gog prophecy (chapters xxxviii. and xxxix.) If one takes with this the Book of Daniel, he can clearly conceive that the apocalypsis, in which finally the ancient spirit of prophecy is submerged, is of Babylonian origin; the Hebrew and the Chaldean geniuses interwoven produced this new phenomenon, as in later days the conflict of the Hebrew and the Greek geniuses produced other phenomena, and foreign to both. It is also well to bear in mind that—what is so frequently noticed in the Talmud—with these last prophets begins the era of casuistry. The prophet's intuitively productive mind having lost most of its buoyancy, comes down to discursive reasoning, as we will see especially in Malachi, and ends in casuistry.

23. The five chapters of Zechariah from ix. to xiii. are certainly not the production of the post-exilic Zechariah. They begin in two instances with *Massa* (ix. and xii.), like Isaiah and his immediate successors, announcing divine oracles to the Gentiles; and this prophet addresses his first *Massa* to Syria, and the second to Israel, then the enemies of Jerusalem and Judah. This points at once to the invasion by Pekah and Rezin in the time of King Ahaz. He speaks of no enemies besides those coming from Syria, Tyre, Zidon, Philistia and the Greek slave-traders (ix. 2, 5, 6, 13), as did also Joel (see above, chapter iv. 3, c.) No Assyrian, no Babylonian, no Egyptian enemy, not even hostile Edom, Ammon and Moab, are known to the prophet, exactly as in the days of Joel. He speaks of the Kingdom of Ephraim and Joseph (ix. 10; x. 6) as a living reality. He knows no Hebrew exiles in Assyria, except those from the East Jordan land and the Lebanon, and a few of them in

Egypt, when both these countries are still in their power
and glory (x. 10, 11). He speaks of three shepherds being
vanquished in one month, which could refer only to Ahaz,
Pekah and Rezin (xi. 8, 9). He describes the prophets with
the hoary garments and "wounds between their hands"
(xiii. 3-6), not as they did appear at any time after,
but as they appear prior to the exile, in the days
of Elijah and Elishah, and contemns them exactly as
did Michah (iii. 5-7). He calls the princes *Alluphei Jehudah*,
and after the captivity they were called *Chorim, Seganim*,
never *Alluphim*. He speaks of the Crown Prince Hezekiah
(ix. 9) as did Michah in his time (v. 1-3), and changes
Michah's *Ki attoh yigdal ad Aphsei Aretz* into *Umoshelo miyam
ad yam*, etc., which means the same.* Besides all this the
diction, rhythm, phraseology and prophetical buoyancy in
these five chapters are entirely different from the Zechariah
style, and sound fully like the classical Isaiah time. It
seems, therefore, evident that these five chapters belong to
the earlier Zechariah, son of Berachiah, mentioned in Isaiah
and Chronicles, and were attached to the second Zechariah
by mistake, as was attached the second Isaiah to the first,
not by the compilers of the Canon, but by later transcribers.

24. Malachi is before us in three chapters of fifty-five
verses. With him begins the polemic dialogue against
skepticism, so well perfected in Job and Ecclesiastes.
It sounds like a distant echo from the prophetical cata-
ract. The temple is built, all its institutions are there;

---

* *Vehibbitu aili eth asher dakaru* xii. 10 refers to to the *Yosheb
Yerusholaim* in the same verse, therefore he changed the *aili* into
eilav. In verse eleven the prophet speaks of the mourning over
Hadadrimon in the valley of Megidon. This ceremony identical with
that mentioned in Ezekiel xii. 11, the women of Jerusalem wept over
the sungod Tammuz, and Hadadrimon being identical with Hadad,
the sungod of the North Syrian tribes, could not possibly have been
observed in the valley of Megido in the time of Zechariah, when all
paganism had disappeared in Judah. It is distinct reference to an
older Zechariah, when such pagan practices still could be imagined
as existent in Judah.

they are already old and damaged by the neglect and skepticism of the priests and corruption among the people. He
begins with an old *Massa* once addressed to Israel and
Edom (i. 1–5), which is his text, basing upon which he
conducts his polemics against the levity and corruption of
priest and people.

He describes the ideal priest (ii. 4–8) and compares with
him the low and despised priesthood of that day. He
threatens them with the sudden approach of the master in
his palace, whom he calls the angel or messenger of the
covenant, and considers himself the forerunner of him who
will purify the palace and its servants. In the thirty-second
year of Artaxerxes Longimanus, Nehemiah returned to
Susa, and remained there nine years. He returned to
Jerusalem and found everything in a state of anarchy
(Nehemiah xiii.). He enforced again the Law and the Ezra
reforms with his own, described vividly in the closing chapter of Nehemiah. Shortly before the return of Nehemiah
to Jerusalem Malachi must have delivered his incisive dis-
courses. If Nehemiah came first to Jerusalem in 445 B. C.,
remained there twelve years, and then again nine years in
Susa, he came the second time to Jerusalem 424 B. C., after
the death of Artaxerxes. Then Malachi must have spoken,
in the years 426 and 425 B. C., the last echoes from the
prophetical lyre. The closing verses of this book (iii. 22–
24), it is maintained, are the solemn words of the compilers
of the prophetical Canon, to connect all with the Thorah of
Moses which God commanded him at Horeb for all Israel,
and to remind the reader that zealous prophets like Elijah
always came and always will come to bring back to God the
hearts of the parents with the children. That is to say, the
right man in proper time always appeared, and always will
appear, to enforce the Thorah of Moses. This refers princi-
pally to the regular and uninterrupted succession of
prophets from Moses to Malachi, one thousand years and
more of prophetical inspiration.

CHAPTER V

HAGIOGRAPHY.

THE nine (or thirteen) books of Scriptures called "Hagiography," or sacred writing, mentioned as such in
the translator's introduction to Ben Sirah's book and in
Josephus, are called in the Talmud plainly כתובים writings or scriptures, and in the later Hebrew works כתבי
קודש holy writings or holy scriptures, and it is maintained
כתובים נאמרו ברוח הקודש "These writings were said
(or written) under the influence of the holy spirit." This
is the degree inferior to the nine degrees of prophecy. In
none of these books is it stated that God said or spoke to
the poet or commanded him, except in Job, and in Daniel
which is apocalyptic, angels take the place of the voice of
God. Psalms, Song of Songs and Lamentations are purely
lyric; Proverbs, Job and Ecclesiastes (also some Psalms)
are didactic; Ruth, Esther, Ezra, Nehemiah and Chronicles
are historiographic, without any attempt or even pretension
at prophecy. In the first Christian century some of the
Rabbis proposed to take out of the Canon Proverbs, Song of
Songs, Ecclesiastes and Esther, but did not succeed, as was
the case also with the Book of Ezekiel. The three books of
Psalms, Proverbs and Job, called by the Massorites א׳מ׳ת
in reversed order, the initial letters of *Thillim*, *Mishlei* and
Iyob—are provided with signs of accentuation different
from other books of the Bible, which point to a chant in
ancient time peculiar to these books, as they are also different in rhythm and parallelism, being regularly divided
in verses of two or three parallel lines, each line of three or
four words, exceptionally of two or five words.

2. The five books of Psalms are five collections made at
different times. The last compiler, connecting the five into

one book, did not obliterate the conclusion of each book, nor did he make any other changes in the text. This last compilation appears to have been accomplished in the time of the Maccabean prince and high priest Simon. Each book except the first contains psalms of different poets and anonymous hymns, without reference to chronology, from David, or even Moses (Psalm xc.), down to the Maccabean age (ibid. cxviii.). The first book, with the exception of the four anonymous psalms, i., ii., x. and xxxii., are all ascribed, or inscribed, to David. The second book opens with eight psalms of the sons of Korah, followed by one of Asaph, then follow again Davidian psalms from Psalm l. to lxx., with one anonymous psalm (lxxi.), which appears to belong to the previous one, closing with the psalm addressed to Solomon, the doxology and the remarkable words. " The prayers of David, son of Jesse, are finished." This state-ment, which was there in most ancient times (*Pesachim* 117*a*) shows that the compiler of the second book knew the first and preceded those of three following books, as in each there are Davidian psalms. The third book opens with ten Asaph psalms, followed by two of the sons of Korah, then one of David, and two more of the sons of Korah, and closes with the psalm of Ethan, the Ezrahite, and a simple doxology. The fourth book consists, besides the prayer of Moses (xc.) and two psalms of David (ci. and ciii.), of anonymous psalms exclusively. The fifth book again con-tains fourteen Davidian and one Solomonic among its forty-eight psalms.

3. The fact that some of the finest psalms are anonymous —and some of them, like Psalms cxxxv. and cxxxvi., are evidently very old—proves that the headings were found as they are by the compilers, who must have verily believed that those psalms, ascribed or inscribed to David and Solo-mon, were, in fact, their own literary productions, as is cer-tainly the case with Psalm xviii.; or at least that they were written by contemporaries of those kings. Fifty-nine head-ings of psalms, also the musical instruments and the close of chapters are quoted and discussed in the Talmud by

teachers, reaching up into the first Christian century (see *Toldoth Aaron*), hence the same headings were there then as now in the Massoretic Bible. The only difference is that Psalms was divided then in 147 chapters and now in 150.*

This fact is also apparent in the *Shir ham-Maaloth* chapters (Ps. cxx. to cxxxiv.), five of which are ascribed to David, one to Solomon, and nine are anonymous. The same is evident from the *hallel* psalms. These are the hymns chanted by the Levites in the temple every feast and new moon day as part of the divine service. All of these psalms are anonymous, although certainly very old, as the origin of the custom even is beyond the traditions of the Hebrews. There are two sets of this *hallel*, one consisting of Psalms cxxxv. and cxxxvi., which is called *hallel haggadol* in the Talmud, "the great or rather the older hallel," and the other is called *hallel hamitzri*, "the lesser or younger hallel," consisting of Ps. cxiii. to cxviii. A cursory inspection of these two *hallel* convinces the reader that the second is an elaboration and amplification of the first and replaced it in the temple service.†

---

* The reason of this 150 division may have been liturgical, to finish the whole Psalm book annually twice, reciting one daily, Sabbath excepted, for which the psalm was specially marked (Psalm xcii.), making twenty-five every month, and may have been made at the end of the third century. We know that the Levites sang daily in the temple the *Mizmor shel Yom*, "the psalm of the day" (*Mishnah Thamid* vii. 4). The particular psalms noted there may have been taken from an extant list, intended for any particular week. Traces of the group of five are still there, as, for instance, the *Shigayou* Psalm v., the *Lammah* Psalm x., the five festive *hallel* Psalms cxiii.-cxvii. (cxviii. was added later), the five anonymous *Lechu Nerannenah* hymns xcv.-xcix., the fifteen *Shir ham Maaloth* hymns cxx.-cxxxiv., and the five Hallelujah hymns closing the whole book. It is custom yet with many to read five psalms daily, except on Sabbath, for which was made a special collection.

† 1 Chronicles xvi. 8–36, identical with Psalms cv. 1–15 and xcv. is also an elaboration and amplification of this first hallel, and is therefore anonymous in both cases.

Yet not even the rabbis knew the time of the origin of the lesser *hallel*, and differ in opinion on the subject from the time of Moses to the Babylonian exile. (See Talmud in *Pesachim* 117 and 118.)* This lesser hallel contains no reference to any event by which the approximate date of its origin could be fixed. The older hallel, however, clearly and distinctly points to the earliest days of the Hebrews' first commonwealth, to Solomon's temple, or even to the tabernacle of Shiloh. It is primitive in form with its unison responses of "His goodness endureth forever" without including the name of God. It praises God, without the use of any abstract terms, for his grace manifested in the creation of the world, the wonders he wrought for Israel in Egypt, and in the conquest of Sihon and Og and all Canaan. Then it deprecates idols and idolatry and admonishes Israel to praise and worship Jehovah. The only mention of Zion is in the last verse of the one hundred and thirty-fifth chapter, and this is also omitted in the one hundred and thirty-sixth. There is no mention of any event beyond the conquest of Canaan. The antiquity of these *hallel* psalms can not be doubted, and yet the compilers left them anonymous, as they found them. No more proof is necessary, all *a priori* speculations notwithstanding, that the compilers of Psalms invented no headings; they found them so and exactly so in the MSS. which they compiled. The accusation of pious fraud and pseudonymousness would certainly be in the wrong place here, where no reason is imaginable inducing anybody to falsify a religious people's prayers, hymns and anthems, especially if the best of them are without name or date. Criticism will have to accept the headings of the Psalms as genuine and authentic, even if there is a discrepancy in the heading of Ps. lxxxv. Nor is it legitimate to doubt that King David was the author of Psalms. The poet and musician, as represented by the authors of Nehemiah (xii. 46)

---

* In Shir Hashirim Rabbah כמנדל דוד Ezra is mentioned as one of the ten authors of Psalms.

and of Chronicles (1 Chronicles xv. 28; 2 Chronicles vii. 6; xxix. 16, 17, and elsewhere), if we know that he surely did write Ps. xviii. (see 2 Samuel xxii.), and is noticed as the sacred bard in 2 Samuel xxiii.; Amos vi. 5; Ben Sirah xlvii. 8-9; 2 Maccabees ii. 13, besides 2 Samuel xxii.*

4. The argument that the Psalms were corrected, reshaped and rewritten by the *Menazeach*, or "Chief Musician," and hence that we are not in possession of the original text after all, does not invalidate their authenticity. For this suspicion attaches only to those Psalms which are headed *Lamnazeach*, "to the chief musician," and concerning them we possess documentary evidence that euphonious changes only and none of sense or phrase were made, as is the case also with the *Tikkun Sopherim* and *Ittur Sopherim* in the Thorah. The *Menazeach* fitted the text to his chorus, melody or orchestra, which sometimes required rhythmical or euphonious improvements of the text. By comparing carefully Psalms xviii. with 2 Samuel xxii.; Psalms xiv. and liii. (or Isaiah xxxvi -xxxviii. with 2 Kings xviii 17 to xx. 19; or 2 Samuel vii. with 1 Chronicles xvii.; 1 Kings viii. and 2 Chronicles vi.); or the passages in Psalms cxliv. taken from Psalms xviii., viii. and xl.—and these are actual cases of transcriptions and no *a priori* suppositions—faithful adherence to the original texts is proved, and the changes made by the transcribers are without the least import to the sense of any passage.

5. The various compilers of Psalms evidently betray their intentions to put together lyric devotional compositions of former days. The close of the second book offers proof that it was compiled after the first and before the third. In this

---

* It is remarkable that Psalms begins with the word אשרי, which word in the plural and in this sense occurs nowhere in Scriptures prior to this time, except in the concluding verse of Deuteronomy (xxxiii. 29), so that Psalms certainly points back to the Thorah. (See *Midrash Thehilim* to Psalm cxix.) The same seems to be the case in Proverbs, which begins משלי, a word found nowhere in Scriptures prior to this time, except in Numbers xxiii. and xxiv.

third book, especially Psalms lxxiv.* and lxxix., the
destruction of Jerusalem and the burning of the temple are
noticed, and in the chapter closing this book the end of the
Davidian dynasty is lamented; the throne, like the altar, is
crushed. Although there are in this book, as in every
other, very ancient psalms (lxxx. to lxxxviii.), it could not
have been compiled prior to the destruction of Jerusalem.
This, however, shows that the two former books were compiled prior to that catastrophe. The fourth book (Psalms
xc. to cvi.) is again a cheerful and joyful collection of
excellent hymns and prayers, entirely different in tone from
the third book. The compiler tells us in clear words at the
end of his little book that he flourished after the restoration,
evidently in the time of Artaxerxes Longimanus. Although
it is very difficult to show with any degree of certainty that
any psalm was written as late as the time of the Maccabees,
yet the fifth and last book contains, with very ancient
psalms, also the latest compositions of this kind, like the
six *hallel* psalms, Psalm cxix , which is certainly the text
book from the boys' school, the five closing Hallelujah
psalms, certainly hymns from the second temple, and
others, so that its compilation could not well have been
accomplished long before the Maccabean time, when the
third Canon was fixed. The first two books, however,
belong to Israel's first commonwealth. The first, being the
Davidian psalm book with the loftiest hymns, like Psalms
viii., xix., xxiv., xxix., xxxiii , full of re-echoes from nature's
secret shrine and the spirit of holiness and devotion, is
certainly the oldest. It is completely Jehavistic, while the
second book is mostly Elohistic.†

---

*Psalm lxxviii. was certainly written before the exile, as were
most all chapters of the third collection.

†That the divine names, Jehovah and Elohim, do not point to
different authors or ages, is especially evident from Psalms. The
Davidian Psalms in Book I. are Jehavistic, and in Book II., with
others, mostly Elohistic. There must be another reason for the
frequency of this or that divine name.

The masters of song and the musical instruments are different in the two books. In Book I. the King is yet called the Messiah, and David is twice called the servant of the Lord; in Book II. there is the King only and no longer Messiah. Book I. refers continually to the house of the Lord, to Zion, and to the Thorah, all of which disappears in Book II. The hapless Levite (Psalms xlii. and xliii.) laments his absence and distance from the house of God, which is far beyond his reach. Book I. mentions historical events from the advanced age of David, and Book II. refers only to the earlier days of David. Summing up these criteria, we can but come to the conclusion that Book I. was compiled in Judah, when Zion and Moriah were in their highest glory; and Book II. was compiled in the Kingdom of Israel when its decline had come, mostly from the products of lamenting Levites, who by the schism of Jeroboam had lost their sacerdotal dignity. The Levites had their fifty-two cities in Israel, and the priests their thirty-two cities in Judah (1 Chronicles vi.). However, there is no chapter in Book II. that could be proved to reach beyond the reign of Jeroboam II., and none in Book I. that reaches beyond the earlier days of King Solomon. In Book I. are the main hymns of David, written in his advanced age and for the use of the Levites in public worship; therefore the tetragrammaton is used, as in all other psalms intended for that purpose. In Book II. are such psalms of David which he wrote in his younger days, not intended to be recited in public worship; therefore the term Elohim is used in place of the tetragrammaton. They being omitted in the first collection, the compiler of the second book added them to the psalms of the sons of Korah, which are from the Levites of the Northern Kingdom, and seem to have been used in the worship at the altars on the Heights, *Bamoth* of the faithful, that did not worship at the altars of Jeroboam. It is safe, therefore, to date the compilation of the five books of Psalms thus:

Book I. 900 B. C.

Book II. 800 B. C.

Book III. 550 B C.

Book IV. 450 B. C.

Book V. 140 B. C., when the present canon was closed.

6. The Book of Psalms, as before us in the Massoretic text, consists of one hundred and fifty chapters, divided into 2,527 verses. Psalm lxxxviii. 36, is marked as half of the book in the number of verses. These Psalms have become the substance of the civilized nations' devotional literature and imposed their phraseology on most all modern languages. They breathe stirring religious inspiration in the simple, often childlike, language of nature, and give sympathetic expression to every form of human woe—now tears crystallized in plaintive words, then soothing consolation rising to triumphant hope, and jubilant anthem, soaring aloft, with the strains from a heavenly lyre, from the dark valley of misery to the very throne of the ineffable Deity. Words, human language, appear inadequate to the psalmist to utter the praise and glory of the Almighty, and he invokes all nature, the quick and the dead, to sing and shout Hallelujah; all nature is roused from its deathlike slumber to proclaim aloud the glory of its Maker. It is the loftiest species of poetry; the pinions of the highest genius could soar no higher, and none did, because the ideal of the psalmist is the most sublime; few could reach, none surpass it. The psalmic tropes, metaphors, similes and parables, personifications and apostrophes are linked to nature, its immutable forms and phenomena; there is no artificial imagery in them. Therefore, they are felt and understood universally, and impress equally forcibly the illiterate child of nature and the man of culture, if they are not too much estranged to nature and piety. This is perhaps the main cause of their universal adoption. Most important, however, is the collection of odes, hymns, didactic poems, *Shir*, *Michtham* and *Maskil*, as a text-book of theology. It presents to us what those ancient Israelites during a period of eight centuries believed, prayed, hoped, what they sang and what they felt, how they rejoiced and how they wept; the soul of a whole people, with all its mysteries, is unveiled

before our eyes, not in the dry formulas of dogmatics, nor yet in the abstract definitions of philosophy, but in the animate and non-deceptive language of prayer and adoration.

7. The theological doctrine represented in Psalms is beyond any doubt the religion of the ancient Israel. Whatever were the laws, rites and cults, and however they changed, these were the well established and fixed beliefs, well rooted in the hearts and souls of the people. Reducing these doctrines to principles, which are apparent in all the oldest and latest psalms, in the prayer of Moses, the psalms of David, the oldest *hallel* and the last hallelujah, we arrive at the following:

(*a*) The stern and uncompromising monotheism; it is the one, and sole God who is worshiped; no angel, no saint, no mediator, no savior, no hypostasis, no kind of fetish, idol, object or force of nature, passion or handiwork of man. God alone and absolute is the sole object of worship and adoration, the hope and trust of man, the rock of salvation.

(*b*) The lofty position ascribed in the dispensations of Providence to virtue, righteousness, purity and holiness in God and man, as the very points in which they meet and which contain the *summum bonum*.

(*c*) The nearness of God to man and man to God, so that the intimate relations, sympathy and love are but faintly expressed in the vulgar phrase of the fatherhood of God and the sonship of man.

(*d*) Man appears in the brightest sunlight of omnipresent Deity, and God is manifested with the most tender affections—almost too anthropomorphous—of the noblest humanity.

These principles are not given in Psalms as something new or just discovered; they are there as old, self-understood and universally cherished heritages—the common good of the common people, Levite, priest, prophet and prince included. The poet can not sing what the popular mind has not priorily conceived; nor does a people pray what is not rooted in its beliefs. It is evident, therefore, that these great principles are older, much older than the oldest psalm; and that they were always present in the mind of Israel. It must also be admitted that the pagan worship and aberrations, which prophets and chroniclers so loudly bewail and so emphatically condemn, were rebellious exceptions in Israel; and the religion with these principles was the general rule and state of the people. This brings us face to face with the question: Where is the source, the origin of these principles? The Psalms reply for themselves: the origin is in the Thorah.

8. Proverbs, the second book of Hagiography, called *Mishlei Shelomoh*, contains thirty-one chapters and 915 verses, each of two—seldom three—parallel lines of three or four words, in rhythm and diction like Psalms. It is a compilation of didactic poems, some as short as two stanzas. The substance of these poems is ethical, the ethics of the Hebrews in the rhythmical form; the practical philosophy in the form of popular proverbs, evidently intended to be committed to memory, especially by the young, to whom it is addressed by the author, who always speaks to בְּנִי, "my son." In form the whole book is like Psalm cxix., which, by its alphabetic acrostic—eight stanzas to each letter of the alphabet—betrays the author's intention to assist the memory of young learners, only that this psalm is addressed to the נַעַר, "lad," the younger learner, and is, according to its diction, of a more recent origin than Proverbs. In Proverbs it is the uniform rhythm, and the rhyme of sense instead of sound, in the parallel lines, either explanatory or supplementary, which assist the memory; while Psalm cxix., intended for younger learners, has, in addition to these mnemonic arrangements, also the eightfold alphabetical acrostic. The authors of Koheleth, especially in the seventh chapter, and after him Joshua ben Sirah (second century B. C.) essayed to imitate the Solomonic rhythm, evidently to the same purpose, but did not exactly succeed. The author of the Book of Job succeeded better.

9. According to its headings Proverbs consists of three parts. It is headed (i. 1) "Proverbs (poems) of Solomon,

son of David, King of Israel;" then chapter x., "Proverbs of Solomon;" then chapter xxv., "Also these are Proverbs of Solomon, which the men of Hezekiah, King of Judah, compiled."* To this come yet chapter xxx., headed "The words of Agur, son of Jakeh, the *Massah;*" and chapter xxxi., "the words of Lemuel, the king, a *Massah*," closing with the golden alphabet of woman. The fact that the first heading is explicit, adding to Solomon's name, "son of David, King of Israel," which is omitted in the two following headings, shows that the two following parts were added to the first, being before that a separate book. In the third heading the words, גם אלה, "also these," admit of different interpretations; they may be understood that only the third part was authenticated as Solomonic by the men of Hezekiah, or that also the second part was authenticated by them. In the latter case, however, this heading ought to be over the second part, and the repetitions in the third part from the second would be inexplicable. Therefore it seems correct that the third part was a separate manuscript, which the men of Hezekiah ascertained to be Solomonic, and added it to the book. Chapter xxx. may well be a *Massah* addressed to Solomon by one who assumed the fictitious name of Agur, as we shall see below; and chapter xxxi. may also be addressed to Solomon, in behalf of his mother, by a Syrian seer, to which he responds with the golden alphabet closing the book. At any rate the Talmudical tradition, that the men of Hezekiah wrote or authenticated the whole book of Proverbs, is not supported by any explicit

---

* העתיקו the Hiphil of עתק was used in the New Hebrew for translating, from its primary sense of "transposing," which could not be its meaning here, as these chapters contain literal quotations from former chapters, as, for instance, xxviii. 13, 14. It must be understood in the sense as used in Proverbs viii. 18, "dignified, permanent, lasting," and in the hiphil form to make something so. The men of Hezekiah authenticated, dignified and made permanent these chapters to be also of Solomonic origin, and added them to this book.

statement in the book itself.* There can be no doubt
that Solomon was a writer especially of *Meshalim* (1 Kings
v. 9–14). His book, or books, *Sepher Dibrei Shelomoh*, was
extant in the time when the Book of Kings was written
(ibid. xi. 41), to which also Joshua ben Sirah testifies in his
book (xlvii. 12–17). It is as certain a fact as it is that he
built the temple, the cities of Tadmor, Balbec and Ezion
Geber, that he wrote the first part of the Proverbs in the
earlier days of his reign, for there is laid down the Solomonic policy and standpoint as the head of the royalistic
theocracy, to which he adhered almost to the end of his
reign.   It must be borne in mind that the theocracy as
established by Moses was democratic, and remained so for
nearly four centuries.   With the ascension of King Saul it
became royalistic.   In its first form the prophet was the
head of the State (Deuter. xviii. 15); the Council of Elders,
among them also priests and Levites, the high priest presiding, and the judges were the head of the law (ibid. xvii. 8–
13); the priests' functions were limited to the altar and
public teaching (Leviticus x. 8–11; Deut. xxxiii. 8–11). The
transition from the democratic to the royalistic theocracy
was not easy.   Jeroboam succeeded in abolishing the traditional priesthood, but did not succeed in extinguishing
the authority of the prophet.   Under Saul and David the
authority of the prophet remained superior even to the
king's.   Solomon attempted, successfully for a time, to set
aside entirely the prophet's authority and establish his own
as the sovereign head of the theocracy.   During the reign of
Solomon, to the very last years thereof, no prophet's voice

---

* The ingenious suggestion, that " King Alkum " (xxx. 81) refers
to the high priest Alcymos, successor of Menelaus in the Maccabean time, and the " lion " (verse 30) refers to Judah, or his successor, Jonathan, is not impossible, as the compilers of the third
Canon, in the time of Simon, may have added this passage, as they
added Maccabean psalms to the Psalm book; but then the " king "
must be omitted from " King of Alcymos," as the latter was no king.
But there is no necessity for this allegation, and nothing to
prove it.

is heard, and when heard again it is that of the stern opposition to the wise king (1 Kings xi. 29–39). The temple is built and pompously dedicated and no prophet is heard. The king does all the praying, receives himself the messages from On High, and conjures down from heaven the fire upon the altar. There is no prophet anywhere. In the writings of the prophets in aftertimes it is David and Zion that are glorified; Solomon's name is not mentioned any more. Solomon opposed effectually the authority of the prophets, to establish his own as the sovereign head of the theocracy. On what did he base his claim of superiority to the prophets? The historical sources reply, he based his claim on superior wisdom, which God himself is said to have bestowed on him as it was given to no other mortal (1 Kings iii. 5–28; v. 9–14).* The difference, however, between Solomon's and the prophetical wisdom is that Solomon's was simply his own, the natural product of his mind, and the prophetical was by inspiration, special messages from On High. It was this prophetical prerogative which Solomon opposed. With this knowledge derived from history we open the Book of Proverbs to find in it the entire exclusion of all special prophecy. Wisdom, reason, understanding, knowledge, prudence, intelligent device, forethought and counsel are personified, apostrophized and glorified in all possible variations, especially chapters. i.–x., of song and eloquence.† David sings the praise of God, Solomon sings the praise of wisdom. David listens with awe and reverence to the prophet's message. Solomon receives none and wants none; wisdom is his highest authority.

---

* It is instructive to read 2 Chronicles i. 7–13, how that author who glorifies the temple builder otherwise modifies his wisdom to a much lower degree and omits much of what the author of Kings wrote before him.

† The oldest commentary on the nature of Solomon's wisdom is in the apocryphal Wisdom of Solomon, chapter viii., and there it is plain enough that it was intended as a poetical personification, and no hypostasis like the Gnostic Sophia.

The whole Book of Proverbs, without an exception, is written in this very spirit, and must, therefore, be the genuine work of Solomon.   There was no time after the Solomonic age (certainly not the time of King Hezekiah) down to the time beyond the Macedonian Alexander, when such a spirit domineered in Israel. We must also take into consideration that in the whole book there is no complaint of and no allusion to any national mishap, war, idolatry, moral corruption or any suffering at all, except the poverty of individuals, everything is lovely, peaceful, with plenty of wealth and sufficiency of protection. It was evidently the Solomonic age, with its advanced state of culture, peace and wealth, which produced the book.

10. The Solomonic ethics as laid down in Proverbs is in substance the ethics of Moses, as Psalms is the lyric exposition of the theology of Moses. The ethical principles of Moses are reduced to practical precepts, and in this respect it matters not whether all passages of Proverbs are of Solomonic origin; all of them are in full consonance with the plan and principle of the book, hence if not by Solomon they are all in the spirit of the wise king. It is admitted in the Talmud that Solomon furnished the handle or ears to the closed urn of the Thorah (*Erubin* 21b.)* But it is also stated there (*Taanith* 8) by the chief Massorite of Tiberias, Rabbi Jochanan, that there is nothing in Proverbs, or even in all Hagiography, which is not suggested in the Thorah, and he discovers Proverbs xix. 3 suggested in Genesis xlii. 21. Those ancient expounders of the law credit Solomon with a number of ritual laws which he is said to have ordained, and yet at one time proposed to remove from the Canon Proverbs, Song of Songs and Ecclesiastes, because "It is merely the wisdom of Solomon" (*Meguillah*), who sought to be like Moses, for which the *Bath Kol* rebuked him (*Rosh Hashona* 21), and did not heed the warning of the Thorah in Deuter. xvii. 14-20, concerning the conduct of the king

* בתהלה היתה תורה דומה לכפיפה שאין לה אזנים עד שבא שלמה
ועשה לה אזנים.

(*Sanhedrin* 21). They entertained no very high opinion of Solomon's moral character (נאה דורש ואינו נאה מקיים) and held the very highest opinion of his wisdom (בחכמתו אמר שלמה). Only in a few instances Solomon is placed higher than the prominent savant.* Thus is maintained (*Maccoth* 23) that the Holy Spirit was poured out in Solomon's court of justice; and furthermore (*Sotah* 41) that "Former Prophets" means David, Samuel and Solomon. This difference of opinions among the ancient sages would be inexplicable, if we would not know already that the policy of Solomon was anti-prophetical as far, anyhow, as the "judging" and "governing" was concerned, claiming for himself unlimited sovereignty by virtue of his superior wisdom, and that on the other hand, his ethics, in Proverbs, anyhow, is no more and no less than the principles of the Mosaic ethics reduced to practical precepts to meet the variety of vicissitudes and emergencies in the life of the individual and society. Some of those ancient rabbis did hold, as did also the author of the apocryphal book, "Wisdom of Solomon," "the wise man is superior to the prophet," which others did not admit. This explains the difference of opinions among the ancient rabbis on Solomon and his ethics.

11. The Solomonic ethics is a commentary on the Mosaic ethics, as by reason understood. This is evident from the principle laid down in Proverbs i. 7: "The fear of Jehovah is the beginning of knowledge," the spontaneous knowledge of the good, the beautiful and the true in all particular cases. This is further explained thus (Prov. ix. 10): "The fear of Jehovah is the beginning (efficient cause) of wisdom and

---

* The defense made for this religious character, "Whoever says Solomon sinned is in error," is contradicted in 2 Kings xxiii. 13: for the defense relies on the potential mood of אז יבנה (1 Kings xi. 7) and understands the passage, "Then he intended to build" those altars to the gods of his wives, but did not actually build them; while in 2 Kings it is stated that Joshiah destroyed the *Bamoth* which Solomon had built to those gods.

the knowledge of holiness is understanding."* It produces wisdom, viz : the correct moral judgment and the control over the will by that judgment. This again is explained (Prov. xv. 33) to this effect : " The fear of Jehovah is the correction of wisdom," it directs reason into the proper channel and guides the will to the proper action. It is on this principle that the author exclaims (Prov. xxi. 30), " There is no wisdom nor understanding, nor counsel against Jehovah," contrary to or in conflict with the God idea as known and understood in Israel, as expressed in the word Jehovah ; whatever is contrary to this God-idea or conflicting with it, is not wisdom, not understanding, not counsel. So did the author of Job also understand the fundamental idea of Proverbs. He sings the ode of wisdom (Job xxviii. 22) entirely in the sense of Solomon and closes it, " And he said to man, behold the fear of *Adonai* (equivalent for Jehovah), this is wisdom, and to eschew evil is understanding." This is the touchstone of genuine wisdom, the manifestation of correct understanding. So did also the author of the apocryphal book of the " Wisdom of Solomon " understand and reproduce the Solomonic principle of ethics, as wisdom based upon the fear of Jehovah. None perhaps has expressed it more forcibly than the princely prophet (Isaiah xxxiii. 6) : " The firmness of salvation, wisdom and knowledge shall be the stability of thy time ; the fear of Jehovah is its treasury." What everybody knows need not be proved. Every reader of Moses knows that " Jehovah " is the word which expresses the God idea of the Mosaic scriptures, defined in various passages of the same Pentateuch ; and every one can see for himself that the whole book of Proverbs is exclusively Jehavistic. So everybody who has read Moses must admit that the ethical principle with him is based upon the cogitation and cognition of Jehovah and his nature of grace and holiness, so

---

* *Kedoshim* in this case, like the plurals in many other cases, *Adonim, Chochmoth*, etc., signifies the abstract idea of the terms, holiness, lordship, etc.

that man's knowledge of ethical doctrine is identical with
his knowledge of God's moral attributes, and all moral
obligation has its root in the Mosaic God-idea. This may
be considered unphilosophical, but it is undoubtedly the
Mosaic standpoint, and perfectly identical with the Solomonic standpoint, with whom also *Yirath Jehovah*, the fear,
veneration, worship, cogitation and cognition of God as by
Moses defined and taught, is the foundation and principle
of all ethics and man's moral obligation. The opposition
of the prophets and the objections of the ancient rabbis to
the wise king's teachings finds its explanation in his opposition to the prophets and their supremacy in his time, all
of which, he thought, could be replaced by the superior
wisdom which God had granted him, as far as the government of the nation and the dispensation of justice were
concerned; and as far as the self-government of the individual is concerned, he thought, the same principle was
applicable, wisdom based upon and rooted in the fear of
Jehovah with the revealed material before them was also
all-sufficient, without any further special oracles of any
prophets. This peculiar rationalism which always thereafter had its prominent admirers in Israel, especially among
the kings and princes, brought on him the ire of prophets
and rabbis. The men of Hezekiah in collecting and com-
piling the last portion of Proverbs, which they certainly
believed to be of Solomonic origin, defend the wise king
with the argument that he certainly took his ethical principle from the Thorah of Moses.

12. Proverbs xxviii., the author speaks distinctly of the
Thorah as the code of ethics, the canon of justice, and the
source of religious instruction without any prophetical aid.
He speaks of the *Rasha*, who flees where none pursues, in
imitation of Deut. xxxii. 30, and the *Tzaddik*, fearless and
confident like the lion. He speaks then (verse 4) of the
friends of the wicked, viz : עֹזְבֵי תוֹרָה "Those who forsake
the Thorah, praise the wicked " and שׁוֹמְרֵי תוֹרָה "those
who guard and observe the Thorah content with them," the
former are the אַנְשֵׁי רָע "the men of evil that understand

no justice," because they reject the Thorah, and the latter as
כבכשי "" " those who seek Jehovah (in his Thorah) understand it all." He then speaks (verse 7) of נוצר תורה, " the
guardian of the Thorah is a wise son," and, referring to
Deut. xxi. 18–20, he concludes, " the companion of the
riotous shameth his father," or the father brings such a son
to shame, according to the above law, saying that the opposite of the guardian of the Thorah who spends his time in
reading and searching the Thorah, is the companion of the
riotous, that runs himself and his father into shame.   Then
(verse 9) he speaks of a third class, מסיר אזנו מישמע
תורה, "one who turneth away his ear from hearing the
Thorah," who does not only not observe the Thorah and not
meditate therein, but would not hear of it if others speak
to him of it, " also his prayer is an abomination ;" because it
is not the expression of any honest religious sentiment.   In
this case Thorah can not signify any canon except the well-
known Thorah of Jehovah, for the observer of which is the
parallel in verse 5. "" כבהשי, like Psalms cv. 3 and Isaiah
li. 1, " those that seek Jehovah."   Nor could it refer to a
traditional Thorah, to which the term נוצר is not applicable
and the ישמע in verse 9 would be a mere tautology.   The
author evidently refers to the written and well-known canon
called the Thorah of Jehovah or the Thorah of Elohim.
This reference to the Thorah of Moses is also supported by
the plain statements in Proverbs xiii. and xxii. 17 e. s.; by
the statements of 1 Kings ii. 3 and viii. 36, 37; also 1
Chronicles xxii. 12, 13; and especially by the doctrine contained uniformly in the whole book.

13.   Two objections are urged against this theory.   One
is the manner in which the author speaks of sacrifices,
Proverbs xxi. 3 and 22, and the golden alphabet of woman,
with which the book closes.   In the dedication prayer Solomon does not even mention the sacrificial cult (1 Kings
viii. 22–61); and in the above passages the author merely
repeats the words of the prophet Samuel (1 Samuel xv, 22,
23), as did several prophets and poets of Psalms without
dereliction to the sacrificial cult.   In chapter xxxi. the

author sings the praise not of queens, princesses, concubines
or other ladies of the court; he sings the praise of the plain
citizen's noble spouse. It is a reply to his mother's chas-
tisement, with which the chapter opens. Lemuel, the King's
Massa, is addressed to Solomon, and the golden alphabet of
woman is his excuse for his polygamy and the debauchery
connected with it. He had not found among his thousand
wives and concubines one like this, because he was a king
and not a plain citizen. Besides this he closes his book
with *Yirath Jehovah* as he begins it (i. 7), true religion as
the fundamental principle of human dignity and greatness,
with woman as well as with man, exactly as Moses did.
The very first word of the book "*Mishlei,*" occurs nowhere
before Solomon in this sense except in the Pentateuch
(Numbers xxiii. 18).

There exists no good cause to deprive King Solomon of the
authorship of Proverbs i.–xxv., or to doubt the veracity of
the men of Hezekiah, who compiled the annex to the book.
Consequently it is safe to place the former after 1000 years
B. C. and the completion of the book 700 years B. C.

14. The Book of Job (*Ee-yob*), the third volume of
Hagiography, consists of forty-two chapters, one thousand
and seventy verses, the middle of which is chapter xxii.,
verse 16. Except chapters i., ii. and xlii., which are prosaic,
the book is written in the same meter or rhythm as Proverbs and Psalms, but differs from both in diction, especially by its numerous quotations and imitations of older
scriptures and many new terms.* As a poetical production
it is the master work not only of the Bible, but also of the
ancient world's literature.

It is an *epos*, the hero of which is the man of perfect
righteousness, and is composed of philosophical dialogues.
Job, pain-stricken, bereaved of all his wealth, health and
happiness, with his wife and his dearest friends against
him, in a state of unspeakable misery, discusses with them

---

*Like סלי, ערק, עטיט, עיש, פרע, קםם, קנין, שחין, רנב, רטב, רטה, רטפש
and many others.

the theme of righteousness as the will of God and the duty
of man.   His friends maintain Job must be a grievous sin-
ner, therefore God punished him so severely, and admonish
him to repent his misdeeds and to appeal to God's mercy.
One of them attempts to console Job with the faith of the
pious that are punished here for their sins and receive the
full reward for their righteousness in life eternal.   Again,
another admonishes Job to submit without a murmur to
the inscrutable will and wisdom of God, as man, who is a
mere atom in God's creation, could not go into judgment
with the Lord of the universe.   He could but appeal to his
mercy and grace.   The fourth endeavors to review and
refute the justification of Job and the harshness of his
words uttered in a state of utmost pain of mind and body,
basing upon the moral principle, that it is sinful to speak
as Job did of God and his justice, that the woe-stricken
must not thus cry out his pain and grief before the Father
of man.   Job's wife, worst of all, sarcastically upbraids him
with his stern righteousness, which, she said, had brought
him down to the lowest state of misery, and advised him to
abandon all hope and faith, "Blaspheme God and die."
Job, however, did not sin with his lips.   He sternly rebukes
his wife and argues against his friends—not always, indeed,
in the most proper language, as one less woe-stricken might
have done.   He pleads his perfect innocence; he knows
himself free of sin and guilt; he has done as much good as
any man in his position could; it is not punishment which
is inflicted on him.   He questions even the justice of God,
in bringing such misery on frail man as punishment for
sins committed, as the Maker knows how weak and perish-
able the creature is, and man's misdeeds can not affect God
in anywise.   He argues against the ideas of future reward
as a consolation in his present misery, as that reward was
uncertain in man's mind; hence it could not counterbal-
ance his present misery, which is a certainty and continuous woe to him.   He could not accept the inscrutability
of God's will and wisdom as a consolation in his abject
misery; ignorance is no consolation; his pains are no less

grievous because he knows not why. He steadily maintains his consciousness of justice and righteousness, hence he knows that justice and righteousness are God's will and man's duty; pain or joy, grief or happiness, however or whatever may come upon man and with what degree of intensity they come, man must not desert his own nature, and his nature is also God's nature; he can not and must not desert or abandon justice and righteousness. I know not why I am woe-stricken, Job argues, but I know that justice and righteousness are the rock of humanity, hence also the essentiality of my Maker. God closes the argument (chapters xxxvii. to xl.), and admonishes Job's friends (xlii. 7) "That ye have not spoken of me as properly as my servant Job." Job is also instructed by the Almighty that no mortal comprehends fully the plans and workings of Providence; and he confesses (chapter xl. 1–4 and xlii. 1–6) that he had blindly argued—which the author of the book makes known to the reader in the very beginning by the allegory in heaven—he confesses: "I have heard of thee by the hearing of the ear, but now my eye hath seen thee, wherefore I abhor myself and I repent in dust and ashes.' It is the *epos* of the perfectly righteous man, who in pain and grief changeth not his allegiance to righteousness, and even then reserves his moral fortitude to confess, that he, in his outcry of woe and his groans of pain, had not spoken as it behooves the righteous man. This is acknowledged by one of the oldest authorities mentioned in the Talmud, and mentioned only on account of this, his defense of Job (Sotah 22): "Rabbi Joshua ben Hyrcan said Job worshiped God out of love," which, according to those ancient Rabbis, is the highest degree of piety and moral perfection.

15. The position of the Book of Job in the Canon is that of apologetics. Therefore it was placed after Psalms and Proverbs, although it is older than some Psalms and claims a closer resemblance to prophetical writings than Proverbs. In the course of logical thought there had to follow after the elucidation of theology in Psalms and the

exposition of ethics based on that theology in Proverbs—
where the *Yirath Jehovah* is treated as a well known and
well understood conception—the apologetics of both in the
Book of Job. The hero of the *epos* in the poet's mind may
have been the man Job, the righteous patriarch living in a
foreign country near the borders of the wilderness, whose
consistent piety, in wealth and poverty, health and abject
disease, under all vicissitudes of an eventful and mutable
life, had become the admired pattern of a righteous man,
as he is represented by the prophet Ezekiel, together with
Noah and Daniel (Ezekiel xiv. 24). Or the term *Ee-yob*,
which signifies "one subjected to animosities or persecutions," may be a personification representing the people of
Israel exposed unjustly to the animosities and persecutions
of petulant nations, represented in the allegory by Satan.
The various opinions of Job's friends, against which he
contends, may have been prevalent among different parties
of that time in defense of Providence and the justice of
reward and punishment; and, in fact, they are traceable
in the history of philosophy both in Greece and the Orient.
Or those opinions may have been prevalent among the
Hebrews as the moral cause of Israel's sufferings among
the nations, the dispersion, captivity and restoration; and
these various speculations are traceable in Prophets, especially in Jeremiah, Ezekiel and Deutro-Isaiah, and in some
of the later psalms, as Job's principle is specially illustrated in Isaiah liii. and Psalms 73, 94. Whatever may
have been the plastic subject in that philosophical poet's
mind—it is difficult now to ascertain it—the character of
the book as a philosopheme is not affected by it; it is the
apologetics of the two main doctrines of Moses, viz.:
revelation and righteousness.

(*a*) Revelation, God himself speaking to man, is originally Mosaic. *Vayedabber Yehovah el*, "God SPOKE to Moses,
to Moses and Aaron, to the people of Israel," and not
merely God appeared or said to this or that person in a
dream or vision, by an angel or another vehicle of com-
munication, is the formula of the revelation, peculiar to

Moses only, and is found nowhere else in Scriptures, except once in Joshua xx , which is a quotation from Moses. The necessity of revelation is undoubtedly one of the main points which the author of Job seeks to demonstrate. He begins with a plot in heaven unknown to Job and his friends. He produces their arguments on the cause of Job's sufferings, none of which is the right one, for they are ignorant of the heavenly plot, and are unable to unravel the mystery or to satisfy Job, till at last Jehovah himself appears and enlightens Job on the momentous problem of Providence and righteousness. The author evidently wishes to tell us that without revelation we would not know this doctrine, and knowing it, we would not be able to understand it, as was the case with Job and his friends.*

(*b*) Righteousness is an attribute of God (Deut. xxxii. 4), the fundamental duty and means of salvation to man (Exodus xix. 5, 6), is the substance of revelation, which was unknown to all Pagan religions of antiquity. It is the doctrine of Abraham and Moses only (Genesis xviii. 17-33) and the heritage of the congregation of Jacob It is the foundation upon which the whole Mosaic dispensation rests, viz. : "God is just, he giveth to every man according to his ways and according to the fruits of his deeds." God's mercy, grace, holiness are included in his attribute of justice, and condition the execution thereof on man on account of his numerous imperfections and his free will. This makes righteousness absolutely the duty of man. To doubt the justice of God is identical with doubting the truth of the Abrahamitic and Mosaic revelation. This skepticism, it appears from Malachi, from Psalms lxxiii.

---

* This seems to be the reason that the Talmud maintains Moses wrote the story of Balaam and the Book of Job, both being defenses of revelation, and plenary revelation, giving doctrine and law to man, according to those teachers is ascribed to Moses only. Balaam, the greatest of Gentile prophets, then and there is inconsistent, superstitious, treacherous and immoral (Numbers xxv. 1 ; xxxi. 8-16, and *Sanhedrin* 86) ; he with his wisdom lacks the revelation and proves its necessity.

and xciv., and the closing chapter of Nehemiah, had taken hold on people's minds when the author of Job wrote his apologetics, proving his position in the last chapters with God's own speech, pointing out to Job the power, wisdom, goodness and justice prevailing in the vast domain of nature everywhere; too vast for man to comprehend it all, still clear and evident enough to force upon Job the conclusion that there is an eternal and universal justice and goodness conceivable in the whole of God's creation, although inscrutable and inexplicable in its details, in individual cases.

16   When was this grand book written and who was its author? It is humiliating to confess that so grand and sublime a poet passed away and no trace of his name is left in his book, none in the nation's traditions, so that the oldest authorities had no knowledge of it. The time of this book's origin can be established by the following facts :

(a)   Job was not written in the prophetical period; it is different in substance, method and style from all books of that period. It is not psalmodic like David; not gnomic like Solomon; not predictive like the prophets; it is purely didactic and universal, and in the dialogue form like Plato and portions of the Zendavesta. Besides this, it philosophizes and contends with skepticism; and a prophetical age doubts not, hence reasons not discursively. It is not the free, untrammeled and artless speech of an inspired and vehemently-moved mind; the entire book is carefully and artistically finished; it is a work of art as a whole and in all its details, and contains besides many imitations and quotat'ons from older scriptures. Its horizon embraces the cosmos, which, besides the first chapter of Genesis and Psalm civ., has no precedent in Scriptures; and its speculations on human nature and events are universally human, as none did write or speculate before him in Palestine. Again, in all the dialogues of Job and his friends the tetragrammaton does not occur (except once, xii. 9, in a quotation); the *Shaddi* and *El*, or *E'ovah*, mostly take the place of the ineffable name. The book could not possibly have been written at any time during the prophetical period.

(b) On the other hand, the book presents other peculiarities. It is not prophetical, nor yet is it apocalyptic. It
knows of the *Benai Elohim;* also of Zechariah's Satan, but
they are not even called *Malachim*, "Angels," and may be
taken as poetical fictions. No angels, no visions of unde-
fined allegories, no oracles from on high appear in the dialogues. Only in the introductory and closing chapters,
when God speaks, the terms Elohim and Jehovah occur.
None of the later writers whose products are preserved in
Scriptures would let God speak to man directly; neither
Daniel, Ezra nor Nehemiah rose to that height in his spiritual exaltation, none would thus freely use the tetragrammaton or its next equivalent, *Elohim.* It is, therefore, evident that Job was written nearer to the prophetical age
than those other books, and, according to what we know of
the prevailing skepticism in the time of Malachi, the poet
of Job must have flourished and written during the last
days of Nehemiah or very shortly after, when the prophetical strains still reverberated in the people's souls, the
catholicity of the Deutro-Isaiah had taken root in the popular mind, and an enlarged conception of nature and cosmos pervaded the land from the Chaldeans on the one side
and the Egyptians on the other. Therefore we may take
for granted that the Book of Job was written between 420
and 400 B. C , as the Talmud has it.

17. The fourth book of Hagiography is composed of the
five *Meguilloth* "scrolls," and in this order: Song of Solomon (*Shir Hashshirim*); Ruth, Lamentations (*Aichah*);
Ecclesiastes (*Koheleth*), and Esther. This succession of the
"scrolls" in the volume is of recent date, as noticed before,
and follows the order as they were read in the synagogues,
viz.: *Shir Hashshirim* was read on Passover, when the year
of the Mosaic festivals begins; Ruth was read on Pentecost;
Aichah the ninth day of the month of Ab, the anniversary
day of the destruction of Jerusalem and its temple; *Koheleth*
during the Feast of Booths, and Esther on Purim day.
According to their supposed authors, as fixed in the traditions, their order should be Ruth, Shir Hashshirim, Kohe-

leth, Aichah, Esther, and in this order we must consider them.

18. Ruth consists of four chapters, eighty-five verses, the middle of which is ii. 21. It is an idylic narrative in artless prose, glorifying the ancestress of the royal house of David, whose name was Ruth or Ruoth, "the friendly." She was the mother of Obed, and he was the father of Jesse, who was the father of David (Ruth iv. 17). According to this statement, the story of Boaz and Ruth transpired three generations or a century before the time of David, and so the book begins : "And it came to pass in the days of the Judges." According to the Talmud, Boaz, the hero of the idyl, was identical with Ibzan (Judges xii. 8), of Beth Lehem, who was Judge in Israel after Jephthah. According to 1 Chronicles ii. 9–12, Boaz was a lineal descendant of Nahshon ben Aminadab, the prince of the tribe of Judah in the time of Moses. The character of Ruth, with her filial devotion to her mother-in-law, is almost identical with that of Jephthah's daughter, so that both seem to reflect the spirit of the age. Still it does not give any assurance that it was written prior to the days of David, whose genealogy seems to be the main object of the little volume. The Talmud maintains that Samuel, the author of Judges, was also the author of Ruth. The beginning of the book shows that it was written after the close of the period of the Judges, hence after Samuel's abdication. We might suppose that the story was known with its details in the family of Jesse only, as it was of no particular interest to others; and Samuel when he anointed David, coming in close contact with the family, and being much interested in it, learned its family traditions and wrote this lovely story to gain the popular favor for his favorite, David. The diction of the book hardly differs from that of Judges. But then Samuel must have been quite old, and it does not seem likely that so old, earnest, serious and disappointed a statesman and prophet could have written so light, lovely, simple, sublime an idyl, in which life, love, nature in their most charming simplicity are portrayed so plastically.

Besides, the spirit of the Ruth scroll does not seem to be the same with that of the uncompromising theocratic-democratic and warlike patriot. In Ruth, the daughter of Moab, the enemy of Israel, the worshiper of Chamosh is glorified, graced with the sweetest womanly virtues and charms, and is held up as a plastic pattern of excellent piety and purity to the daughters of Israel. This, like the Book of Jonah, Deutro-Isaiah and Job, betrays a tolerance, catholicity and universal religion, which hardly looks like the time of Samuel. It rather looks as if David in his younger days had written it and Samuel had made it known in favor of the young bard and hero. The language of the whole volume is that of a young, poetical and vivacious writer. There is no expression in the whole narrative which points to an age beyond the Davidian, while that artless simplicity of speech, manners, occupation, food, house, the touching and unconscious innocence of the heroine, the simple urbanity of Boaz, although evidently a prominent aristocrat among his townsmen, point to a high antiquity, evidently to a pre-Davidian age. This is also supported by the frequent use of the tetragrammaton and *Shaddi* in the conversational passages, which no writer after the prophetical millenium would do. It is the frequent reference to the Thorah of Moses which misled critics, and also us in former days, to place the authorship of Ruth after the time of Ezra. But after we do know that in the time of Samuel and David the Thorah was well known, there is no reason whatever why the authorship of the Book of Ruth should not be given to Samuel and David during the last half of the eleventh century B. C.

19. The Song of Solomon or Song of Songs—*Shir Hashirim*—consists of eight chapters divided into one hundred and seventeen verses, the middle of which is iv. 14. In diction and rhythm it is purely Solomonic and Hebraic, as it is in its sceneries and tropes purely Palestinian. There is no allusion in it to a divided country; Jerusalem and Thirzah, Lebanon, Karmel, En Gedi and Baal Hamon are equally delightful, the tower of David and the tower of

Lebanon are of equal distinction, Gilead in the north and the seam of the wilderness in the south are present in the poet's mind. As a profane lyric poem or a collection of poems, an outpouring of the most impetuous passions, a glowing word picture of indomitable love "mighty like death" on the background of all that is beautiful, fragrant, refreshing in motion, shapes and colors, beguiling and intoxicating in human beauty and Palestinian climate and scenery, *Shir Hashirim* ranks highest in the world's literature. And yet with all its enticing and sense-enchanting tropes and almost lascivious descriptions it denies nowhere the chastity and purity of the Hebrew woman, the devotion and self-control of the Hebrew lover, which always outshine and overwhelm the wild fire of passion and the inebriety of sensuality. Nor do all the opulent beauties of nature compressed by the poet in so small a frame form the prominent and plastic presentation of the poem; they are mere background and frame-work, mere ornamentation of the main picture, which is human excellency, love, honor, purity, faithfulness, vehement resistance to seductive sensuality, strength of character and the triumph of a noble womanhood over the very tempting enticements of the world's most envied treasures of happiness. No Greek, no Arab, none but a Hebrew poet could produce such a poetical creation.

20. The story which, with some exceptions, is the subject of the whole *Shir Hashirim* is quite simple. Sulamith (the feminine Solomon), an artless shepherdess, comely though sunburnt, is the object of King Solomon's ardent love. She is brought to Jerusalem, and under the influence of all the dazzling brilliancy of the royal court, the seductive promises of the most extravagant luxury and pomp, the persuasive language of the royal lover, the choruses of the court and the daughters of Jerusalem. Sulamith's best affections, however, belong to the shepherd in her rural home; she clings to him, sings his praise, fancies and dreams of him only, addresses to the absent lover the words of love's liquid fire, remains steadfast and firm in

her affections and forces the poet to the conviction, "Love is strong as death—jealousy is cruel as the grave—the coals thereof are coals of fire, a most vehement flame. Many waters can not quench love, neither can the floods drown it; if a man would give all the substance of his house for love, it would utterly be contemned" (viii. 6, 7). The whole of Song of Songs is a glorification of the daughter of Israel, the triumph of the ideal over the sensual, the moral idea over the voluptuous and sensuous allurements, outside the centers of wealth, luxury and sensuality. Yet the main subject is several times dropped in the book and other songs are inserted (iii. 7–11); iii. 1–5 and the similar v. 2–8 are dreams of Sulamith, as she says (v. 2), which she tells the daughters of Jerusalem; viii. 8–10 and 11–14 are fragments of poems.

21. In this natural signification *Shir Hashirim* may be well taken as the product of King Solomon or at least of the Solomonic age, which, as the Talmud maintains, the Men of King Hezekiah compiled, and the non-Solomonic poems may have been taken into the Solomonic because they had been addressed to him, so that אשר לשלמה in the heading may be intended to express both "by" and "to" Solomon, as in the case in Psalms with the "Le David" and "Li Shelomoh." The fact that Solomon is the rejected lover in the poem does not contradict his authorship. It is the identical case as with the golden alphabet of women in Proverbs. The polygamist Solomon must have well understood that he could never possess a woman's genuine love like the poet's ideal, and so he felt himself rejected by Sulamith. He objectified himself in the poem, as many other poets did, and this is the most touching lyric echo. It is maintained that there are Aramaic or Syriac words in the poem, therefore the conclusion that it must have been written in the Kingdom of Israel, where the Syriac at an early date was interpolated in the Hebrew—for which not the shadow of proof exists; or it was produced in or after the Babylonian captivity, which is impossible. The exile, the mourner, the genius with mortified sentiments among a

mortified and hapless people, could not sing so cheerfully
and joyfully; nature does not appear to him so illuminated,
love not so sublime; the music of the hapless is plaintive,
his song melancholy, and none can rise very high above the
sentiments dominant in his community. In the time of
Solomon, who reigned over the largest portion of Syria, it
could not appear strange to anybody if Syriac terms had
been adopted by Hebrew writers or *vice versa*. Besides this,
however, there exists no proof that the terms pointed out as
Syriac were not Hebrew long before, or that prior to the
adoption of the Aryan terms in the Syriac there was much
difference in the roots of the two languages. This is also
applicable to the song of Deborah.* No word can be called
Syriac, because it was no longer used in the Hebrew and
preserved in the Syriac. Again, that there are fragments
of other poems inserted in the Sulamith poem was not advanced originally by Abraham Ibn Ezra and repeated by
ever so many exegetics down to Moses Mendelssohn, Aaron
Wolfsohn and Joel Levy; the theory appears already in the
Midrash (*Rabbah* to Canticles, I. section), where Rabbi Aibo
maintains that it announces itself as containing at least
three different parts, and this was in the third Christian
century. From this standpoint *Shir Hashirim* becomes intelligible, and especially one of its most striking peculiarities is explicable. God's name is never mentioned in this
book, no reference even to God—except in *Shalhebethjah*, and
here the term *jah* is an adjective expressing strength, power
in the superlative degree—no Providence or any religious
sentiment is met in it. This is without parallel in the Bible,
except the Book of Esther. The only supposition to explain this seems to be, that neither of these books was written for any divine purpose, and those ancient men obeyed

---

* ש *sheh* instead of אשר *asher* is used in both poems, and this could
but prove that the poets used this abbreviation long before it was
adopted in prose composition. The proof is in the heading of *Shir
Hashirim*, which certainly must be younger than the poem, and
there *asher* and not *sheh* is used as the relative pronoun.

very strictly the third commandment; they would not write
or pronounce any name of God in profane song or narrative.
It seems evident from a passage in the Talmud (Sanhedrin
101a) which found its way into the "Zohar" in *Theromah*,
that *Shir Hashirim* was in common use as banquet songs
and at such other symposia, against which, of course, Talmud and Zohar protest,* although in the Mishnah (*Yadaim*
iii. 5 and iv. 6) it is not decided that, as Rabbi Jose maintains, the great poem is endowed with the same grade of
holiness as other holy books.

22. When the question rose, if *Shir Hashirim* is a profane
poem or collection of Solomonic poems, why did the Men
of Hezekiah compile the little volume, and if they did this
in honor or out of particular respect for the king's illus-
trious sire, why did the great Sanhedrin that established
the third canon accept it among those holy books?—then
it was advanced, and especially by Rabbi Akiba ben Joseph
and his supporters, that *Shir Hashirim* was an anagoge.
Its characters are symbolic. Sulamith is the congregation
of Israel; Solomon, except in one passage, represents the
name of God; its tropes are esoteric, its entire structure is
mystic, it discusses the love of God to the congregation of
Israel, that mystic love which the prophets also symbolize
by the love of bridegroom and bride. The main question
might have been answered thus: this grand monument of
a sublime genius deserved careful preservation, and is no
less glorious to the ancestors of the nation than the records
of heroes on the fields of battle, or the wisdom of savants
in the nation's council. Nor is its subject less divine than
the friendship of David and Jonathan so carefully described
in 1 Samuel, or the undying love of Jacob for his son
Joseph; love in any form is a bright reflex of divinity.
Sulamith's faithful and indestructible love is as divine and
as worthy of record as a nation's love of country proven
genuine in trying and distressing struggles. We might
suppose, however, that those earnest, serious, chaste and

---

* תנו רבנן הקורא פסוק ושל ש ה'ש' ועושה אותו כמין זמר וג'

God-fearing men could not well appreciate such arguments. Those savants, however, do not give any reason why just this one production of Solomon should be an anagoge, when all his other writings, as also those of David and Samuel, their contemporaries and immediate successors, are plainly exoteric. It could not be on account of the subject, as the love of God and Israel is fully expressed in the covenant, upon which the whole structure of Israelism was based, and Solomon built the temple and had deposited in its *sanctum sanctorum* the "Ark of the Convenant of Jehovah" (1 Kings viii. 1–11). There was no cause whatever for putting the main and well known conception under a cloud of mysticism, nor does it seem proper to represent the divine love in so sensual a form. Besides all this, Sulamith does not reciprocate the love of Solomon; she rejects him and remains true and faithful to her absent shepherd lover; hence the esoteric idea of the poem would be, that God loves the congregation of Israel, but she loveth best the charms and bliss of nature's gifts, or clings tenaciously to other ideals of happiness. This, indeed, may have been the esoteric idea of the poet, in the opinion of the Akiba school, and thus again Solomon objectifies himself. Anyhow, there is no alternative left; either *Shir Hashirim* is plainly exoteric, the poems were written by Solomon, with some addressed to him, in the tenth century B. C., or it is esoteric and was written under circumstances of national prosperity and happiness similar to the Solomonic age, which never was the case except in the early days of the reign of the Egyptian Ptolemies over Palestine. Then the idea of the Platonic love had reached Palestinian poets, together with the Grecian forms of poetry and the worship of external beauty, so exuberantly displayed in *Shir Hashirim.* Then the struggle of Judaism against alluring Grecism was still young and mild, and seemed so much more dangerous to the former. The highest ideals of the Grecians were beauty, philosophy, poetry and the king, while Judaism clung to Sinai, righteousness, God and his law. The poet, while glorifying the daughter of Israel, well

represents this struggle between two civilizations. Sulamith, the daughter of Sinai, that "cometh up from the
wilderness leaning on her beloved" (viii. 5) well represents
the congregation of Israel, faithful, true to her beloved.
The beloved is the God of Israel, who in the whole poem is
spoken of by Sulamith, but never appears personally on
the stage of the poem; he is the invisible God, whom no
idols can represent. The highest ideals of the Grecian
mind, philosophy and the king, could best be represented
by the philosophical King Solomon, and he is the absent
shepherd's mighty rival. But he is rejected, the wisest of
kings is vanquished by the unshaken faith of the plain
shepherdess; the Grecian ideals can not captivate the
congregation of Israel; she remains faithful to her beloved,
to Sinai, to the God of Israel. Here is the anagoge without
mysticism. It is an allegory.*

We can not decide which is the case, but we know that
only these two are probable: either *Shir Hashirim* is an
exoteric, poetical effusion of King Solomon and some of
his contemporaries, and was compiled by the Men of Hezekiah, as the tradition has it, or it is an allegory and was
written in the time of Ptolemy Euergetes, 221–204 B. C. It
was accepted in the third canon, because it represents so
well the cause of Judaism in its struggle with Grecism.
Because it was written so late it contains no name of God
whatever, and, therefore, it was used as a popular song at
banquets and other symposia.

23. Ecclesiastes (*Koheleth*) consists of twelve chapters,
two hundred and twenty-two verses, the middle of which is
vi. 10. It is a dissertation on the Highest Good (*summum
bonum*) in plain prose, without any attempt at ornamentation or poetical symbolism, an informal philosopheme,
hence without technical terms, and, with the exception of
very few foreign words, purely Hebrew. Tradition gives its
authorship to King Solomon; affirming that it, like the other

---

* See on this point our " History of the Hebrews' Second Commonwealth," p. 80.

works of Solomon, was compiled in its present form by the Men of King Hezekiah in the seventh century B. C. Moses Mendelssohn divides the dissertation into the following thirteen interconnected essays: (1) Chapter i. 1 to i. 11, introduction; (2) from i. 12 to ii. 11; (3) from ii. 12 to ii. 26; (4) from ii. 27 to iv. 3; (5) from iv. 4 to iv. 17; (6) from iv. 18 to v. 19; (7) from vi. 1 to vii. 14; (8) from vii. 15 to viii. 9; (9) from viii. 10 to ix. 12; (10) from ix. 13 to x. 15; (11) from x. 16 to xi. 6; (12) from xi. 7 to xii. 7; (13) from xii. 8 to the end of the book. This division is logical as far as the different parts are concerned; each presents a unity, according to Mendelssohn's interpretation; but the connection of the various parts into one logical unit is not established. This was felt by the Rabbis of the Talmud, who maintain in the name of Aba Areka (*Shabbas* 30*b*) that it was proposed to take *Koheleth* out of the Canon, "because his words contradict one another;" to which is added in *Vayikrah Rabbah* (chapter 28) by Rabbi Levi, a cotemporary of the former: "because some of his words incline to heresy (as if) the bands were loosened; there is no justice and no judge." It was not done, as stated in the Talmud, "because the beginning and the end thereof are words of the Thorah." Evidently those ancient savants did not succeed in discovering a logical unity in *Koheleth*. "The beginning and the end thereof," on the merits of which this book was retained in the Canon, can not refer to the introductory and closing verses of the book, for these do not appear Solomonic. The whole book, from i. 12 to xii. 7, is written in the first person, Koheleth speaking to the reader; while the first twelve and the last seven verses are in the third person, the editor or compiler speaking to the reader. The closing verses, in which *Koheleth*, the proper noun, becomes *hak-Koheleth*, the common noun, and in which the compilers do expressly mention themselves (verse 11) as בעלי אסופות, and warn the young (בני) against making many books (verse 12), could only be the postscript of the Men of Hezekiah, or of the compilers of the third canon. The same seems to be the case with the eleven introductory verses, which consist only of general statements to the one point, that man's deeds are without any effect on nature or mankind; nothing can be changed in the world's process or man's destiny. "There is nothing new under the sun." This, however, is but one point of the many, and not even the main point discussed in Koheleth—the main point is the *summum bonum*. It appears, therefore, that the first editor or compiler of the Koheleth manuscripts knew but those portions thereof which discuss that fatalistic doctrine; and a second editor or compiler added thereto such other Koheleth manuscripts, which complete the work as a philosopheme on the *summum bonum*, and wrote the conclusion of the book. Abraham Ibn Ezra, in his commentary to Koheleth (twelfth Christian century), and after him the philosophical exegetists, Levi ben Gershom, Isaac Abarbanel, Obadiah Seporno, Joseph Ibn Jochiah and others, expounded Koheleth and attempted to harmonize the apparent contradictions of statements and doctrines in the book, without observing, however, that the introduction does not correspond with the whole book, and the conclusion can not be by the author of the book.

24. The cause of the apparent contradictions in Koheleth is that the author either quotes from other documents or reduces to writing such current sentiments which he discusses and contravenes from his standpoint in regard to the *summum bonum*, and either the compiler or the transcriber failed to mark those passages, so they stand now in the text in contradiction to the other passages thereof. The exegetists failed to distinguish the assumed themes from the arguments and conclusions of the author, therefore they failed to harmonize the statements and doctrines of Koheleth. Its author is a firm monotheist, the ha-Elohim is his designation of the Deity. He believes in Providence, which has preordained all things from the beginning, and believes no less in the freedom of man, who may try and do all things which, in his opinion, may lead him to attain the *summum bonum*. He believes in the justice of God, who brings to judgment every deed of man, and laments over the injustice

prevailing in human government in consequence of man's free will. So he believes in creation and the Creator's wisdom, who has made everything beautiful in its time and place and made man upright, perfectly prepared to attain the highest good, and believes no less that many fail in appreciating God's wisdom and their own aim and destiny on account of their ignorance or their submission to the lower passions. The author clings steadfastly to the principle that there is universal necessity in nature and history and individual freedom in both. He believes in personal immortality, "And the spirit returns to God who hath given it." The golden mean in everything is his moral principle, and in this he finds the means to attain the *summum bonum*. He is no fatalist, no pessimist and no pantheist. From the purely religious standpoint of Moses and the Prophets he argues the question against all prevailing beliefs in his time, showing not only their inability to secure the *summum bonum*, but as their last sequences the disirability of suicide, life not being worth living; "all is vanity and windy thought." Yet we feel and know that human nature is imbued with the desire to live and the longing after happiness, consequently he is forced to the conclusion that his standpoint is THE truth from which man can reach the *summum bonum*. Koheleth is apologetic like Job, opposite the philosophical views prevailing in his age, and so in order to understand the book correctly the passages must be divided into the assumed themes and the author's arguments and conclusions.

25. According to traditional beliefs King Solomon is the author of Koheleth, although his name is never mentioned in the book. The heading speaks of Koheleth as a son of David, King of Jerusalem, but this is evidently taken from i. 12, the actual beginning of the book. "I, Koheleth, was King over Israel in Jerusalem," to which "Son of David" is added, and for which no authority is given. The author (i. 16 *et seq.*) speaks of his great wealth, luxury, power and wisdom, which seems to point to King Solomon, yet no name is mentioned, neither Solomon nor a son of David.

" Koheleth " is no name of a person, as is evident from the
" hak-Koheleth" (xii. 8).   There is no evidence in the book
that Solomon was its author or that he was a son of David.
The question always remains unanswered :   If Solomon
was its author, why is his name not given, as in Proverbs
and Song of Songs?   The entire argument of Koheleth is
apologetic of the Solomonic principle laid down in Proverbs,
that the fear of God, the theological postulate, is the safe
foundation upon which wisdom or human intellect must
base its moral doctrine and regulate its conduct in order to
attain the *summum bonum;* only that in Proverbs the principle is advanced especially in regard to the state and the
ruler or rulers thereof, and in Koheleth it is discussed chiefly
with reference to the individual and his means to attain the
highest good.   Therefore, the governing power of wisdom
is here considerably modified and in all problems of morality
the golden mean is recommended.   But all this does not
prove that Solomon or a son of David was its author.   The
King of Israel in Jerusalem may be fictitious, like the word
Koheleth.   Nor is this proved by those passages in the book
which point to Solomon's disappointments toward the close
of his reign, which necessitated a modification of his principle in regard to wisdom ; any other savant or reasoning
prophet may just as well have referred to this fact to
strengthen the argument that the individual wisdom also,
even if based on the fear of God, is insufficient in all cases to
reach the highest good.   On the other hand, the book
affords no direct proof against the authorship of Solomon.
The arguments against certain Grecian philosophemes,
especially against Epicurism, Skepticism, the self-sufficient
Rationalism of Aristotle, and the Pessimism more or less at
the bottom of all Grecian mythology and speculation, is no
proof; as all those speculations may have been and undoubtedly were current in the Orient long before formal philosophy utilized them.   The Syriac and Aryan terms prove
nothing against the time of Solomon, as we have noticed
before.   The absence of the tetragrammaton, the covenant,
and congregation of Israel, everything that is specifically

Hebrew, Judaic or Israelitish throughout this book again proves nothing, as it evidently was not written for Jew or Gentile especially—and Solomon was the king of a large number of non-Israelites; it is an argument of equal force to all monotheists, and was evidently addressed to all and not to the Hebrews only. No prophet and no prophecy is referred to in Koheleth—this again looks like the days of Solomon—because it is a piece of reasoning from principle, fact and analogy, which has nothing in common with prophet or prophecy. It seems, therefore, correct to maintain that the Men of Hezekiah did compile certain writings of the Solomonic age addressed to the congregation called "Koheleth," as the term signifies, because they are addressed to the individuals to unite them in sentiments to a congregation of similar doctrines. The king's name was not given on account of the uncertainty as to the author. Centuries after, during the struggle between Grecism and Hebrewism, at a time when the third canon was compiled, other manuscripts, believed to be by the same author, were added to the older volume, and the present Book of Koheleth received its present form. Then Koheleth received the signification of the congregation of Israel arguing against the encroachments of Grecism; Sinai versus Olympus, monotheism against philosophy, stern righteousness against sensuality, a life of joy and gladness against asceticism, optimism against pessimism, with the golden mean everywhere. If this is correct, the Book of Koheleth received its present form about 200 B. C., in the time of Antiochus the Great in Syria, and the boy king in Egypt, containing materials from the time of Solomon, if not entirely from himself, as compiled by the Men of Hezekiah.

26. The Book or scroll of Lamentations, called by the rabbis *Kinnoth*, was originally called *Aichah*, according to the first word of the same, as it is called now and is designated in all Hebrew manuscripts and prints. It consists of five chapters, three of which begin with the same word *Aichah*, divided into one hundred and fifty-four verses, the middle of which is iii. 34. These five chapters are five

poems apparently independent of one another, the first two
of which are lamentations, and the last three are elegies containing consolation. Their unity is (a) in the subject, the
capture, destruction of Jerusalem and its temple, and overthrow of the country and dissolution of the nation. The
third chapter, although it chiefly laments the sufferings of
the author, according to Abraham Ibn Ezra's commentary,
is also an elegy on the discomfited and exiled Israel; and
(b) in the artistical construction of these poems. Each
chapter consists of twenty-two stanzas, and each stanza in
the first four chapters begins with a letter of the Hebrew
alphabet in the usual order, only in chapters ii. and iv. the
Pai (פ) precedes the Ayim (ע), otherwise the alphabetical
acrostic is perfect. In the third chapter there are three
verses to each letter, beginning with the same letter, and in
the last chapter the alphabetical order is omitted, but the
number twenty-two is preserved. In meter, the first and
second chapters are alike; each stanza, consisting of three
lines, each line of three or two feet (words), or two and
three, or four as an exception. The third chapter with its
threefold alphabet is in meter somewhat different, its lines
—two to each stanza—are mostly of 3-2 or 2-2. The fourth
and fifth chapters also divide each stanza in two lines, each
line in 3-2 or 2-2 feet. It is evident, therefore, that we
have before us in this book or scroll carefully and artistically constructed poetry and no irregular effusion of sentiment and thought as in the books of Jeremiah or Ezekiel.
This is also evident from the numerous metaphors, similes,
apostrophes and personifications in this book. As a poetical production of a high order this book is no less remarkable than it is for the depth and warmth of its patriotic
sentiments and its word painting of the profoundest grief
and affliction over a nation's downfall and a country's
catastrophe. The destruction of neither Troy nor Car-
thage, Nineveh nor Babylon produced an elegaic monument
of similar grandeur and sublimity.

27. Three times before its destruction Jerusalem was
besieged and captured by the Babylonians supported by

Syrians, Edomites, Moabites and Amonites, viz.: under King Jehoiakim (2 Kings xxiv. 1), under King Jehoiachin (ibid., verses 11-16), and from the ninth to the eleventh year of King Zedekiah (ibid. xxv. 1). The second king together with his princes and high dignitaries was carried into captivity (2 Kings xxiv.; 2 Chronicles xxxvi.), and the last king was deprived of his eyesight after his children had been slaughtered, and was then dragged into captivity. All these calamities of the three invasions and their destructive effects together with the destruction of Jerusalem and the temple are lamented in the three chapters of Lamentations, beginning with the word *Aichah*, viz., the first, second and fourth, evidently blended in the poet's mind into one prolonged catastrophe, as if all the disastrous events had happened simultaneously. The third chapter is the elegy of the author written in the first person, in which he sings in melancholy strains his own painful fate in that time of disaster and defeat, destruction and annihilation, together with the sorrow and grief which overwhelmed the wounded patriot at the sight of his people's misery and his country's destruction, rising, however, from under the thick cloud of that double misery to the luminous height of light, consolation and hope, with his trust in God and his grace. It seems that the third and fourth chapters should be reversed, which would make of the four chapters a continuous elegy, setting forth, in the first place, the greatness of the nation's calamity and disaster and its effect on the poet's mind; then his own personal afflictions, which depress and deject his soul; and then, notwithstanding the double grief and the hopeless future before him, his trust in God, his source of consolation, and his unshaken faith in the grace of the Almighty. As the order of the chapters is now, it seems that chapters iv. and v. belong to another author; one who not only mourns over the past events, but also laments in chapter v. the present state of misery and the cheerless future of his vanquished people in the power of a despotic conqueror and fierce enemies; and yet, like the first author, he rises above all disas-

ter and benighting prospect of the future to consolation
and hope by and with his faith and trust in God's loving
kindness, with which the fifth chapter closes so pathetic-
ally. There can hardly be any doubt that the prophet
Jeremiah was the author of the first three chapters of
Lamentations. If the fourth and fifth chapters belong to
another author he must have been a cotemporary of Jeremiah, as none but an eye-witness could produce so vivid
and impressive a description of any event. Therefore, we
may set the date of Lamentations between 586 and 560
B. C., the year of King Jehoiachin's release from prison; for,
after that event, as is evident from Isaiah's orations, the
feeling of pain and grief over the nation's fall and the fate
of the vanquished could not have been as fierce and oppres-
sive any longer as it appears in the closing chapters of
Lamentations. The question, if Jeremiah was its author,
why was it placed in the third and not in the second canon?
is easily answered, viz: because Lamentations are no prophecies, and the second is the prophetical canon. It is no
less easy to tell when he wrote these elegies viz: after the
captors of Jerusalem had taken him from his prison and he
had gone along with other prisoners in chains as far as
Ramah, where Nebuzradan released him and he went back
to Mizpah and staid there with Gedaliah till he was
forced to go with the assassins to Egypt, which was at
least two months after the fall of Jerusalem. In Ramah he
began his lamentations (Jeremiah ix.). There the prophetical lyre was tuned to the melancholy strains of the elegy
(ibid. xxxi. 15). Hence it follows that Jeremiah wrote his
Kinnoth (his former *Kinnoth* were lost, 2 Chronicles xxv.)
in the months of *Abh* and *Elul*, 586 B. C. He may have
written the last chapters after his return from Egypt, when
the effects of the conquest had become most bitterly felt.

28. The book or scroll of Esther consists of ten chapters
of one hundred and sixty-seven verses, the middle of which
is iv. 7. It is a prosaic, well constructed narrative, of which
tradition maintains it was written by the Men of the Great
Synod under the influence of the Holy Spirit. Abraham

Ibn Ezra thinks it is a translation from a Medo–Persian Chronicle. It is just as well possible that it was written in Persia, when Antiochus Epiphanes invaded that country, to encourage the rebellion in Judea, and the Men of the Great Synod adopted it as the authentic narrative of that affair, a number of which were in circulation, as is evident from the Greek version, the two Aramaic versions, and the narrative of Josephus. It contains an episode of the history of Ahasuerus, a Medo-Persian king, who, after executing his wife Vashti, selected as his consort out of many maidens a daughter of the tribe of Benjamin, whose name was *Esther* (a star) and also *Hadassa* (a myrtle). She was an orphan adopted by her uncle, Mordechai, and, like him, a scion of the ancient family of Kish, who was also the father of King Saul. Ahasuerus knew not that she was a Jewess, nor that she was the niece of Mordechai, who stood in some intimate connection with the royal court. The king had a favorite minister whose name was Haman, a scion of the royal house of extinguished Amalek. He came in conflict with Mordechai, who would not show the demanded honors to the mighty minister. He contracted such a revengeful hatred against Mordechai and his race that he obtained a decree of the king that on a certain day in the month of Adar all Hebrews should be slain by the populace and their property to be free booty te the murderers. The decree was published, and, according to the laws of that country, could never be revoked. By the influence, however, of Mordechai upon Queen Esther, and by her intercession with the king, the murderous scheme was defeated, the mighty misister was deposed and put to death, and the Hebrews were enabled to defend themselves against their assailants. The excited populace, with a prospect of rich booty, rose on that given day, according to the king's decree, to slaughter and spoliate the unprotected Hebrews, who, however, were prepared to meet their enemies. and made a great slaughter among them in the city of Susa, and chiefly in the adjacent provinces Mordechai became the prime minister of the king; in consequence thereof, and perhaps chiefly on account of their heroic defense, the Jews became much more respected among the populace than before. The day after this, viz., the 14th day of Adar, and in the city of Susa also the 15th day of Adar, were made days of festivities and rejoicings, called "Purim." By order and request of Esther and Mordechai the Purim was established among all the Israelites in all countries. That the Purim existed before the book of Esther was written is evident from the book itself (ix. 9-32.) That this day of feasting and rejoicing was generally celebrated among the Israelites is evident from 2 Maccabees i., the account of Josephus, its mention in *Meguilloth Thanith*, quoted also in the Talmud (*Thanith* 18*b* and *Meguillah* 5*c*), and from the rabbis of the first century, from and after Rabbi Jochanan ben Saccai, who knew of special laws and regulations concerning the *Purim* day, and the reading of the Esther book on that day. The feast itself is considerable testimony in favor of the fact related in the book, as feasts, like fasts instituted by a nation, especially by Israel, always commemorate a historical occurrence. Yet if the Purim had been instituted soon after Ezra and Nehemiah, it might be maintained that it was adopted from the Persian heathens; but when the Hebrews had become most zealous and scrupulous observers of the laws of Moses in every detail, as they certainly were from and after the fourth century B. C., such an adoption was clearly impossible. The occurrence narrated in this book could not have happened prior to Darius Hystaspis, because under his reign the institution of the "Seven Princes of Persia and Media" (Esther i. 14) was established. It could not have occurred under Darius, Xerxes or Artaxerxes, as the authors of the books of Ezra, Nehemiah and Chronicles must have noticed the important event and prominent persons. The next following three kings of Persia reigned together but twenty years, with none of whom the dates of Esther correspond, nor do they correspond to the reign of the two last kings who reigned together but two years. There are left but Artaxerxes Mnemon, 404 to 359 B. C., and Darius Ochus, 359 to 338 B. C. We know of the former that during the last ten years of his reign a fine of fifty shekels for each lamb sacrificed in the temple was imposed upon the Hebrews, and that was certainly not the Ahasuerus of Esther who was so much influenced by Mordechai and Esther.* Therefore Darius Ochus only could be that Ahasuerus. To him and his character every line and date fits exactly. He was an enemy of the Hebrews and Phœnicians in the first year of his reign. He made the feasts described in Esther, slew eighty of his brothers, and became the indolent, sensuous and foolish despot, Ahasuerus. Besides, he did not call himself Darius; he called himself Artaxerxes, son of Artaxerxes, and so does the Syriac translator call (Esther i.) Ahasuerus. The Purim story could not have occurred prior to 345 B. C., and then there was no longer the barest possibility for Hebrews to adopt a Heathen festival, nor to invent such a story on the Persian court. If it had been a fiction it must have been located in India, Ethiopia or the Desert of Arabia. Susa, the Persian court, and all about them were too well known in Jerusalem to be thus misrepresented. It is certain, from the book itself, that the Haman edict was of a local nature, not for the 127 provinces, and the whole occurrence transpired in Susa and adjacent country. Therefore, nothing was known about it in Jerusalem or the other cities and provinces, and so the Purim feast was instituted in Susa first and then by the influence of Queen Esther and Mordechai also in Jerusalem, and from thence it spread all over the dispersed Israel after the advent of Alexander the Great. The book of Esther, however, it seems was written about 160 B. C.

29. The Book of Daniel is before us in twelve chapters (modern division), seven *Sedarim* (ancient division), 357 verses, the half of which is v. 30. It is Hebrew from i. 1 to ii. 4 and viii. to the end of the book; the part from ii. 4 to vii. 28 in Aramaic, as it is called there (ii. 4), or Eastern Syriac. Two peculiarities of this book are, that from i. to vii. it records disconnected events, one in every chapter,

---

*See our History of the Hebrews' Second Commonwealth, p. 29-31.

and each is a miracle; and from viii. to xii. it is a record of apocalyptic prophecies. In the first part the author speaks of Daniel in the third person, and in the second part Daniel appears as the author, and always speaks of himself in the first person. This, aside from the two languages of the book, suggests that it was not written by one author.

There could be no doubt that Daniel really existed in Babylon during the exile, a great and wise man, as outside of this book we find his name in Ezekiel (xiv. 14 and xxviii. 3) among the most righteous and the wisest of his age, and in the Grecian version of his book, in connection with the narratives of Susanna and Bel and the Dragon. Nor could it well be doubted that this Daniel did write, when Josephus reports (Antiq. x. viii. 5), that one of Daniel's books was shown in the temple of Jerusalem to Alexander the Great, and further on (x. xi. 7) speaks of several books of Daniel, which, it appears, had been extant in the time of Josephus. The question would only be, did he write this book, or any parts thereof? The Talmud states, the men of the Great Synod wrote it, but this we know may refer only to the compilation of the book as in the case of Ezekiel.

The narrative part of Daniel was certainly not written in Judea, it being in diction and description by far superior to any Aramaic production of Palestine. It was certainly written where that language was the vernacular and had skilled literati, which was the case in Babylon before its fall. Each of those episodes closes with a special glorification of the God of Israel, so that they appear to be myths, legends or allegories based on facts, to impress the reader with the special information that Nebuchadnezzar, Belshazzar and Darius praised and glorified the God of Israel, seeing as they did that the Lord wrought such extraordinary miracles for his people, seemingly abandoned in captivity. Taken in this sense, Daniel may have written these and many similar episodes, as the author of the book of Jonah did with similar good, humane and patriotic intentions. The Talmud in *Chelek* takes a similar view, at least in one case, the three men thrown into the fiery furnace, and the dead that

Ezekiel revived in the same valley of Dura.   This view of
the subject anyhow accounts for the strange accident, that
none of the authors of that or any subsequent age refers to
those astounding miracles, and that Nebuchadnezzar, who
thus glorified the God of Israel, did not release King Jehoiachin from his prison.

The prophetical portion of Daniel, from chapter viii. to xi.,
was certainly not written in Babylon.   Had it been written
there during the captivity it must have become known
among the exiles and its author must have taken a high rank
among the prophets as well as Ezekiel, Haggai, Zechariah
and Malachi did, when the prophetical Canon was established by the Men of the Great Synod, and the book could
not have been placed among the volumes of Hagiography, as
was actually done.   This part of the book, together with
the first chapter to ii. 4, which is an introduction, and chapter xii., which is a *resume* and conclusion of it, bears strong
imprints of Essenean doctrine, as reported by Josephus.
This sect at its inception was certainly identical with the
Hassidim of 1 Maccabees, the main support of the Maccabees in their great struggle against Syria.   This leads us
directly to the time when the Hebrew portion of Daniel
was written, to the occurrences of which in the time of
Antiochus Epiphanes and the victories of the Maccabees,
all those prophecies point.*

30.   The seventh chapter of Daniel reports a dream of the
author which one of the bystanders (verse 16) in that dream
expounded.   Both the dream and its explanation are so
sublime, picturesque and mystic that almost any part of
history, or the entire historical process of humanity, could

---

* The seventy weeks of Daniel, about which so much was guessed
and written, begin with the first exile of the Israelites to Babylon,
when King Menassah was carried to Babylon a vanquished captive
(2 Chronicles xxxiii. 11).   That was the beginning of Israel's downfall and loss of independence and nationality, from which it never
recovered till after the victories of the Maccabees, which established
again the independence of Israel, in round numbers seven times
seventy years after that first catastrophe.

be discovered in it, although the author evidently intended
to prophesy no more than the end of Babylon's power and
sovereignty.   This is undoubtedly the part of the book of
Daniel shown to Alexander in the temple in which the
priests discovered the prophecy of the Macedonians'
victories and conquests. This very fact may have started
the belief among the expounders of the ancient oracles
that Daniel's predictions in that chapter reach to and far
beyond Alexander. When Antiochus Epiphanes began his
work of oppression, and schemed extermination in Judea, one
of the Essenean or Hassidim patriots, perhaps the deposed
high priest, Onias, or Mattathia himself, or his younger cotemporary, Jose ben Joezer, wrote the introduction and the
Hebrew commentary to the book of Daniel, showing that
his prophecies refer to this age and its calamities, this
struggle and its victorious outcome, the fall and the rise of
Israel, the desecration and the consecration of its sanctuary
and priesthood — he calls the high priest Messiah and
prince—the end of servitude and the resurrection of Israel's
sovereignty. With this commentary, introduction and conclusion, the book was circulated among the patriots, to fire
the souls with glowing patriotism and courage, and it was received and read with enthusiasm, and did well its intended
work. This procured for the book of Daniel in this form a
place in the Canon among the Hagiography, which was established after this event. We place, therefore, the Aramic
portion into the year 540 B. C., and the Hebrew portion
into the year 170 B. C., with Daniel as the author of the former and perhaps Jose ben Joezer of the latter. He being at
the head of the Synod the tradition correctly maintains
that the Men of the Great Synod wrote or rather finished and
edited the book of Daniel.

31. Ezra and Nehemiah were taken as one book also by
the authors of the Massorah. The two books, as they are
before us, consist of Ezra, ten chapters, and Nehemiah,
thirteen chapters (modern division). In the Massorah
both books are quoted together as having ten *Sedarim*
(ancient division), 688 verses, the middle of which is Nehe-

miah iii. 32. The Septuagint has three Esdras, viz.: i.
Esdras which is apocryphal and is neither mentioned nor
quoted in any of the Biblical or Rabbinical sources; ii.
Esdras (in some MSS. of the Septuagint i. Esdras) is
identical with the canonical Ezra, and iii. Esdras with the
canonical Nehemiah.   That this division in the Septuagint
is recent is evident from the fact that neither the Massorah
nor the Talmud knew of it.   Chapters iii. and iv. of the
apocryphal book are original, were adopted by Josephus
(Antiquities xiv. 5 and xi. 2) and contain sufficient internal
evidence, that the author was an African Hebrew, perhaps
identical with the author of II. Maccabees, or with that
Aristobul who wrote commentaries for a king of Egypt in
the second century B. C.*

32. The contents of Ezra and Nehemiah are episodes of
Israel's history 536 to 423 B. C., as follows:

Chapter i. (Ezra) begins with the closing verses of
Chronicles, the proclamation of Cyrus to the exiled Hebrews
to return to their ancient homes and to rebuild the temple
of Jerusalem, those remaining in the Medo-Persian Empire
to furnish them with substantial means, and the vessels of
gold and silver taken from the temple now returned to them.

Chapter ii. A register of the families returning with Zerubabel and Joshua, the high priest, their arrival in Palestine.

Chapter iii. The erection of the altar in Jerusalem;
reintroduction of the Mosaic cult; celebration of the feasts
on the first and fifteenth days of the seventh month; prepa-
rations for the building of the temple and placing the
foundation stone.

Chapter iv. The Samaritans being refused co-operation
in the rebuilding of the temple, succeed in obtaining an
interdict from the Persian court under Cyrus and his suc-

---

* See our History of the Hebrews' Second Commonwealth, pp.
89, 131 e. s.   There exists in Latin a fourth book of Ezra, or Revelations of Ezra, which belongs to the apocalyptic literature in the
time of the destruction of Jerusalem, without any claim to historical authenticity.

cessors, Cambyses and Smerdes,* and the work was inter-
rupted.

Chapter v. Haggai and Zechariah, the prophets, encourage Zerubabel and Joshua to proceed with the building,
beginning of the reign of Darius II., they do; Tatnai and
others oppose it and write a letter to Darius to enforce the
interdiction.

Chapter vi. Darius finds in Ecbatana the original edict
of Cyrus, ordains the completion of the temple, which is
completed the third day of Adar in the sixth year of Darius
II.; the temple is dedicated; the first Passover is celebrated
by the returning exiles. This ends the first part of the
book. The second part begins fifty-eight years later.

Chapter vii Artaxerxes sends Ezra with a second
colony, and gifts for the temple, to Jerusalem, appoints him
Chief Judge and promulgator of the Law in all provinces
west of the Euphrates, with sufficient executive authority.

Chapter viii. Register of the families returning with
Ezra, their journey and arrival in Jerusalem, delivery of
the holy vessels and gifts.

Chapter ix. The princes accuse their brethren of having
taken foreign wives; Ezra's prayer and address.

Chapter x. Ezra convenes a general meeting, to remedy
this evil, a representative body is appointed; the names of
the main persons guilty of that transgression are ascertained
and registered. Here the book of Ezra closes abruptly.

Nehemiah i. opens thirteen years after Ezra's coming to
Jerusalem with Hanani reporting to Nehemiah the deplor-
able condition of Jerusalem; Nehemiah's prayer.

Chapter ii. He asks permission of the king to visit his
country; he is appointed Pasha, and starts on his journey,
arrives in Jerusalem, inspects at night the walls of the city,

---

* Verses 6 and 7 they are called אחשורוש and ארתחששתא, and the
former can not be identical with his namesake in the book of
Esther, nor the latter with ארתחשסתא or Artaxerxes in chapter 7.
It seems, therefore, that those kings had different names in the
Aramaic and Persian, as is evident partly from the Persian sources
and the inscriptions, and Herodotus Grecised the one or the other.

tells the rulers his mission, is scorned by Sanbelat, Tobiah and Geshem.

Chapter III. The building of the walls of Jerusalem.

Chapter IV. Tribulations and hostilities against which he contended.

Chapter V. Liberating the poor and enslaved; his own disinterestedness and self-sacrificing work.

Chapter VI. Dissensions, tribulations and hostilities at home and from abroad are overcome.

Chapter VII. Military organization and orders for the protection of the city; reviewing and completing the register of the families that had returned from Babylon.

Chapter VIII. Presenting, reading and expounding to the people the Law of Moses on the first day of the seventh month by Ezra and Nehemiah; celebration of the Feast of Tabernacles.

Chapter IX. Second public meeting and reading of the Law; address of the Levites.

Chapter X. Solemn acceptance of the Law of Moses as the law of the newly organized State, a document signed by the representative Levites, Rulers and Priests, and confirmed by an oath; ordinances added to the Law by Ezra and Nehemiah.

Chapter XI. The names of the men who moved from the country into Jerusalem; organization of the Levites; appointment of Patachiah as the king's agent; the districts of the country.

Chapter XII. Another and later register of priests and Levites; the dedication of the walls of Jerusalem. This ends the account of Nehemiah's twelve years' administration. He returns to Susa, comes back to Jerusalem in 424 or 423 and then occurs what is narrated in chapter xiii.

33. The language in these two books is the plain Hebrew prose with the exception of the official documents from the Persian court or addressed to it, which are Aramaic. Very few Aramisms are in the Hebrew portions, except the names of persons, places, coins, official documents and offices. Some of the Hebrew pieces like Ezra ix 6-15; Nehemiah

i. 5–11 ; ix. 8–37, although full of reminiscences, sound classically pure. The diction gives us no points on hand to ascertain when these books were written.* It is certain that the first part of Ezra, including the seventh chapter to verse 27, was written prior to the next part. It is a mere compilation of documents which must have been preserved in the temple. It is written all in the third person, the author never speaks of himself. He narrates briefly in chapter vii. 1–10, what is actually narrated in chapter viii., so that it does not seem that one author wrote both, and besides, he describes and lauds Ezra (vii. 6, 10) in a manner which Ezra would not have said of himself. He makes Ezra a son of Sheraiah, the last high priest in the Temple of Solomon, slain after its destruction by Nebuchadnezzar (2 Kings xxv. 18; Jeremiah lii. 24), whose great grandson he could hardly have been, as Ezra came to Jerusalem 128 years after the death of Sheraiah. Whether it was the intention of the writer to suggest that Ezra was the descendant of the last high priest and the lawful heir by the right of primogeniture and the Joshua dynasty was a second line by Jehozadek; or whatever other intention he had; thus much is sure that Ezra would not have denied his father. The same author does a similar thing, and it seems for the same reason, with Zerubabel, whom he calls son of Shealthiel, when he actually was the son of Pedaiah, but the former was the second son of King Jehoiachin, Assur was the first born (1 Chron. iii. 17, 18).

The next parts of Ezra and Nehemiah, from vii. 5 to the end of the second book, are purely Hebrew and in the

---

*The supposition of some critics, that the King of Persia is called (Ezra vi. 22) "King of Ashshur" (Assyria), points to the time of the Seleucidic kings—provided "Ashshur" signifies Syria, which is never the case—is a mistaken notion, as Cyrus was also King of Assyria, and in that passage is also referred to the exiles of the children of Israel from Assyria and the proselytized Gentiles (verse 21) after the exiles from Babylon in verse 19; the author calls Cyrus King of Assyria. It must be borne in mind that many of the northern tribes also returned with Judah and Benjamin.

first person, the authors narrate their own stories in their own words. These portions of the book present themselves as the original writings of Ezra and Nehemiah, and there exists no reason whatever to doubt it. Nehemiah vii. 5 e. s. is not identical with Ezra ii., the two accounts differ in the various numbers of the men belonging to each family returning from Babylon, although they agree in giving the sum total, yet it seems evident that both accounts could not have been written by the same author. Nehemiah viii., ix. and x., different entirely in diction from the rest of the book, is an official document, written by an eye-witness of that important affair (See אֹבְנוּ and the following verbs in chapter x.). Chapter xiii. is again Nehemiah's own.

34. It is evident that the first part of Ezra (i.–vii.) was compiled by an earlier historian than the rest of Ezra and Nehemiah, and not long after the arrival of Ezra in Jerusalem. It can not belong to the author of Chronicles, although this latter book was known when Nehemiah xii. 23 was written, the *Sepher Dibre Hayamim* is expressly referred to. Nor can it be questionable that the author of Nehemiah xi. and xii. was the compiler of the books of Ezra and Nehemiah, as they are now in the Canon. This compiler must have flourished about 350 B. C., as he mentions the six high priests from Joshua to Jaddua (xii. 10, 11), and we know that the third was in office in the time of Nehemiah (iii. 20), and from Josephus that the last was still alive when Alexander the Great appeared before the walls of Jerusalem. In the Talmud, however, it is maintained that Simon the Just was that high priest. If this passage is not a later addition, the two books could not have been compiled long before 350 B. C., about sixty to seventy years after the death of Nehemiah, in the time of Darius Ochus, whose name seems especially to be mentioned xi. 22, and he reigned from 359–337 B. C. But then it seems strange that this compiler betrays no knowledge of the three great events which occurred prior to 350 B. C., viz : the building of the temple on Mt. Guerizim, the high priest John slaying his brother Jesus in the temple, and the

Haman persecution under King Ahasueros.   It would seem, therefore, that the Darius in Nehemiah refers to Darius Nothus, who reigned from 423 to 404 B. C., and the passage of the six high priests is either a later addition, or the Talmud has the correct tradition, viz : that the grandson of Jaddua, Simon the Just, was the high priest who received Alexander the Great.   Simon died 292 B C., after a reign of forty years.   His father reigned thirty years ; this brings Jaddua down to the year 362 B. C.   If so, Ezra and Nehemiah were compiled during the life-time of Jaddua at any time between 390 and 360 B. C., within a few decades after the death of Nehemiah, prior to the fratricide in the temple which occurred in 372.

35. Chronicles i. and ii. is before us in 29 and 36 chapters (modern division), 25 *Sedarim* (ancient division), 1,656 verses, the half of which is I. Chronicles xxvii. 25.   The contents of this book are I. Chronicles i. to viii., the genealogy of the principal families in Israel, beginning with Adam and continuing to the Babylonian exile, with many historical notes not found elsewhere in the Bible.

1 Chronicles ix.   The families living in Jerusalem before its destruction, together with the offices of the various Levitical families, and closing with the genealogy of King Saul.

1 Chronicles x.   The end of King Saul according to the Book of Samuel.

1 Chronicles xi. to xxix. is the history of David as King of all Israel, according to the Book of Samuel, with many additions and omissions, but no contradiction of facts.

2 Chronicles i. to ix. is the history of Solomon according to the Book of Kings, with many additions and omissions, and no contradiction of facts.

2 Chronicles x.   The division of the kingdom in Judah and Israel, Rehoboam and Jeroboam.

2 Chronicles xi. to the end of the book narrates the history of the Kings of Judah to 586 B. C., omitting the history of the prophets and the Kings of Israel, adding to the history of the temple and its priesthood, and closing with a

brief reference to the Babylonian captivity and the edict of Cyrus 536 B. C.

As the author of Kings wrote chiefly the history of Israel and the prophets with mere references to the Kings of Judah, the temple and its servants, so the author of Chronicles wrote chiefly that part of history which the former omitted. He evinces no animosity to Israel, and even records of it deeds of magnanimity (2 Chron. xxv. 17-24; xxviii. 8-15). He accounts for his additions to the books of Samuel and Kings by pointing to the ancient documents before him in their original form as they were before the authors of the former historical books, the public records and the books and scrolls of prophets as well, to which he invariably refers, except in the historical notes contained in the genealogies (chapter i.–viii). This part of the book, however, is ascribed to Ezra, and must be considered separately. That his additions are historically correct is proved by his story of King Manassah's captivity in Babylon,* which is omitted in Kings, and was found noticed in the Babylonian inscriptions.

36. Characteristic of Chronicles' additions to Samuel and Kings is:

(a) The author's endeavors to rouse patriotism in the hearts of his people, encouraging the exiles to return to Palestine, and the returned to be faithful and hopeful in their work of reconstruction. In this particular point he re-echoes the prophecies of Jeremiah (xxx. and xxxi.), and he makes mention of him (2 Chron. xxxv. 25) and of his prophecies (ibid. xxxvi. 21, 22). He re-echoes also the prophecies of Ezekiel (xxxvi. and xxxvii. especially) and does not mention him nor Daniel, who must have flourished prior to the issue of the edict of Cyrus, with reference to which Chronicles closes. This omission only proves that its author writing from existing written records and books only, to which he always refers, had no knowledge of the

---

* See Schrader's " Die Keilinschriften und das Alte Testament," page 366.

books of Daniel and Ezekiel, as in the case of the latter the Talmudical record maintains, to have been compiled and edited by the men of the Great Synod.

(b) The center and symbol of this patriotism, faith and hope is in the temple on Mount Moriah, its cult, rites, priesthood, builders and supporters. He glorifies David and Solomon, the builders of the temple, by numerous additions, and also by characteristic omission of incidents which mar their glory; as the story of Uriah and Bath Sheba, the rebellions of Absalom and Sheba, his conduct toward Saul and his descendants in the case of David; and the idolatry favored by Solomon, the rebellions occurring in his days, the prophecies of Ahiah, the Shilonite, in the case of Solomon. He is less partial and more severe on the dynasty, except those kings who did something for the temple, the promulgation of the Thorah among the people, or the glorification of priests and Levites. He narrates the faults and shortcomings also of the best kings, like Asa, Jehoshaphat, Jotham and Hezekiah.

(c) About the priesthood and the temple service the Chronist's additions are most profuse in his accounts of the organizations of the priests and Levites, the psalmody, the musical instruments, the musicians and singers, especially of the ancient families of Asaph, Heiman and Ethan. He pays much less attention to the sacrifices and the priests than he does to music, song and psalmody. The Levites occupy the foreground in all his additions to the books of Samuel and Kings.

This entitles us to the conclusion that the Chronist had three main objects in view, viz: to produce a detailed history of the kings; to glorify the temple as the center of Israel's pride and patriotism; and to enhance and beautify the temple service by the reintroduction of Davidian psalmody and orchestras, Levitical choruses, stately guards and ministers; all of which disappeared among the last of the prophets from their speeches, especially in Ezekiel's vision of the future temple, and had no prominent place in the earlier prophets' writings. The fort of this historian is in urging this reform, this addition to the sacrificial polity, and to prove from the documents at his command that this psalmody, orchestras and choruses, always were the most important part of the temple service, and also prior to that in the time of David and Samuel. The decline of the temple service at different times, especially after the reign of Jehoshaphat and later on after Hezekiah, was chiefly in the reduction and neglect of the poetical and musical departments, and the concentration of all piety and worship in the sacrificial rites, as is evident from the objections urged by prophets and psalmists against the sacrifices.

37. The diction of the Chronist is a clear prose without any attempt at ornamentation, the popular style of the narrative in his days. So the people in the author s time spoke and wrote. In doctrine and historical data he is in perfect harmony with all the other books of the Bible. His peculiarities consist of the following points:

(*a*) The Aramaic forms in grammar, phraseology, terms, names of persons, places and things, use of adverbs and prepositions, the addition of letters in the middle of a name, changing the Hebrew *Hai* (ה) into the Aramaic *Aleph* at the end of a word, transposing the *Yeho* (יְהוֹ) from the beginning of a name to its end or changing into *El*, transliterating, abbreviating or replacing letters by others similar in sound then and there, are chief characteristics of Chronicles, much more so than of any other book of the Bible.

(*b*) New nouns and verbs derived from Hebrew or also Aramaic roots abound in this book.

(*c*) The silent or Hebrew vowel letters הוי *Hai, Vav, Yud,* are frequently added in words, in which in older books they are omitted. Many of the *Keri* and *Kethib* marked in marginal notes of Samuel and Kings are replaced by the correct *Keri* in the text; and a number of obscure or incorrect passages in those books are corrected in Chronicles.

Point *c* shows that Chronicles was written later than the books of Samuel and Kings, and even then none dared make any correction, any kind of change in those ancient books.

Points *a* and *b* prove that Chronicles was written where and when the people's language had been Aramized to a large extent, and the correct pronunciation of Hebrew words, even popular names like that of David required the assistance of vowel letters.

This could have been the case only in Babylon among the exiles, or very shortly after their return to Palestine. After their return they rapidly improved in the Hebrew language, as is evident not only from the books and psalms written then, but also from the notes of Ezra and Nehemiah and the speeches of the prophet Haggai, which were certainly addressed to the general public. The complaint of Nehemiah (xiii. 24) that the children of alien mothers did not know how to speak Hebrew, only proves that all others could and did speak the Hebrew well. Chronicles must have been written before Ezra and Nehemiah came to Palestine, or if by Ezra, which the Talmudical tradition maintains not, he certainly wrote it in the earlier days of his life in Babylon. There is nothing in the body of the book, i. e., from 1 Chronicles x. to the end of 2 Chronicles, which points to any time later than Zerubabel's return to Palestine ; but there are in the first part (i. to ix.) traces of a later time, which must be considered.

38. The nine chapters in the beginning of Chronicles are ascribed to Ezra in the Talmudical tradition. In the main they are transcripts from genealogies recorded in Pentateuch, Joshua, Samuel and Kings, to which are added genealogies especially of the tribes of Judah, Levy, Benjamin, the transjordanic tribes, with short notices on the tribes of Ephraim, Simeon and Dan, all of which was compiled from works no longer extant, to establish the claims of those families to purity of blood and right of possession in their different districts and towns, founded originally by their ancestors. The reason for this imperfect record—only a small number of families and founders of towns are mentioned—is obvious. Ezra's work was intended to establish the legal claims of such families that either had never left (not all members thereof did) their original possessions

in Palestine, or had returned from the exile prior to or cotemporary with Ezra (1 Chronicles iv. 41–43 and v. 16–22). Chapter vi. is an ancient document, which may have been written in the time of King David or Solomon, if it begins v. 27 as maintained in the Septuagint. It was placed here to give prominence to the purely Levitical families, especially of Heiman and Asaf, and the priestly line from Phineas, their titles to certain towns and districts, which had been deserted by some of them already in the time of Jeroboam (2 Chronicles xi. 14), and many more of them in course of time abandoned their vocation and neglected their genealogies (Ezekiel xliv. 9–24; Ezra ii. 59–63). Chapter ix. is a record of families that lived in Jerusalem prior to the exile, and Nehemiah xi. reports the inhabitants of Jerusalem after their return from the exile. Only one passage in 1 Chronicles iii. 19–24 is pointed out to prove that it must have been written after Ezra, and that is a mistake. We find there the genealogy of Zerubabel, the lineal descendant of the Davidian kings, by Pedaiah, son of Shealthiel, son of King Jehoiachin, or Jechoniah. Then verses 19 and 20 are given the eight children of Zerubabel. Verse 21 are given the names of two grandsons of Zerubabel, and four side families of the Davidian house, and again three generations of one of these families (Shechaniah's). Without any good reason these four families are taken as descendants of Zerubabel, and they with their descendants, and following the descendants of Zerubabel would make seven generations and bring the author of this passage to 200 years after Zerubabel, about 300 B. C., while in fact Ezra and Nehemiah flourished in the third generation of Zerubabel (Nehemiah iii. 4; vi. 18, 30). There is no cause to gainsay the Talmudical tradition that Ezra wrote the Book of Genealogies to himself עֶזְרָ לוֹ. Nor can there be any doubt he wrote from authentic written sources, old official records lost to us. This is evident from the historical notices reaching as far back as to the sons of Ephraim and Benjamin in the land of Goshen (1 Chronicles vi. 21–23; viii. 13); Jabez and the city of scribes in the early days of the Judges (ibid. ii. 55; iv. 9); one of the house of Kaleb, who had for a wife Bithiah, the daughter of Pharaoh (ibid. iv. 18); the exploits of the sons of Simeon before and during the life-time of King Hezekiah (ibid. iv. 39–42); the exploits of the Reubenites in the time of King Saul (ibid. v. 6, 19); the inhabitants of Gilead had been counted and registered in the time of King Jotham and Jeroboam II. (ibid. v. 17); that a granddaughter of Ephraim, Shearah, built three towns (ibid. vi. 24); of all of which we have no notice in any other book. The author tells us (ibid. ix. 1) that all Israel had been carefully registered in the book of the Kings of Israel and of Judah, before they were exiled to Babylonia, which tells us one of his sources, and also the reason for not going into any further details.

39. We have in fact before us four books:

(a) The book of Chronicles proper from 1 Chronicles x. to the end of 2 Chronicles, written in Babylonia or very shortly after the return from the exile, written by a reformatory prophet or Levite in that period about 500 B. C.

(b) The nine chapters of genealogy, written by Ezra before his return to Palestine about 460 B. C.

(c) The documentary history of Zerubabel and his time with the arrival of Ezra in Palestine, written about 457 B. C., now Ezra i.–vi.

(d) The notes of Ezra and Nehemiah, written by themselves between 458 and 423 B. C., compiled in one book, the main book of Ezra and Nehemiah about 360 B. C.

The Men of the Great Synod connected these four books into Chronicles and Ezra in chronological order.

The difficulties in these books are the extravagant numbers, which occur frequently, and the change of names for the same persons, for which it is easier to account, but there is none in the narrative except 2 Chronicles xxii., where it is stated that King Ahaziah was forty-two years old on mounting the throne of Judah as immediate successor of his father, Jehoram, of whom it is stated three verses before that he was forty years old when he died. This is evidently a mistake, not made by the author, but by some transcriber

who mistook the *kaf* (20) for a *mem* (40) without seeing
that in 2 Kings Ahaziah is said to have been twenty-two
years old, and almost the whole account in 2 Kings viii. 26
is literally copied in Chronicles with the addition of " the
youngest son " of Joram.

CHAPTER VI.

THE traditions of the Hebrew people and documentary evidence before us preclude the theory of that school of modern criticism which places the Pentateuch at or near the close of the prophetical millenium, as the product of historical development. Prior to Abraham Ibn Ezra, in the twelfth century, none expressed any doubt that Moses was the author of the entire book, excepting only the closing passage of Deuteronomy, which some rabbis in the Talmud ascribe to Joshua; and he merely suggests that a few historical notes must be of later origin than the body of the book. They may have been added by transcribers or copyists as marginal notes first, which were then amalgamated with the text. After him some other passages of the same kind were pointed out—one by Moses Nachmanides—but neither of them changed the traditional belief in the authen· ticity of the Pentateuch, so that this very day the minister, taking out the Scroll of the Law from the ark during divine service, tells his congregation : " This is the Thorah which Moses put before the children of Israel." The exceptions are but few and recent. The entire post-biblical literature, both the apocryphal and rabbinical, reaching in some of its parts as far back as to the days of Ezra and Nehemiah, and down to the sixth Christian century, records the universal existence of this tradition in Israel, independent of the same records in the Greco-Judaic and the early Christian literature.

2. The documentary evidence is either direct or indirect. The direct evidence is the following :

(a) The statement in the Pentateuch : Genesis v. 1, the *Sepher Tholedoth Adam* is noticed ; and *Sepher* signifies a

book, a something written by somebody. *Tholedoth* is usually rendered " genealogies," but it signifies also the birth
of events, the narration of facts,* so that the narrative
of every prominent progenitor begins with the same words,
Eleh Tholedoth, also without speaking of descendency,
as in xxv. 19 and xxxvii. 2. There can be no doubt
that the author of Genesis intended to inform us that he
had before him written records of genealogies and events,
which he adopted, or adapted. Exodus xvii. 14, we are informed that Moses began to write the Book of the Wars of
Jehovah (see above Chapter II., p. 28). Ibid. xxiv. 12 and
xxxiv. 1 we are told that God wrote for Moses the inscriptions
on the two tablets of stone, also Thorah and commandment.
Ibid. xxiv. 4 and xxxiv., we are informed that Moses wrote
the Book of the Covenant and a special copy of the Decalogue. From Numbers xi. 26 we learn that the names of
seventy-two elders were written down, who were most likely
the heads of tribes and the heads of family groups mentioned by name elsewhere in Numbers. Then writing is
mentioned again, xvi. 17–18. Ibid. xxxiii. 2 we are told expressly that Moses wrote the book, or scroll, of the " Sojourns," *Eleh Massei*, which, it appears from the context,
contained also the history of the exodus and the events
which occurred in the wilderness. The practice of writing
as a religious duty is commanded not only to the priest
(Numbers v. 23), to the presumptive king (Deuteronomy
xvii. 18), to the leaders of the people crossing the Jordan
ibid. xxvii. 3–8) and to the Judges (ibid. xxiv. 1), but also
to every occupant of any house (ibid. vi. 9 and xi. 20).
Then it is noticed again that God wrote the inscriptions
on the two tables of stone (ibid. x. 2–4); that Moses has
commanded " to read" this Thorah publicly at stated times
(ibid xxxi. 11); that he wrote Deuteronomy and delivered it
to the priests and all the elders of the people (ibid. xxxi. 9–
24); and that he wrote another Book of the Thorah, which
he delivered to the Levites, the bearers of the ark of the

---

* Genesis vi. 9; ix. 1; xi. 10; xxv. 12–19; xxxvi. 1; xxxvii. 2.

covenant, to be placed as a testimony at the side of the ark (ibid. verse 25). Then again we are informed (ibid. verses 19 and 21) that Moses began also to write the Book of Jashar (see above Chapter II., p. 28), and commanded the people to copy and commit to memory his last song. These direct statements of facts can not legitimately be explained away as metaphoric or symbolic language. They can not be disposed of as interpolations, as they are not in contradiction with the known origin of alphabetical writing and literature among the Shemites of Asia or Africa. In order to bring the Pentateuch down to post-prophetical times, or any time after Moses, all these and many more passages must be declared fraudulent interpolations, willful deceptions, which is certainly an illegitimate verdict in this case, when the entire book treats on the loftiest ideals of humanity and spirituality, without any selfish motive or any attempt in favor of any person, community or nation, and without any contradiction to reason, or the experience of mankind. This excludes every possible motive of fraud and willful deception. All that can be derived from these various statements against the authenticity of the Pentateuch is that the repetition of these statements in those particular places of the book may prove that not all in that book was written by Moses; but also this seems to conflict with Deuteronomy xxxi. 25, and it would only remain to be proved that the entire Pentateuch as now before us is of Mosaic origin.

(b) The word " Thorah," with prefixes or suffixes, or with Jehovah, Elohim or Moses connected with it, occurs in the Bible no less than two hundred and forty-six times, as every reader can see in any Hebrew concordance. The frequent recurrence of this word in the historical books (except in Judges and Samuel), in Prophets from Amos to Malachi, in Psalms, Proverbs, Job, throughout the entire Biblical literature, although in some instances it may not refer to the written Thorah, certainly proves that something real and authoritative must have always existed, generally known as " Thorah," so that prophets and psalmists could in some instances call also their own teachings Thorah. Recurring some fifty times with the definite article (ה) in *hat-Thora*, *bat-Thorah* and *kat-Thorah*, it must evidently refer to a reality, and not to the mere preaching of this or that prophet. Appearing with the word *Sepher*, "book," or *ka-kathub*, "as it is written," before it, we know that it is a book written. Again, the term Thorah appearing in connection with *Mitzvah*, "commandment," or *Chukkim*, "statutes," or *Mishpatim*, "ordinances," we know it is a book in which also commandments, statutes and ordinances occur. If we then find this written book qualified as the Thorah of Jehovah, the Thorah of Elohim and the Thorah of Moses, we know that this term refers to a well-known book which contains also commandments, statutes and ordinances, which according to the records was always known and believed to be of God and written by Moses. That the word Thorah appears in Holy Writ in all the connections noticed is evident from any Hebrew concordance. If in any special case the word Thorah refers to the teaching of any prophet or psalmist, it must be proved, in every instance, after we know that generally it means the Thorah of Moses.

That the authors of Judges and Samuel had no occasion to mention the Thorah does not invalidate the argument. For in the oldest piece in the book of Judges, the revelation on Mount Sinai is mentioned, viz.: In the song of Deborah (Judges v. 4, 5),* besides which there are in both these books frequent references to the Thorah, as shall be noticed below. In Samuel, to which belongs also the first, second and part of the third chapter of Kings, the Thorah is very explicitly mentioned (1 Kings ii. 4), to which is referred also in Psalms i. 2; xviii. 31; and xix. 8. Again the book of Joshua was written prior to Judges and Samuel (see Chap. III. pp. 39–41), in which the Thorah is mentioned too often and too explicitly to doubt its existence then; the

---

* This is taken from Deuter. xxxiii. 2. The song of Deborah has become the text to the ancient Davidian *Shir*, Psalm lxviii., where Judah only is added to the tribes praised by Deborah for patriotism and heroism.

Davidian Psalms and the Solomonic Proverbs shortly after the book of Samuel testify no less than Joshua to the existence of the Thorah then; hence the absence of the word Thorah in those two books could be but accidental, unless it be maintained that in the interim the Thorah was suspended, neglected, violated and forgotten, which does not gainsay the authenticity of the Pentateuch, and can not be sustained in the face of the facts that there are in the books of Judges and Samuel numerous quotations from and references to the Thorah, both its historical and juridical portions and its poetical tropes.

The position, that those historical books, Psalms and Proverbs, were written or rewritten with fraudulent intentions during the Babylonian exile or thereafter, has been disposed of in the former chapters of this book. What was written during or close to that exile besides Ezekiel, the first part of Daniel, and parts of the twelve Minor Prophets, is the main portion of the book of Chronicles; and this proves beyond any doubt that in its time the antiquity of the historical books was so well established that no corrections of mistakes even would be permitted in those old monuments.

(c) The origin of the fundamental institutions and apparatuses, inseparable from the political and ecclesiastical life and the historical process of the ancient Israel, is described in the Thorah only; and in all other books of Holy Writ not even a remote intimation of the origin of those institutions and apparatuses can be discovered. This demonstrates at once the existence of the Thorah prior to all other books of the Bible. Such institutions are:

A. The division and organization of the nation in thirteen tribes, the sons of Joseph as two tribes, each with its own *Nassi* or prince of the tribe, each tribe divided into family groups, and each group into natural families, two and a half of those tribes located east of the Jordan River, and ten and a half tribes west of the Jordan located in their exact districts to the very end of their national existence, where they were, when Deborah and Barak in the century after

Joshua sang their celebrated hymn, and then this tribal
division and location was already a matter of history. The
origin is noticed in the Thorah only. (Genesis xlviii. 5;
xlix. 28; Exodus xxviii. 6–30; Numbers i. and vii.; xxvi.
11–65; xxxii. and xxxiv.; Joshua xiii.–xxii.; compare
1 Chronicles ii. to ix.)

B. The fundamental institution of the Seventy Elders
with all the ideas of the federal and representative form of
government, which, according to the unanimous testimony
of the Bible, Josephus and the Talmud always existed in
Israel unless momentarily suspended by some despotic
king; and yet there is no mention or intimation of its origin
except in Numbers xi. and Deuter. xvii. 8; yet they are
there in Joshua xiv.; Judges xxi.; 1 Samuel viii. 4; 2
Samuel iii. 17 and v. 3; 1 Kings viii. 3; at every important national event down to the prophet Jeremiah's time.

C. The continuous existence of prophets from Moses to
Nehemiah for one thousand years (see Chapter IV., p. 61)
with precisely the same pretensions of being the messengers and mouthpieces of the same God, with the same
religious principles and ethical doctrine, the very same
system of righteousness which the Thorah prescribes and
defines, without yielding or even inclining at any time
to any foreign doctrine and without advancing or even
intimating anywhere that any one of them taught any doctrine, principle or law not known before to the Hebrews;
so that the Talmud could maintain that forty-eight prophets
and seven prophetesses prophesied, and they added naught
and took naught away from what is written in the Thorah.
(*Meguillah* 14a.) If this God-idea, these principles and
doctrines, this particular system of righteousness had not
been established authoritatively before the very first as
before the last of these prophets, their unanimity would
have been a matter of impossibility, as the history of
Grecian philosophy proves.

D. The sameness of the polity with the same Levitical
priests, upon the *Bamoth* or heights, as prescribed by Moses

(Exodus xx. 19, 23) and in the national sanctuary* (Numbers xxviii.) in Shiloh, Nob, Gibeon and Jerusalem† from the days of Joshua nearly fifteen hundred years, without any intimation anywhere or of any one having introduced or changed the same—points undeniably to an authoritative Thorah prior to Joshua.

E. The Ark of the Covenant (אָרוֹן), containing the two tables of stone, the "Testimony" (עֵדוּת), covered with the golden lid and the two cherubim, (כַּפּוֹרֶת) was there and is noticed in the Biblical books at all times from Joshua to Jeremiah; and yet outside of the Thorah the origin of this historical monument, this very heart and soul of the Mosaic dispensation, doctrine and law, is noticed nowhere by statement or intimation. No less than one hundred and forty-five times the Ark of the Covenant is expressly noticed after the Pentateuch in the books of Joshua, Judges, Samuel,

---

*Moses evidently permits the sacrificing upon *Bamoth* or altars of earth or rough stone upon heights, not in the wilderness but in the land of Canaan (Exodus xx. 20-23). This passage is further expounded in Deuteronomy xii. where באחד שבטיך signifies in any one of thy tribes or wherever the prophet will point out the place, that God will cause his name to be mentioned. Yet in after times there was a continual difference between the prophets who opposed the *Bamoth* and the kings and people who sustained them. The law was undoubtedly there. This is evident from 2 Kings v. 17, where it is reported that the Syrian captain, Naaman, being converted to worship Jehovah, asked for earth to take along to his country, to build of it an altar to Jehovah. It seems that then the letter of the law in Exodus, verse 21, was understood literally that the earth for the altar must be from Palestinean soil. Being permitted by the law and having become universal custom, the people and also the most pious kings clung to it (See 2 Chronicles xxxiii. 17). Having become in many instances pagan altars the prophets opposed the *Bamoth*, but never succeeded in overcoming the practice, because the law permitted it. Had the Thorah been written or revised at a late date by any of the prophets this passage in Exodus must necessarily have been omitted together with Deuteronomy xii.

† The sanctuary of Shiloh, with the uninterrupted continuation of the same sacrificial polity, can not be doubted. It is mentioned

Kings, Chronicles and Jeremiah, in connection with historical events and always as a reality, being actually there when
such event or events occurred, as may be seen in any Hebrew concordance. It is described as the "Ark of the Covenant," the "Ark of Jehovah," the "Ark of Elohim," the "Ark
of the Covenant of Jehovah," the "Ark of the Covenant of
Elohim," the "Ark of the God of Israel," and the "Ark of
the Covenant of Jehovah Zabaoth," with the same *Baddim*,
or two bars in the rings on its two sides, and containing the
same two tables of stone in the time of King Solomon when
it was placed into the *sanctum sanctorum* of the temple,
where it certainly remained unchanged, the same until
Jeremiah, prior to the destruction of the temple, hid it,
together with the golden altar and the Mosaic tabernacle in
a cave on Mount Nebo (2 Maccabees ii. 4-6) ; or, as the Talmud and Maimonides have it, it was hid under the temple
in a secret chamber by King Joshiah (See Art. "Aron" in
Pachad Yitzchak).*

3. The indirect evidence to the authenticity of the Pentateuch consists of the following points :

(a) The laws and institutions on which critics agree that

---

first as the presumptive capital of Canaan (Genesis xlix. 10), then
as the capital of Canaan and the place of the national sanctuary
(Joshua xviii. 1; xix. 51), and is that yet in the time of Phineas
(Judges xxi. 19). It is mentioned again as such in 1 Samuel; then
in Psalms lxxviii. 60, and in Jeremiah vii. 12-14, where its destruction is noticed. It was situated in Ephraim (Joshua xvi. 6).
In the Talmud (*Sebachim*) the tradition is recorded that the sanctuary at Shiloh consisted of a stone structure, on the top of which
the tabernacle of Moses was pitched. The tabernacle itself was
not destroyed; it was tranferred from Shiloh to Nob (?) and then
to Gibeon (1 Chronicles xvi. 37–42) and finally by Solomon to Jerusalem (2 Chronicles v. 5; 2 Kings viii. 4). Those critics who must
prove the non-existence of any Thorah at the start of Israel
in Canaan, make it easy for themselves by simply denying all
this documentary testimony concerning Shiloh and the Mosaic
tabernacle.

* Most objectionable in this connection is the assumption of some
radical critics, that the "Ark" was the god or idol worshiped by

they were adopted into the Pentateuch from the Egyptians, as is also the case with the Egyptian words and names in the Book, and the fact that its author and the people to whom he spoke knew more of Egypt than of Canaan. These points being sufficiently discussed, require no further support; it is for the negative side to show how this could have been the case if the book had been written after the time of Moses. In connection therewith it must be borne in mind that there is no trace in the Pentateuch of Zoroasterism, which we know also from Isaiah (xlv. 6, 7) that it existed in his time; no knowledge of the city of Babylon, no more than that one of the four provinces over which Nimrod reigned in the land of Shinear was called Babel (Genesis x. 10 and xi. 2)* no knowledge of a land called Assyria or a capital called Nineveh, Ashshur is yet the name of a man and Resen is the " Great City " (Genesis x. 11, 12), not even in the time of Abraham (ibid. xiv.), and the Ashshur in the poem of Balaam (Numbers xxiv.) seems yet to be taken as the name of a man and not of a country. The Pentateuch betrays no knowledge of any country except Egypt and

the ancient Hebrews, to which others add that the stones kept therein were those gods or idols, in support of which the Scriptural texts offer no more argument than reason and experience offer in support of the assumption that human beings at any time worshiped stock, stone, or any other object of nature, box, idol, image, or any other work of art, otherwise than as presentations of ideas or conceptions of divinity preceding the objects of nature or the works of art adopted to represent those previous ideas or conceptions. Only when the original ideas were forgotten, thoughtless multitudes continued to worship those objects. It is an outrage on human nature to reverse the order and entirely contrary to experience. The ark and the tablets, if they were ever worshiped in Israel, must necessarily first have represented ideas of divinity, which could but be the inscriptions on those stones and the character of that ark as testimony of the covenant. Those radical critics, however, admit the existence of the ark and tablets at all times after Moses; hence their assumption does not invalidate our argument in this connection.

* Also in Joshua vii. 21 we find the Adereth Shinear.

Arabia. It has not even the city of Tyre, and besides Damascus and Haran in Mesopotamia, none in Syria. In the East it knows only of Ur of the Chaldeans.

(b)   There are in the Pentateuch a number of laws and narrations which could have been written only during the sojourn of Israel in the wilderness prior to taking possession of the land of Canaan ; as the laws concerning the Year of Jubilee and the Year of Release (Leviticus xxv.). In no land and among no people in possession of the soil such laws of possession could be ordained with any prospect of success. They could be prospective only and ordained before the Israelites possessed the land of Canaan, as conditions *sine qua non* under which God gives them possession of the land (Leviticus xxvi. 33–35, 43). It is evident that the law of possession, as ordained in Moses, existed among the Israelites at all times (Ruth i. 9 to ii. 10; Jeremiah xxxii. 1–12; xxxiv. 1–27; Ezekiel xlvi. 17), so that not even wicked Ahab dared to violate it (2 Kings xxi.); and when the exiles returned from Babylon, the family groups were carefully noticed to return each to its own. It is not certain that the Year of Jubilee was enforced at any time; so much the more it must have been a prospective legislation, which, like many others of the same kind, were never reduced to practice. If it had been enacted at any time in Canaan it must have left a trace of its origin.*

(c)   Among other chapters of Leviticus and Numbers

---

*Jeremiah xxxiv. gives us to understand that he refers to the Thorah. He uses the terms חפשי and דרור for free and freedom, exactly like Moses in Exodus and Leviticus, which none after him had used except Jeremiah, and connects them with the same verbs as Moses did לקרא דרור לשלח חפשי. In verse 14 he begins with the words of Moses in Deuteronomy (xv. 1), and continues with the Mosaic words in (Exodus xxi. 27), and like Moses he places the verb ימכר *yimmocher* in the passive voice, showing that he knows and refers to all the laws of Moses on this subject, and refers only to persons that had been sold as a punishment for crimes committed, as Exodus xxii. 2, to whom alone Exodus xxi. 2 refers. No other bondsman went out free with the seventh year of his servitude unless such was his special compact

which refer especially to the sojourn in the wilderness, Leviticus xvii. contains the plainest evidence of having been written there, and even in the beginning of that period, soon after the tabernacle had been erected, which applies also to chapters xviii.–xx., wherein the peculiarity of addressing the commandments to אִישׁ אִישׁ or אִישׁ recurs frequently.* These are special laws expressed in concrete cases, without abstraction of general laws, as in Exodus xxi. and xxii., which is certainly the form of primitive legislation. Besides, this chapter closes thus: "And every person that eateth that which hath died of itself, or that which was torn by beasts, be this one born in your own country, or a stranger, shall both wash his clothes, and bathe himself in water, and be unclean until the evening, when he shall be clean. But if he wash (them) not, nor bathe his flesh, then shall he bear his iniquity." This was certainly written prior to Leviticus xi., where the eating, touching or carrying any unclean carcass is prohibited with much more emphasis than prescribing for the transgressor no other punishment or means of atonement than washing his body and garments, so that the sin is not in eating the forbidden food, but in not washing if one ate it. This passage can only be a continuation of Exodus xxii. 30, which it supplements. The whole of this chapter refers to matters in the wilderness and at that special time. There is no reason imaginable why it should have been written at any other time. This is also evident from Deuteronomy xii. 15, 16, 20–23. It prohibits the killing of sheep, goats or cattle otherwise than at the altar, where the blood is to be sprinkled and part of the fat to be burned, for which the reason is given in verse 7, "that they make no sacrifices to the *Se'irim*," the demons of the wilderness, besides which there was also an economical reason not stated in the text, all referring to the sojourn in the wilderness. Then in verse 13 the exception to this rule is stated in regard to game, which may be freely used for

---

*Also in Numbers v. 6 to vi. 31 and ix. 9–18.

food, but the blood must be covered with dust or ashes.
This again, was only for the wilderness, a sanitary measure,
and is not repeated in Deuteronomy xii. 16, 24, because it
referred to the wilderness only. No motive is imaginable
that could have induced any author, after or before Moses,
to write this chapter xvii. of Leviticus. The same is the
case with the story of the golden calf, made in the wilderness, in which Aaron is placed in so unfavorable a light
(Deut. ix. 20), to which Leviticus xvii. evidently refers. It
was certainly not written when the descendants of Aaron
were the highest aristocracy of the nation, as was always
the case, at least from and after the time of King Solomon.
The same seems to be the case with all Pentateuchal passages referring to the conquest of Canaan and the subjuga-
tion or even extermination of the aborigines, when they had
ceased to exist, and none disputed the right and claim of
the Israelites to their land;* on the contrary, those passages sound so harshly and so contrary to the Mosaic principle of humanism that no author of a later date would
have written them, and if one had done so, no compiler
would have inserted them in the Thorah.

There are also a number, especially of penal laws, in the
Pentateuch which, if tested by the general principles and
standard of Pentateuchal ethics, could have been intended
for Israel's sojourn in the wilderness only. To this class
might be taken the thirty-six cases in the Thorah, the commission (in two cases omission) of which to be punished
with *Karath*, " cut off " (*Mishna Kerithuth I.*), the transgressor

---

*The passage in Ezra ix. 1 does not say that those nationalities
existed in his time; it only tells that in taking foreign women for
wives, they did כתועבתיהם " like their abominations " which their
ancestors did in marrying the daughters of those nations. The
להם in verse 2, refers to עמי ארצות in verse one. Their practice now, it says, was as abominable as it was in former days,
when Hebrews took in marriage the daughters of other nations,
referring to historical data, as is evident according to the Talmud
in regard to Ammonites and Moabites and according to the Law as
regards the Egyptians, mentioned in Ezra.

to be cut off, and it is said nowhere from what he is to be cut off. The rabbinical expounders, therefore, were in doubt as to what to make of this kind of punishment, and some made of it a divine punishment executed by the Almighty in time or eternity.* This esoteric conception of the term *Karath* is not its primary meaning. It could but be intended to convey the idea to cut off from the tribe or from the main body. This was a severe punishment in the wilderness only, and was inflicted on transgressors among many other tribes similarly located. The same seems to be the case with the punishment of death for the Sabbath-breaker (Exodus xxxi. 13-17; Numbers xv. 32-36) and all penalties of death in Leviticus xx., all of which are justifiable from the ethical standpoint of Moses, as temporary measures in the wilderness only, where such heroic and rigorous laws were necessary, to break down the pagan practices, to maintain moral purity among the hundred thousands of men and women encamped in close approximation in the heart of a wide waste, and to introduce effectually the laws, then new, like the Sabbath, the sexual relations and the anti-pagan practices. As measures in the wilderness, they are harsh and rigorous, but justifiable by prevailing circumstances; as laws enacted at any time in the land of Israel, they are unjustifiable, almost unthinkable in connection with the Mosaic standard of ethics. These must be legislations from and for the wilderness, and are, therefore, not repeated in Deuteronomy, nor by prophets, psalmists or chronographers.

(d) The body of doctrine, the institutions connected therewith and the conception of righteousness as advanced in the Pentateuch re-echo from all parts of the Bible from first chapter of Josuha to the last of Chronicles. It is not only the same Jehovah-Elohim, but also the same Creator, Preserver and Governor of the world, the same sole Sovereign of heaven and earth, and in his relations to man the same Holy God of mercy, benevolence, long suffering and of abso-

---

*See *Siphri* to Numbers xv. 30, 31, and Talmud *Sanhedrin* 99 and *Targum Yerushalmi*.

lute grace and truth, who preserves and extends the good and
the true to the thousandth generation and permits evil to
exist only to the fourth, and forgives iniquity, sin and transgression.   So God is revealed from the summit of Sinai, so
Moses defines and proclaims Jehovah (Exodus xx. 5; xxxiv.
6–7; Numbers xiv. 17–20; Deuter. x. 17; iv. 35, 39; vii. 9;
xxxii.3,4). So did David praise him in Psalms ciii. and many
other psalms; so God's name and glory resounds and re-
echoes in the speeches of all prophets, the songs and hymns
of all psalmists and the narrators of every episode of
Israel's history. And yet none of those inspired men maintains that God revealed himself to him in this full majesty
of his glory; none added any new idea to this sublime
cognition of the Most High, and none was able up to this
day to add to it.   The same is the case with the lofty conception of human nature which Moses proclaims (Genesis i.) and David sings in inspired lays (Psalms viii.); the
threefold covenant, viz., with man (Genesis ix. 8–17), with
Abraham (ibid. xvii.) and with Israel (Exodus xix. and
xxiv.), which re-echoes so from all books of the Bible that
the term *Berith*, " covenant," recurs no less than two hundred
and fifty times, and none maintains that he advanced this
doctrine, or added anything to it.   The same is the case with
the institutions connected with it, viz., circumcision, Sabbath, New Moon, the three high feasts, the duty of righteousness, holiness and worship.   All this we find present in
the mind of every author that contributed to the collection
called Holy Writ, without any claim to originality in all
these matters, and these taken together make the essentiality
of Israel's religion; hence the outspoken confession that the
Thorah of Moses preceded all other books and parts of books.

(e) The main historical data narrated in the Pentateuch
also recur in the scriptural records.   There is none which
alludes not to the fact that the Hebrews were the descendants of Abraham, Isaac and Jacob.   Also that Jacob went to
Aram, served Laban for his daughter, and was then called
Israel, is mentioned by the prophet Hosea (xii.).   The fact
of Israel's sojourn in Egypt, the exodus and remaining forty

years in the wilderness re-echoes from most all books, as also the story of Baal Peor (Numbers xxv.), and of Balak and Balaam (ibid. xxiii. and xxiv.), especially from Hosea (xi. 1; xii. 10; xiii. 4), Amos (ii. 10)* and Micah (v. 1-5), and mentions especially Moses, Aaron and Miriam. The occurrences in the wilderness toward the end of Moses' life are re-told by Yiphthach in Judges xi. 12-28. The fact that Aaron was appointed a *Nabi* in Egypt, and afterward the Cohen, is referred to in 1 Samuel ii. 27, 28 by the Man of Elohim. 1 Samuel xii. it is this prophet who repeats the story of Jacob going to Egypt and of Moses and Aaron leading them out of that country. 1 Kings ii., the Thorah of Moses as a written book containing ordinances, commandments and testimonies, as also in Psalms xix., are reported, so that as far as facts are concerned we need go no further, although we might refer to many more passages, as for instance, the Asaph chapters (Psalms lxxviii., lxxx., lxxxi.), and especially Psalms cxxxvi. This suffices to establish the fact advanced at the head of this paragraph.

4. There are a number of arguments *e silentio* in support of the antiquity and authenticity of the Pentateuch which in connection with the foregoing are of considerable weight. Mark the following : .

(*a*) About eleven hundred and fifty Hebrew roots, and no less new formations of words from existing roots occur in Prophets and Hagiography, which are not found in the Pentateuch. Take away the Aramaic portions in Daniel and Ezra, and the Pentateuch will be found to contain much more than one-fourth of the Hebrew of the whole Bible. This marks the progress of the Hebrew language after the five books of Moses had been written, most visible in the books of Isaiah, Micah, Psalms, Proverbs and Job, and points directly to the antiquity of the Pentateuch.

(*b*) The failure of all critics not only to fix with any degree of certainty the time when the Pentateuch, or any

---

*Amos also knows the story of Sodom and Gomorrah, and tells it with the same unusual verb וַיַּהְפֹּךְ as Moses did. See Amos iv. 2.

part thereof, was written—simply because the history of the Hebrew language is unknown to them—but also to discover any anthropological, geographical or topographical error, as far as Egypt, Arabia and Palestine are concerned, in the whole Pentateuch. This, as well as the exact location of places and the life-like descriptions of persons and events points undoubtedly to an author cotemporary with the events and perfectly at home in those localities. For instances of this kind we may point especially to the addresses and songs of Moses in Deuteronomy and Exodus xv., and the prayer of Moses (Psalms xc. and xci.). It is not merely the antique form of the poetry and the concrete terms, it is the clearness and exactness of the contents which exclude any idea of a later author, especially in the above psalms, in which the last days of Moses in the wilderness, with all the horrors of the wilderness, the death of a whole generation before his mind, with a small band of sur-vivors approaching their end, are so vividly described.

(c) The entire disregard in the Pentateuch to the Later Prophets is characteristic. No notice is taken of the un-favorable sentiments of prophets and psalmists to the sacri-ficial cults in general, to the *Bamoth*, the altars on the heights in particular, and to all the innovations proposed by the prophet Ezekiel. This could not be the case, if the Thorah had been written late in the prophetical millenium. Nor could those passages and penal laws pointed out above have been accepted in the law—in spirit so contrary to the teach-ings of the prophets and psalmists—if it had been revised and re-edited at a later date. Not even the musical reforms pressed so emphatically by those who returned from Baby-lon, as is evident from Chronicles and Ezra, were given a support in the law.

(d) The absence of any fixed doctrinal formula of im-mortality of the soul or resurrection of the body with any kind of future reward and punishment is proof positive almost of the antiquity of the Pentateuch. The indefi-nite ideas of eschatological matters correspond only with ancient Egypt, by no means with the Zabaism or Zoroas-

terism of the East, not even with the older prophets and
psalmists in Israel whose ideas of an immortal soul are
much clearer and definite, as is evident from 1 Kings xvii.
17-24; 2 Kings iv. 20-37; Psalms viii. xvi. and xlix.; Isaiah
xxvi. 19 further illustrated in Ezekiel xxxvii. Had the Pentateuch been written or rewritten at a later date none can
doubt that a fixed formula of this doctrine would be in it.

5. Last, although no less important, the direct testimony
to the antiquity of the Pentateuch from Chronicles, Ezra
and Malachi must be considered. The main portion of
Chronicles, we have seen in the previous chapter, was
written before the advent of Ezra, nearer to the Babylonian
captivity than any other book besides the three last
prophets. There can be no doubt that the chronist had
before him the written Thorah of Moses, which, he states,
existed in the time of King David (1 Chron xvi. 9) at the
first occasion he had to refer to it. He refers again and
again to it in the time of David (ibid. xxii. 12; xxix. 19),
of Solomon (2 Chron. viii. 13), of Rehabeam (xii. 1), of Asa
(xiv. 3), of Jehoshaphat, who appointed teachers to
visit the cities of Judah with "the book of the Thorah of
Jehovah," and they did teach it publicly (xvii. 7-9). He
reports then again the Thorah in the time of King Hezekiah
(xxx. 16). When he reports that "the book of the Thorah"
was found in the sanctuary (xxxiv. 14, 15), which he further
on calls "the book of the Covenant" (verse 30), he certainly
could not intend to say that a new book, one unknown
before, was discovered. No author will thus contradict his
own statements. There is no cause to suspect the chronist
of false reports. Still, however this may be, he proves to a
certainty that the Pentateuch as it is existed in his time,
was known as the Thorah of Jehovah, the book of Moses,
and was generally believed to have existed in the same
form at least up to the time of King David. Later on the
prophet Malachi closes his prophecy with the same solemn
testimony: "Remember the Thorah of Moses, my servant,
which I commanded him at Horeb upon all Israel ordinances and statutes." There comes to all this the solemn

testimony of Ezra, Nehemiah, the elders, priests and Levites,
of all the people assembled in holy convocation at Jerusalem, from the first to the twenty-fourth day of the
seventh month, when the Thorah was read and expounded
to them, and all of them acknowledged it as the genuine
Thorah of Jehovah Elohim (Nehemiah ix. 3) given by
Moses on Mount Sinai (verses 13 and 14 and x. 30), confirmed it with two solemn affirmations, by the oath, and
signing their names to the document to convey all this to
posterity; all of which is preserved in the viii. ix. and x.
chapters of Nehemiah. All speculations, however ingenious and plausible to contradict this fact, are worthless.
In the time of Ezra, Nehemiah, Malachi and the Chronist
the Pentateuch was generally known and firmly believed
to be the Thorah of Jehovah, the Thorah of Moses,
the Thorah revealed on Mount Sinai. The groundless
hypothesis, that Ezra wrote, amended or interpolated the
Thorah, is a forlorn hope and can not be sustained by any
known fact. His cotemporaries solemnly swore that it is
the Thorah of Moses and not of Ezra. The Samaritans,
who did not accept any of the Ezra and Nehemiah reforms, not even the other books of Scriptures, accepted the
Thorah in the ancient writing. In the post-biblical literature prior to the Talmud, Ezra is not mentioned any more,
not even in the forty-ninth chapter of Ben Sira's book,
where the prophets Zerubabel, Joshua and Nehemiah are
glorified. Josephus and Philo know nothing of Ezra as
author or lawgiver.* All this would be impossible if Ezra
had written the Thorah or even any part thereof. Therefore
we know from all foregoing arguments of this chapter, that
there always was a Thorah; a written Thorah, a Thorah of

---

*All anybody knows of or about Ezra must be from that book or
the traditions recorded in the Talmud, and these two only sources
never intimate that he, in regard to the Thorah, was any more
than a learned scribe and expounder, who in a very few instances
filled up a defective passage, which he marked by points above the
letters. (See Numbers Rabba 37, 24 to לָמָה נֻקַּד עַל לָנוּ and *Tikkun
Sopherim*, of which we speak in the next chapter.

Jehovah, a Thorah of Moses, prior to all other biblical books, that the contents of that Thorah were in doctrines and narratives in the main at least identical with the one before us; but we know not yet their perfect identity, nor do we know yet when and by whom it was cast in the form as it is before us. We must continue the investigation.

6. The three middle books of the Pentateuch were certainly not edited in the time of Kings in Israel or Judah. They are strenuously democratic-theocratic in all their provisions and narrations. No room is left to a king, no prerogative is given to any, no sphere for the exercise of the royal authority is intimated. This democratic spirit is so clearly expressed—and this is to be especially remembered—that God is never called "King" in all the Pentateuch, nowhere before Samuel (xii. 12). Such a code could not have been written or edited in any country governed by a king. That these three books were not written after that time is evident from the foregoing arguments in this chapter. Some of the negative critics admit this, when they maintain that the book of the Thorah found in the temple by Hilkiah, the high priest, and brought to King Joshiah (2 Kings xxiii.; 2 Chronicles xxxiv.) was Deuteronomy, which the prophet Jeremiah forged, and in conspiracy with the priest, imposed on the king as the work of Moses. Before arguing this point it must be taken into consideration that if this is so then the three middle books of the Pentateuch must be much older than Deuteronomy. There could be no reason to forge that book nine centuries after the death of Moses upon his name; had he not been known as the redeemer, lawgiver and founder of the institutions extant in the time of Jeremiah. It can not be maintained that the name also was an invention, because either it was used to give authority to the book, then the name must have been identified with this authority, or the invention was foolish, as historical names of high authority like Samuel, David, Solomon, Elijah, Isaiah, must have been well known then, and any one of them would have conferred a higher authority upon the pseudonymous book than the unknown

and foreign Moses. If Moses was known as the redeemer,
lawgiver and founder of the institutions, it could not have
been by tradition nine centuries *post festum*, there must have
existed documents to this effect. These documents — the
evidence is too overwhelming—must have been besides the
three middle books of the Thorah, also Genesis, or such other
documents in which the subject matter of Deuteronomy was
contained, to which it literally refers in almost every chapter, in narration, doctrine and law.* However, there exists
no passage and no intimation in any book of the Bible or elsewhere to justify the ungenerous and unethical hypothesis, that
Jeremiah or any other prophet or priest in Israel committed
literary forgery, pious fraud or impious dissimulation; or to
assume that Deuteronomy was the book found in the days of
King Joshiah. The books of Kings and Chronicles were written undoubtedly by authors of ability, who would not contradict themselves in matters of facts in the same book. And
yet in 2 Kings xiv. and 2 Chronicles xxv.—besides many
other passages—the existence and authority of Deuteronomy
is expressly acknowledged by quoting from it literally verse
6 in Kings and verse 4 in Chronicles. Still further on, in
Kings xvii. and Chronicles xxx. and xxxi., in the time of
King Hezekiah, the existence and authority of the whole

---

* As most striking reference of this kind compare Deuteronomy
i. 9–18 to Exodus xviii. 26; Moses being omitted in the Deuteronomy passage which closes, "And I commanded you then all the
words which ye shall do." Compare Deuteronomy i. to iii. with
the corresponding passages in Numbers; also iv. 1–3 to Numbers
xxv. 1–9; ibid. iv. 9–13 to Exodus xix.; ibid. three times כאשר צוך "
in Deuteronomy v., and after verse 19 compare to Exodus xx. 15–19;
ibid. Deuteronomy xiv. and Leviticus xi.; Deuteronomy xxviii. to
Leviticus xxvi., and so on throughout the book with numerous
references to Genesis. The difference of expressions in the Decalogue and some laws prove that Moses was the author of Deuteronomy, as none else would have attempted these changes and
emendations. The defectiveness of some laws, as in Deuteronomy
xxiii. 1–3 points most distinctly to laws of prior existence, in this
case Leviticus xviii. as the emendations to other laws again demonstrate the authorship of Moses.

Thorah is expressly acknowledged. Anyway, no fair critic can presume that two pages beyond the author or compiler contradicts all that and meant to say there that Deuteronomy or any part of the Pentateuch, then unknown, was produced or found in the temple. Besides Kings and Chronicles inform us expressly that סֵפֶר הַתּוֹרָה THE book of the Thorah, viz., the main book of the Thorah, was found in the temple, which in both sources is called then סֵפֶר הַבְּרִית "THE Book of the Covenant," which we know from Exodus xxiv. 4–7 was the principal book written by Moses. There exists not the least cause to maintain that it was any other book except an ancient manuscript supposed, perhaps, to be the original book written by Moses. In hearing the contents of the book the king rent his garments, and sent to the prophetess Huldah—not to Jeremiah, who was not known yet as a prophet and was a very young man—to inquire of the Lord as to what evil would come over the land, "because our fathers hearkened not to the words of this book to do like all that is written concerning us." This is repeated in clearer language in 2 Chronicles. Hence it was not a new book or one not known or not observed at that time, it is only the fathers, meaning Menasseh and Amon, who did not do as prescribed in the said book. The cause of the terror which the book struck was simply that the Book of the Covenant closed with Leviticus xxv. and xxvi., and the latter chapter contains the prophecies of Moses concerning all the evils to befall the people breaking the covenant and deserting their God and his law. To this the message of the prophetess Huldah refers, which is also stated extensively in the name of many prophets in 2 Kings xxi. 10–17, and is repeated in Jeremiah in most all of his messages. All this, no doubt, was known in the days of King Joshiah, but it was not believed to be the genuine prophecy of Moses. The ancient manuscript found in the temple proved to them that such was the prophecy of Moses, and this struck terror into the hearts and started Jeremiah on his prophetical mission of, " the end approaches," taken from Amos' בָּא הַקֵּץ (viii.

2), announced to Israel, " I will hasten my word to perform it."*

7. The existence and authority of the Thorah are traceable up to the time of Samuel in the historical books, the oldest prophets, Proverbs and Psalms. In regard to the older prophets attention is called to the following special points:

(a) The main events narrated in the Thorah are noticed in these books. Such are the origin of the Hebrew people and its religion from Abraham, Isaac and Jacob (Micah vii. 20; Hosea xii. 4, 5; Amos vii. 16); the destruction of Sodom and Gomorrah with the same exceptional term of כמהפכת ויהפוך ההפכה as in Genesis xix. (Amos iv. 11; Isaiah i. 9, 10, also iii. 9 and xiii. 19); Israel's sojourn in Egypt, the redemption by Moses, Aaron and Miriam and the forty years in the wilderness (Amos ii. 10; iii. 1; v. 25,) where also the prophets and Nazirites are noticed (Hosea ii. 17; xi. 1; xii. 14; xiv. 5; Micah vi. 4); the story of Balak and Bileam (Micah vi. 6) and the location where it occurred; so also the story at Baal Peor (Hosea ix. 10).

(b) The imitations and quotations from the Pentateuch. Such are Joel ii. 13 like Exodus xxxiv. 6; ii. 16 like Deuteronomy viii. 10; ii. 17; and iv. 17 like Numbers xv. 41 אני יי ; אלהיכם ; Amos iii. 14 like Exodus xxxii. 34 ביום פקדי; iv. 6–11 is an abstract of Leviticus xxvi. the phrase אם לא תשמעו לי changed into the refrain ולא שבתם עדי; Hosea i. 7 והושעתים ביי like Deuteronomy xxxii. 19; i. 9 is like Deuteronomy xxvi. 16–19; ii. 1 is like Genesis xiii. 16 and xxi. 17; v. 8 is like Numbers x. 1–10 with the identical words of שופר, חצוצרה and והריעו; v. 10 is like Deuteronomy xxvii. 37, with the identical מסיג גבול; xii. 10 and xiii. 4 are literally the first verse of the Decalogue. Isaiah i. 2 is an imitation of Deuteronomy xxxii. 1. Besides all of them repeated the words of Moses (Deuteronomy xxx. 3),

---

*The prophecy of Jeremiah that the Babylonian captivity would last seventy years, was based upon the prophecy of Moses (Leviticus xxvi. 32-34). The number seventy must be understood as the ordinary lifetime of a man.

ושב יי אלהיך את שבותך (Joel iii. 4; Amos ix. 14; Hosea
vi. 11.) This phrase passed into almost every book of the
Bible.

Hosea (iv. 15) informs us that the people also in the
kingdom of Israel swore חי יי by the Living God of Israel.
They speak of the "Covenant" by which Israel became a
kingdom of priests (Hosea iv. 6; viii. 1; Isaiah xxiv. 5); so
Micah speaks of the grace and truth, or the love and faithfulness which God has sworn to our ancestors from ancient
days (vii. 20). They speak of the sacrificial polity, the
altar, the priesthood, the sacrifices as ancient institutions,
not as a form of Pagan worship (Joel i. 13; ii. 17), and
Amos brings in connection with *Chaggim* "feasts," *Atzeroth*,
generally rendered "feast of conclusion," which word in this
signification occurs in the Pentateuch only.

They make mention of תורת יי וחקיו "the Thorah of
Jehovah and his statutes" (Amos ii. 4); תורת אלהיך "the
Thorah of thy Elohim," and ברית ותורה "the Covenant
and the Thorah" (Hosea iv. 6 and viii. 1), תורת אלהינו
"the Thorah of our Elohim" (Isaiah i. 10) in parallel with
דבר יי "The Word of Jehovah," of which he, like Micah,
knows that the Thorah will go forth from Zion and the word
of God from Jerusalem to all nations (ii. 3). He knows
that the Thorah is not the *Theudah* or prediction (viii. 20)
and that it consists of more than one book which stands in
connection with *Chok* or statute, and *Berith* or covenant
(xxiv. 5), and that his people refuse to obey the תורת יי
"The Thorah of Jehovah" (xxx. 8). He speaks of *Sepher*
a book (xxix. 11, 12), and even of two kinds of Holy Writs,
the *Luach Ithom* and the *Sepher Chuckoh*, and tells us expressly (xxxiv. 16), "Inquire ye from the Book of Jehovah"; hence we must conclude that the Thorah was written
a *Sepher Chuckoh*. We know it was the Thorah which
stands in connection with *Berith*, the covenant, which, to
the best of our knowledge, was the Pentateuch only

8. It seems, therefore, probable that the three middle
books of the Pentateuch were recast in their present form

from the Mosaic documents, by editors from the period of
the Judges. In this period there are but two ages when
such an important work might have been accomplished ; (1)
from and after the conquest and occupation of Canaan by
Joshua to the time of Deborah and Barak, which we may
call the Phineas age ; and (2) the time of Samuel and his
immediate disciples, the first *Bene Hannebiim*. In regard to
the Phineas age, we read in Joshua xxiv. 31 and Judges ii.
7, "And Israel served God all the days of Joshua, and all
the elders that lived long after Joshua, who had known all
the (great) works of God, that he had done for Israel."
This age of piety and knowledge re-echoes yet in the Deborah song, and it appears from there (Judges v. 6) to have
reached into the time of Shamgar ben Anoth, the immediate predecessor of Deborah. It was evidently a literary age
when laws were written (ibid. verses 9 and 14) "to ennoble
the people," and men were searching into the law to establish justice (verse 10) and there were expert scribes in Zebulon (verse 14). It is probable that then, even by the
immediate disciples of Moses, like Phineas, Othniel ben
Kenaz and their cotemporaries, the Mosaic material was
recast for the benefit of priests and people into the more
practical form of Exodus and Leviticus, as these two books
contain nothing which points to a date after the Deborah
age, and after that came the retrogression into the rude
ages of Jephthah and Samson, arrested by Samuel and his
disciples. The prophet Samuel, according to Psalms xcix.
6, 7 ranks with Moses and Aaron, among those who proclaimed God's name, who cried to God and he responded to
them : "In a pillar of cloud would he speak to them ; they
guarded his testimonies and he gave them statutes." This
sounds very much like placing Samuel among the law-
givers, so that the Talmud could maintain שקול שמואל
כנגד משה ואהרן "Samuel equipoises Moses and Aaron."
The next consideration is that Samuel was the author of
the book of Judges, taken from the " Book of the Wars of
Jehovah," and after Judges opens a new method of histori-
ography and a new epoch of Hebrew language and litera-

ture; as if the old Mosaic and post-Mosaic records had been closed, after the material for Pentateuch, Joshua and Judges had been transcribed from them, new records were opened and continued thereafter by the prophets and the Scribes and Chancellors of the royal court. Besides all this, it appears that Judges and the first part of Samuel are in spirit closer to Numbers than to any other book, and several passages in Numbers have their counterparts in Judges, as for instance Judges i. 17 and Numbers x. 3–5, also Deuteronomy iii. 14; Judges x. 3–5; Numbers xxx. 39–42; Judges xi. 11, 12–28, and Numbers xxxi.; Judges xiii. 7 and Numbers vi. 1–5, while none reach beyond the time of Samuel. The last of the Balaam's poems (Numbers xxiv. 15–24) bears the imprint of Samuel, and some maintain also his name. There must be added to all this, that from and after Samuel we have before us detailed history; if at any time after Samuel such an important literary monument as the Pentateuch had been erected, some notice of it must have been left in chronographers, psalmists or prophets, which, however, is not the case. Thus we are again obliged to admit that the recasting of the Mosaic documents could not have taken place after the days of Samuel.

9. The question arises, do the documents before us compel us to admit that the Mosaic documents were edited after the death of Moses? In this connection the following points must be considered:

(a) There are anachronistic passages in the Pentateuch. Exodus xvi. 35 and 36 closes the narrative of the manna and the first falling of quail in the wilderness of Zin, thus: "The children of Israel ate the manna forty years, till they came to the inhabited land; they ate the manna till they came into the borders of the land of Canaan. An omer is the tenth part of an ephah." This could have been written only after they had come into the land, and had a different measure of capacity; hence after the death of Moses. Leviticus xxi. is headed, "Say to the priests, sons of Aaron," contrary to all similar passages, which open invariably, "*Speak* (and not say) to Aaron and his sons." Then verse 10 occurs, "And the priest greater than his brothers." These verses could have been written only after the death of Aaron, as the latter had no brother priests, hence could not be called the greatest of them. Numbers xiii. 24 is an explanatory note, giving the reason why that place was called Nahol Eshcol, called so by "the children of Israel" in after times, not by the spies, but after the death of Moses. The same is the case with Numbers xxii. 20 and 27–30; xxxiii. 34–42, as quoted above. The only anachronism in Deuteronomy xvii. 14–20, the law concerning the king, which is in dissonance with the whole Mosaic legislation, also may be ascribed to Samuel, as the last chapter, in which the death of Moses is narrated, is given to Joshua. We notice no passages in Genesis that must necessarily have been written after Moses. It has been stated before that all land west of the Euphrates was called by the Eastern nations ARAB, "the West," and by the Egyptians EBER, the other side of the Red Sea and the Isthmus, hence all that country was called "Land of the Ebrim," or Hebrews. The supposed anachronism of והכנעני אז בארץ " the Canaanite was then in the land," is none with the author of Genesis, and would be none even if Abraham was supposed to have said it, as it means as well: "And the Canaanite had just then come into the interior of the land," viz., when Abraham came, as its actual home was at the western and southern borders of the land (Genesis x. 19; Numbers xiii. 29). Genesis xxxvi. 31–39 is not necessarily an anachronism. It begins: "These are the kings which reigned in the land of Edom before a king reigned (or a government was established) to the children of Israel." Then eight kings, all foreigners, are named, evidently successive conquerors, or governors, placed there by the Pharaohs. All of them may have reigned over the Horites and the children of Esau before the latter achieved superiority and independence, and gave kings to the land. From the emigration of Esau to Seir to the exodus of Israel 300 years elapsed—too long a time almost for eight successive kings. The מלך־מלך with its peculiar construc-

tion, preserved also in Chronicles, does not necessarily signify any king; it means also a government organized. In
this sense we find in Deuter. xxxiii. 5, Moses is called King
of Jeshurun, "he having gathered around himself the heads
of the people, uniting the tribes of Israel," i. e., establish the
government whose head he was. In the Samaritan Joshua,
Moses, Joshua and others are plainly called kings.

(*b*) There are, Exodus xxxiv. 29–33 and Numbers xii. 3,
two passages speaking of Moses in so laudatory a manner
that it seems not Moses had written them. No man of that
eminence will write of himself how his face was shining
and beaming so that Aaron and the people were afraid to
look at him; or that he was the meekest of all men.

(*c*) There are in the Pentateuch definitions of names of
persons which are not deemed correct, and point to a later
hand.

(*d*) There are numerous repetitions in the Pentateuch
which could not be the work of one writer, it is maintained.
This point, however, is not well taken. As regards the repetition of laws, the ancient expounders, as recorded in the
Talmud, established that the repetition of any law contains
an amendment, especially in Deuteronomy, which maintains to have the object of באר את התורה הזאת "expounding this Thorah" (i. 5). For instance, Deut. xiv. begins with amending Leviticus xi., adding thereto that such
may be given to the resident alien or sold to the transient
foreigner, they being not bound to observe those dietary
laws. Then from verse 22 the law of tithe is repeated, to
add thereto that the part of the tithe which the owner is
commanded to consume at "the place where the Lord thy
God will choose" may be sold at home and the money used
to that purpose. Then chapter xv., the law concerning the
year of release, in order to add thereto that debts must not
be collected during the Sabbath year (the rabbis held all debts
were canceled) and that the transient foreigner was not included in this law. Such is the case with every repetition
of law, except כאחד הבאים כתובים שני. Where narrations are repeated, as the same having happened to two

different persons, it must be borne in mind that this is by
no means impossible. Besides, repetitions of this kind
occur only in Genesis, whose author may have had before
him double traditions or documents in those particular
cases.

(*e*) The only book written in the first person is Deuteronomy, the others are written in the third person, as though
another author had written the whole from older records
before him or from traditions.

(*f*) We find there but scanty outlines of Israel's
history in Goshen, and none from thirty-seven years'
sojourning in the wilderness, viz., from the second to the
fortieth year, a few episodes in Numbers excepted. And yet
we know from Hosea ix. 10; x. 1, 2; xi. 1–4; xiii. 5, 6; Amos
v. 25, 26; Ezekiel xx.; Psalms lxxviii.; lxxxi. xcv., that we
possess but a small part of the history in the wilderness in
Exodus and Numbers. In regard to Goshen we learn from
1 Chronicles how little we know of its history; as for
instance iv. 19–23; vi. 20–24; viii. 11–13. It seems even
from some of these notices that many of the Hebrews possessed estates and towns in Canaan, while their people were
in Goshen. It seems, therefore, that the historical portion
of the three middle books is a mere abstract from older and
more extensive records.

(*g*) There is no chronological order in the first four
books (אֵין מוּקְדָם וּמְאוּחָר בַּתּוֹרָה) as the Talmud admits,
nor a logical connection in the order of the sections of laws
(אֵין דּוֹרְשִׁין סְמִיכוּת), except in Deuteronomy; the fourth
book is fragmentary and contains pieces which belong
either to the preceding books or also to Deuteronomy.

Therefore we are bound to admit:

A. That the Thorah with all its principles, doctrines,
laws, institutions, political, social and ecclesiastical, and the
cotemporary history as laid down in the original documents
of Moses, was always known in Israel and was always canon
to the nation, notwithstanding despotic kings and princes
had sought to override the Law, and paganizing multitudes,

that went astray after other gods and the immoral practices undermining reason, freedom and justice.

B. Exodus and Leviticus were edited after the death of Moses—in the Phineas age—from the original documents and contain few of the editor's additions and many omissions (perhaps also exaggerations) in the historical portions.

C. Numbers was edited later on, from fragments omitted by the former and parts originally belonging to Deuteronomy.

D. Genesis and Deuteronomy are the original works of Moses, with some very few later additions in Deuteronomy.

E. Numbers bears the imprints of the prophet Samuel, by whom and his school it must have been edited, it bears no traces of any later date, to connect Leviticus with Deuteronomy. The additions to Deuteronomy also do not reach beyond the time of Samuel.

F. Exodus and Leviticus may have been edited any time after the conquest—they contain nothing pointing to a later date—and no later than the time of the prophetess Deborah.

The question may arise, why do we insist upon this system, and not rather yield to the fragmentists, Jahvists and Elohists, with whom the Thorah is composed of a number of fragments from various authors of unknown times? To this we reply :

(*a*) Because we possess no documentary evidence whatever of the origin or existence of any such fragments at any time ; but we have such evidence of the origin and existence of the Mosaic documents, in contradiction of which speculation is of no value.

(*b*) Because the whole Thorah is of one and the same spirit in principle, doctrine, precept and law, which must necessarily come from one author, and not possibly from a number of authors.

(*c*) Had such fragments existed at any time, the biblical records being so particular with registering of names, must have taken notice of them, which is not the case, while the Mosaic records are specifically mentioned.

(*d*) Because the entire fabric of speculation basing upon

the Jahvistic and Elohistic criteria of authorship is *eo ipso* false and worthless.

10.   The theories advanced, that the Thorah was compiled of a number of older books written by various authors at different times, with or without Mosaic portions, are based upon the first hypothesis, that there are portions in Holy Writ, in which God is called Jehovah and others in which he is called Elohim.   This it was assumed—certainly on no holding ground—points to different authors.   Then on the strength of grammatical niceties and supposed repetitions and contradictions in the different books, the division into original fragments was pressed to an unreasonable number, although it is evident that casual grammatical deviations in such small portions of literature are no evidence for different authors, as by a rigid application of the same method, any book, ancient or modern, could be split into fragments from different authors.   The very fact that with this method the Pentateuch was split in twenty-five slices, each of a different author, proves the fallacy of that method, anyhow to any critical reader of the original.   This method, however, like all others, to prove that the Thorah was not of Moses and the historical books were re-edited and interpolated, started originally from the Jahvistic-Elohistic hypothesis and in support thereof; this being refuted, all those theories fall with it.   This hypothesis, however, is without foundation for the following reasons :

(*a*)   Every book of the Bible was written by a Jahvist, none besides the second and a part of the third book of Psalms is Elohistic (Psalms xlii.–lxxxiii.), that is, the Elohim predominates in all of them.   Here is the documentary evidence that the different names of God do not point to different authors.   The same David who is credited with the purely Jahvistic psalms (especially Psalms viii. xviii.) is also credited with the Elohistic psalms (Psalms li.–lxi. and lxiii. lxxi); the same sons of Korah at the heads of Elohistic psalms (Psalms xlii.–xlix.) are also credited with the Jahvistic (Psalms lxxxiv., lxxxv., lxxxvii. and lxxxviii.).   Our theory, for which we have some Scriptural support, is

that the hymns of David were written for public worship
at the advanced age of the King, after the ark had been
brought to Zion, therefore they are Jahvistic, as he only in
his last words calls himself author of the *Zemiroth Israel* (2
Samuel xxiii.). His Elohistic psalms were considered productions of his earlier days, as all the headings show and
as the compiler of the second book confirms by calling them
Thephilloth (Psalms lxxii. 20) and not *Zemiroth*, in them he
omitted the tetragrammaton. The Elohistic psalms of the
Sons of Korah and Asaph psalms, together with those of
David, were only used at the *Bamoth* worship outside of Zion,
and the tetragrammaton is omitted in them, replaced by Elohim. The few Elohistic pieces in Genesis have been accounted
for as old documents partly adopted and partly adapted by
the Jahvistic author. *Elohim* like *El Shaddi* are purely
Hebraic and monotheistic, marking distinctly the age of
transition from the worship of the natural forces to the
cognition of the absolute and infinite Deity, and the end of
that transition period with Abraham.

(*b*) The oldest poetical parts of Scriptures are mainly
Jahvistic with the term Elohim used alternately. These are
the songs of Moses, the poems of Balaam, the blessing of
Moses, the song of Deborah, the prayer of Hannah, Psalms
xviii. cxxxvi., and in all of the Prophets. This frequent
alternation, in each case of Elohim with the tetragrammaton
in the oldest poetical pieces, which could impossibly be cut
into fragments and given to a number of different authors—
if even the headings of psalms are taken to be of later origin
—offer proof positive that the Jahvistic-Elohistic hopothesis
is a fallacy. This is so much more evident from such pieces
which were actually transcribed, like the eighteenth psalm
from 2 Samuel xxii., or Psalms cxv. from cxxxv., or cxliv.
from three older psalms, or even in Chronicles from Samuel
and Psalms, the names of God are never changed except
once in Psalms xviii., where Elohim is put instead of the
tetragrammaton ; hence the transcribing hypothesis is also
worthless. All other objections raised against the authenticity of the Pentateuch and the historical books, the David-

ian Psalms and the Solomonic Proverbs prove a failure and
can only be taken as the products of misunderstanding or
misinterpretation of Biblical passages, if it is admitted that
documentary evidence opposite speculations is conclusive,
which none can justly doubt. If we add thereto that Exodus
and Leviticus received their present form in the Phineas
time, when also Joshua was edited, and Numbers in the time
of Samuel, for which we have documentary intimations anyhow, also the anachronistic objections fall away, and we are
entitled to the conclusion that the main laws of Moses, with
as much of history as was deemed necessary to understand
them correctly, was recast in the Exodus-Leviticus canon—
originally one book—as early as it was necessary for government, priests and people to have it, and this was at the very
beginning of the occupation of Canaan. When a new literary
period dawned in Israel with the Prophet Samuel, other
laws and portions of history which the former had not considered, but were there in the ancient Mosaic records, were
compiled in the book of Numbers, which, with the former,
exhausted the laws of Moses, although not also the history,
which was not considered of equal importance. Therefore,
we have no history of Goshen and none of the wilderness
fragments excepted from the second to the fortieth year.
This gives us the following dates :

Genesis, Deuteronomy (with some Samuel additions) and
the entire material of the three middle books of the Penta-
teuch date from the first half of the fifteenth century B. C.,
Exodus, Leviticus and Joshua, fourteenth century B. C.,
Numbers, also Judges and part of Samuel, eleventh century
B. C.

With this argument established, those advanced against
the authenticity of the historical books have become worthless. For they were originally construed in support of the
hypothesis, that no Thorah existed, and its production was
a fraud and forgery ; in support thereof another and still
more flagrant fraud and forgery was perpetrated, viz.: the
historical records were falsified to make it appear that the
Thorah existed from the days of Moses. That hypothesis

being overthrown, the whole series of arguments in its support is useless and worthless, and truth is re-enthroned.

11. Ezra, the Scribe, a scion of the last high priest in the
Temple of Solomon, was born in Babylonia toward the
close of the reign of the Medo-Persian King, Darius Hysta-
pis (521–485 B. C.). All that is known of the life and work
of Ezra is taken from the books of Ezra and Nehemiah and
the traditions preserved in Talmud and *Midrash*. Outside
thereof that great Scribe is not mentioned, not even in the
Mishnah; where (Aboth I. 1) his name is most naturally
expected, it is omitted, and the chain of tradition is stated
thus: "Moses received the Thorah from Sinah, delivered it
to Joshua, Joshua to the Elders, the Elders to the Prophets
and the Prophets to the Men of the Great Synod;" although
elsewhere he is counted a bearer of traditions and a disciple
of Baruch ben Neriah, who was the scribe of the prophet
Jeremiah. The theory advanced by modern critics, that Ezra
was the author or the editor or compiler of the Thorah,
and the historical books of Former Prophets, is based upon
no kind of documentary evidence; it is the product of speculation, contrary to all written accounts of the great scribe,
who, according to one statement in the Talmud, was identical with the prophet Malachi (*Meguillah* 15). This, however, was not generally accepted, as he is always called the
scribe, the *Hasid* and *Anav* (pious and meek) like Moses,
the twenty-second bearer of the traditions after Moses, but
he is never called a prophet. He is supposed (*Sanhedrin*
21) to have been competent that the Thorah had been given
through him, if Moses had not preceded him. The Talmud
(*Succah* 20) contains also this statement: "At first when
the Thorah had been forgotten in Israel Ezra came up (from
Babylon) and established it;" but the same thing is said
of Hillel (100 B. C.) on the same page of the Talmud, which
proves that Thorah in this connection refers to the oral law
only, and not to the written Law of Moses.

12. What Ezra actually did is reported in the books of
Ezra and Nehemiah, and in the ancient Rabbinical literature, thus:

(a) Ezra viii., the oldest chronist, reports that Ezra was an "expert *Scribe* in the Thorah of Moses," (verse 6) and "had put his heart into the inquiry in the Thorah of Jehovah, and to do and to teach in Israel ordinance and judgment," was appointed by King Artaxerxes, Supreme *Judge* and *Teacher* of the "Law of the God of Heaven" (verses 12 and 21), also to appoint judges of all grades for all people west of the Euphrates (verse 25), "that they may judge in all Syria and Palestine" (1 Esdras viii. 23). He was given almost absolute power to carry into effect the provisions of the king's decree (verse 26), and he made use of his authority (Ezra x. 7, 8). He was also appointed carrier of the treasures sent to the Temple of Jerusalem and head of the colony led to Palestine. The term of *Sopher*, rendered "Scribe," we know from the use of this term ever after Ezra, signifies "a writer" or copyist (and not an author), and an "expounder" of any existing book or books, or existing traditions. The terms of the edict in verse 25 (also 21), that Ezra's powers should extend "to all people" west of the Euphrates, or according to the apocryphal Esra all "Syria and Palestine," where the non-Israelites were certainly predominant in numbers, proves that it was not purely religious or ritual laws which Ezra was to teach and enforce, all of which existed in Palestine before the advent of Ezra; it was the political and social law, חוק ומישפט (verse 10), which was to be introduced and enforced. This had been suspended, of course, during the Babylonian captivity and was not restored to the Zerubabel colony in Palestine and at no other time prior to the seventh year of King Artaxerxes; he decreed the conversion of the Medo-Persian colony in Palestine into a state organization with its own law and jurisdiction. This was accomplished by Ezra and Nehemiah. This is evident also from the fact that Ezra never interfered with any purely religious institution, and with Nehemiah never went beyond the sphere of political and social law. This appears from Nehemiah ix. 36, 37 and x. 30, 40.

In Jerusalem the books inform us, that Ezra, on complaint by the princes, convened a general meeting of all people of Judah and Benjamin together with the priests and Levites, in order to adopt measures against the evil of misalliance and polygamy. The general meeting demanded the construction of a representative body (Ezra x. 12, 15). This, it is justly supposed, was the origin of that representative body, called in the Talmud "the Men of the Great Synod," of which we treat further on. Then again Ezra appears before the assembled people, by order of Nehemiah, with "the book of the Thorah of Moses, which Jehovah commanded Israel" (Nehemiah viii.). On that memorable first day of the seventh month Ezra read the Thorah up to noon time of that day before the assembled people, and the Levites expounded, or perhaps also translated it to those from foreign countries. These readings were then continued especially during the days of the feast of tabernacles (verses 13 and 18). On the twenty-fourth day of the seventh month, the Thorah was proclaimed as the law of the land, the assembled people swore the oath of allegiance, the princes signed the document to this effect, and additional laws were promulgated (ibid. ix. and x.). This and nothing more is narrated of the work of Ezra in the two books.

(b) In the two Talmuds and the *Midrash* Ezra is reported as the author of new rules (תקנות) mostly referring to the administration of political and social laws; some referring to writing and reading of the Thorah; and the interdiction of intermarriage with the *Nethinim* (Ezra viii. 20) assistants of the Levites in the temple service, appointed to it by King David, supposed to be descendants of the Gibeonites that came to Joshua to which belonged also the "Sons of the Servants of Solomon." The supposition that Ezra was the author of any *Thargum*, Syriac or Aramaic version of the Thorah, is erroneous. In the Talmud (*Nedarim* 37 and *Megillah* 3), on which this supposition is based, it is stated in advance, that *Onkelos* was the author of the *Targum* to the Thorah, and Jonathan ben Uziel wrote the *Targum* of Prophets. The Targumist of Hagiography, Rabbi Joseph the Blind, is mentioned later on. Against this statement of fact, an exposition of Abba Areka on Nehemiah viii. 8, is cited, where the word כפרים‎ is understood to signify "translation" or Targum. This verse, however, refers not to Ezra at all, it refers to the Levites, who expounded the Thorah to the people, some of them may have spoken Aramaic to the foreigners in that assembly, and this, as is stated there in the Talmud, was forgotten. In the same passage it is stated also that the Levites promulgated then among the people the *Massorah*, the division of verses, and the disjunctive accentual signs (פסקי טעמים‎). As no writing was done there, we can but understand this passage to convey the idea that the Levites repeated the passages of the Thorah so subdivided in verses and the verses in phrases, with the same accentuation, stress and emphasis, as they heard it from Ezra; but it does not say that he invented anything. It is maintained elsewhere that the main portion of the *Massorah* (not the vocal and accentual signs) were as old as the Thorah itself, to which is added (*Taanith* 27b and *Meguillah* 22a) that the verses were originally established by Moses. Therefore Abba Areka could not have thought of crediting Ezra with this work. The *Sopherim*, "Scribes," succeeding Ezra, are given credit only for counting every letter in the Thorah (*Kiddushin* 30a).

13. One invention is ascribed to Ezra, and this is the Hebrew square-letter alphabet, called the כתב אשורית‎, now the only style of the Hebrew Bible, the Aramaic portions included. The oldest Hebrew alphabet, extant in coins and inscriptions, is like the Phœnician, original Greek, Syrian, Samaritan and other Shemites. With Ezra that new alphabet was brought into Palestine, and he transcribed the Thorah in these characters. After him the Great Synod transcribed all books of Holy Writ in the same manner. The oldest alphabet was henceforth used for ordinary purposes (*Sanhedrin* 21b and *Yeru-halmi Meguillah* first Perek). It is maintained that Daniel was the inventor of the new alphabet, the *Menai Men ii* was written on the wall in these

characters, therefore only Daniel could read the ominous inscription on the wall, and Ezra learned it from him. Nothing similar to these letters, except in the inscriptions of Palmyra, has been discovered anywhere; certainly nothing anyway like them in the cuneiform letters of Assyrian origin. Therefore the rabbis of the Talmud differ as to the signification of the term *Kethab Ashurith*. While some maintain it was called so because it came with Ezra from Assyria, others define the term שהוא מיאושר בכהתבו " it was an improved writing," more distinct and more beautiful; while others again maintain it was the original Hebrew alphabet which in course of time had fallen in disuse and was restored by Ezra. All agree, however, that the *Sepher Ezra*, the Scroll, preserved in the temple as the authentic copy of the Thorah, from which all scrolls of the Thorah used in synagogue, school or hall of justice had to be an exact copy, was written in this *Kethab Ashurith* by Ezra the Scribe.

14. Connected with this translettering of the Thorah was the critical authentication of the text from the various manuscripts and the bearers of the traditions. The latter were supposed to know every word of the Thorah, with its proper vocalization and accentuation and every letter of every word, by heart, of which class Ezra is represented the highest expert. Wherever the two authorities deviated from one another, the differences were noted in the following manner: קרייין ולא כתבין כתבין ולא קרייין קרי כתיב חסר וכלא תקון ספרים ועטור ספרים viz., the letters or words as found in the manuscripts were retained in the text, and the deviations of the tradionalists were noticed in marginal notes. The authenticated copy of the Thorah required also protection against the mistakes of transcribers or willful interpolators; to this end other parts of the *Massorah* were established referring to writing. One of the most important rules in this connection is that none of the sacred books must be written from memory; it must be copied word by word and letter by letter from an authentic copy. Other rules of this kind are large letters and small letters in cer-

tain fixed words (א' ב' רבתא וזוטא) the exact space to
be left between words and verses, major and minor paragraphs (פתוחות וסתומות) that certain pages must begin
with certain words; the exceptional lineal arrangement for
writing the poetical portions of Scriptures, and many other
rules compiled in the rabbinical code of Maimonides, by
which the authentic copies could be recognized *prima vista*.
All these rules and exceptions are noticed in Talmud and
Midrash centuries before the *Massorites* of the sixth Christian century invented the vowel and accentual signs; hence
as far as the Thorah is concerned may be ascribed to Ezra,
as is always presupposed in the Talmud. This, however, is
all that can legitimately be ascribed to Ezra in connection
with the Thorah. There exists no documentary evidence
beyond this of Ezra's work, and these suffice to establish
beyond a reasonable doubt that after him no change whatever could be made in the text of the Thorah.

15. The Men of the Great Synod (אנשי כנסת הגדולה)
consisted of 120 members, viz., 44 *Horim*, 44 *Seganim*, 22
Levites, 8 priests, all heads of family groups, high priest
and scribe as presiding officers, up to the time after the conquests of Alexander the Great. After this time the number
of the body was changed to 70, and was called "The Beth
Din of the High Priests," from Simon the Just to Judah
Maccabee, and "The Beth Din of the Maccabees" up to the
reign of John Hyrcan, when the character and name of that
body was changed into Synedrion or Sanhedrin, no longer
presided over by high priest and scribe. Prior to this
change the body was called, generally, the Great Synod.
This body continued the work of Ezra in accordance with
his rules and regulations applied to all books of Holy Writ,
authenticated critically, translettered into *Kethab Ashurith*
(some books they compiled from defective manuscripts) and
established official copies for the temple archives, which remained the exemplary copy for all copyists. In course of
time it seems Former Prophets came first, then Later Prophets, then Hagiography, of which Psalms, Koheleth and
Shir Hashirim came last. There were in the temple salaried

correctors of copies made from the books kept in the
archives (*Yerushalmi*). They were called *Zophim* and
Hachraim, only the names of the two last officers are preserved, viz., Rabbi Joshua ben Chananiah and Rabbi Eliezer
ben Hyrcan, under whose direction Onkelos or Aquila translated the Thorah (ibid. *Megillah* first Perek),* the correct
pronunciation and accentuation of each word and phrase
was the particular care of the scribes and teachers of the
young (*Nedarim* 37a), and the main science of the profession. The Massorites could invent no more in their time
than the vowel and accentual signs to represent the sounds
known to every man of knowledge in Israel. The Maso-
retic notes only refer to exceptions, the rule of reading correctly the text was always well known, as is evident from
the ancient Rabbinical literature, the ancient translations,
Greek, Aramaic, Syriac, Latin, Samaritan and Gothic. Thus
not only the manuscripts but also the pronunciation and
accentuation of each syllable of Holy Writ were preserved
intact, alike in all ages and in all parts of the world, as is
evident from the ancient manuscripts extant and especially
from the still more ancient commentaries and the united
testimony of the Karaites and the Christians of the first
centuries. There exists no solid ground on which to base
any doubt in the authenticity of any book of Holy Writ.

---

* The story of R. Simeon ben Lakish in *Sopherim* vi. 4, and in
Yerushalmi that scrolls of the Law found in the temple court were
rejected by a majority rule, because two had it so and one otherwise, the one always was rejected, is certainly a mistake of the
copyist, because no such rule in this connection is given in the
Talmud. The passage is suspicious anyhow by its number three
and in three cases. The mistake of the transcriber is perhaps that
he turned the statement to tell the very opposite of what was the
case, viz., although two were incorrect and one correct, yet the two
were rejected.

THE END.

www.ingramcontent.com/pod-product-compliance
Lightning Source LLC
Chambersburg PA
CBHW030553040726
47497CB00008B/2703